Praise for the Bear Collector's Mysteries

"Has the potential to quickly turn into a favorite series of many."
—*The Mystery Reader*

"Don't be fooled . . . [these] mysteries are full-bodied . . . the identity of the primary villain will come as a real surprise."
—*Richmond Times-Dispatch*

"A page-turner . . . [with] plenty of action. This is an original, refreshing change in the overcrowded amateur-sleuth genre."
—*Romantic Times*

"Be warned that if you pick this book up, you won't put it down until you've finished reading it . . . You'll want to read every one of the books in the series—and jump into the world of teddy bear collecting, murder, and intriguing mystery."
—*Armchair Interviews*

"The story skips along with plenty of humor, interesting and unusual characters, recognizable scenery, and quick-paced action."
—*The Fredericksburg (VA) Free Lance-Star*

"Full of interesting information on teddy bear lore (including a profile of a genuine teddy bear artisan at the end of each novel), a complex and interesting mystery, and a macabre and twisted sense of humor."
—*Gumshoe Review*

continued . . .

The False-Hearted Teddy

"With a quick-moving plot that's neither too cozy nor too hard-boiled, a likable sleuth, and an original premise, Lamb has another honey of a mystery."

—*Richmond Times-Dispatch*

"A quirky but surprising read, and one that readers who prefer a little plush to gore should relish."

—*The Carlisle (PA) Sentinel*

"A fast-paced trip . . . Mystery fans will follow the twists and turns of this tightly woven tale with pleasure."

—*Teddy Bear and Friends*

"A fast and fun romp into murder and mayhem . . . An enjoyable read."

—*Armchair Interviews*

"Both story and dialogue are fast paced . . . I finished *The False-Hearted Teddy* in one lazy afternoon because I couldn't put it down."

—*Cozy Library*

"John J. Lamb will drive you absolutely ursine with his series of Bear Collector's Mysteries."

—*Raleigh News & Observer*

"*The False-Hearted Teddy* can't help but make you smile and want to read more of this series."

—*Reviewing the Evidence*

The Mournful Teddy

"Once you start, you can't bear to miss a teddy mystery."

—Rita Mae Brown, *New York Times* bestselling author of the Mrs. Murphy Mysteries

"A smart debut."

—*Mystery Scene*

Berkley Prime Crime titles by John J. Lamb

THE MOURNFUL TEDDY
THE FALSE-HEARTED TEDDY
THE CRAFTY TEDDY
THE CLOCKWORK TEDDY

THE
CLOCKWORK TEDDY

John J. Lamb

BERKLEY PRIME CRIME, NEW YORK

THE BERKLEY PUBLISHING GROUP
Published by the Penguin Group
Penguin Group (USA) Inc.
375 Hudson Street, New York, New York 10014, USA
Penguin Group (Canada), 90 Eglinton Avenue East, Suite 700, Toronto, Ontario M4P 2Y3, Canada
(a division of Pearson Penguin Canada Inc.)
Penguin Books Ltd., 80 Strand, London WC2R 0RL, England
Penguin Group Ireland, 25 St. Stephen's Green, Dublin 2, Ireland (a division of Penguin Books Ltd.)
Penguin Group (Australia), 250 Camberwell Road, Camberwell, Victoria 3124, Australia
(a division of Pearson Australia Group Pty. Ltd.)
Penguin Books India Pvt. Ltd., 11 Community Centre, Panchsheel Park, New Delhi—110 017, India
Penguin Group (NZ), 67 Apollo Drive, Rosedale, North Shore 0632, New Zealand
(a division of Pearson New Zealand Ltd.)
Penguin Books (South Africa) (Pty.) Ltd., 24 Sturdee Avenue, Rosebank, Johannesburg 2196,
South Africa

Penguin Books Ltd., Registered Offices: 80 Strand, London WC2R 0RL, England

This is a work of fiction. Names, characters, places, and incidents either are the product of the author's imagination or are used fictitiously, and any resemblance to actual persons, living or dead, business establishments, events, or locales is entirely coincidental. The publisher does not have any control over and does not assume any responsibility for author or third-party websites or their content.

THE CLOCKWORK TEDDY

A Berkley Prime Crime Book / published by arrangement with the author

PRINTING HISTORY
Berkley Prime Crime mass-market edition / October 2008

Copyright © 2008 by John J. Lamb.
Cover illustration by Jeff Crosby.
Cover design by Annette Fiore Defex.

ISBN: 978-0-425-22429-8

BERKLEY® PRIME CRIME
Berkley Prime Crime Books are published by The Berkley Publishing Group,
a division of Penguin Group (USA) Inc.,
375 Hudson Street, New York, New York 10014.
BERKLEY PRIME CRIME and the BERKLEY PRIME CRIME design
are trademarks belonging to Penguin Group (USA) Inc.

PRINTED IN THE UNITED STATES OF AMERICA

10 9 8 7 6 5 4 3 2 1

For Daniel Ahrens,
my best friend, my wife's cherished brother,
and the finest backup a cop could ever have

One

I couldn't help but notice that the guy dressed in the furry brown bear costume didn't quite grasp the concept of being a teddy bear show mascot. Instead of playfully interacting with the early-bird attendees and their children, the ersatz Ursa was about as cheerful and communicative as the backside of a gravestone. He plodded down the aisle with his woolly head downcast and swiveling back and forth, peering glumly at the exhibitor's tables.

It was a sunny morning on the first Saturday of September and my wife, Ashleigh, and I were in Sonoma, California, getting ready to present our stuffed animals at the Teddy Bear Flag Republic, one of the most popular bear shows in the country. The annual event attracts participants from all over the world and we had spotted well-known artists from across the U.S., Australia, Japan, and even the Netherlands. The show's venue is unique for being held outside, under the enormous eucalyptus trees of the lovely downtown Plaza. Primarily known now as the capital of California wine country, back in 1846 Sonoma was also the site of some momentous history. That's when American settlers gathered in the square to declare their independence from Mexico and proclaim the establishment of a republic. It was a mostly peaceful revolt and the rebels soon raised over the Plaza their flag, which featured a crude brown silhouette of a grizzly bear—a creature once very common throughout the region—and before long, the new country had a nickname: the Bear Flag Republic. Hence the unusual name for the teddy bear convention.

Using the handle of my blackthorn cane to gesture at the morose bear mascot as he shuffled past, I asked Ash, "What do you suppose his major malfunction is?"

She looked up from the soft-sculpture cougar she was carefully positioning on our table amidst our other more traditional teddy bears. "How can you be sure that's a he?"

"I can't be absolutely certain, but he's taller than me and—"

"He walks with his weight on his heels, like most guys do," said Ash, giving the bear mascot a closer look.

"Good obs, Deputy Lyon," I said, referring to her new status as an auxiliary deputy sheriff, back home in Massanutten County, Virginia. "Now, can you tell me why he's so sulky?"

"Honey, it's probably hot and stuffy inside that costume."

"That's no excuse. And if we're talking hot and stuffy, let me remind you of that time right after I made detective when I was working a stakeout and—"

"Had to dress up like a lobster and stand day after day in front of that seafood restaurant in North Beach?" As usual, Ash had read my mind. She put a hand over her mouth to conceal a smile.

"Which was a much bulkier suit than the one Grumpy Bear there is wearing," I said defensively.

"I think we have a Polaroid of you in that suit in one of the photo albums."

"I don't need a picture to remember it. That costume had a stuffed tail and I could barely move my arms inside those big freaking claws."

"You had cute orange antennae that bobbed up and down."

"And that were attached with hard plastic bolts that scraped my head every time I moved. When they told me that, as the junior man in the detective division, I would have to wear that lobster costume, what did I say?"

"That you were going to throw yourself in front of a BART train."

"But I didn't, did I? No, I wore that ridiculous outfit and did the surveillance while pimping the catch-of-the-day like I was Barney the Dinosaur on crystal meth."

Ash giggled. "All the other detectives said that you were a very animated crustacean. But what does that have to do with that guy in the bear suit?"

I watched as the unhappy bear disappeared around the corner of Sonoma's city hall, a handsome old two-story stone building near the front of the Plaza. Shrugging, I said, "Nothing, I guess. It just bothers me that he's trudging around a teddy bear show looking as if he's on the Bataan Death March."

"I agree. But maybe you're mistaking embarrassment for a bad attitude. For all we know, he's someone's husband or boyfriend who got roped into wearing that costume when he'd rather be out on a golf course."

"I guess that would explain why he's so *fur-lorn*."

Ash rolled her eyes at the bad pun. "Or maybe it's someone's teenaged son."

"And what kid wouldn't enjoy spending his Saturday morning wearing a fuzzy costume and hanging out with a bunch of silly adults who love teddy bears?"

"Exactly. So, if he comes by again, why don't you say something to him? Maybe he just needs a little encouragement."

"But it's way more fun to be grouchy and make snap judgments about strangers."

"That's the Brad I know and love." Ash kissed me on the cheek. "And now I've got to get back to work. The show starts in less than an hour."

Ash and I had attended the Teddy Bear Flag Republic shows religiously back when we still lived in California, but only as collectors. This was our first experience here as exhibitors, which was why she was so focused on making our display of handcrafted stuffed animals look perfect. I also knew that the best way I could help was to stay out of her way and keep quiet. So I sat down in one of our folding chairs and watched her work, a more than satisfying pastime given that my wife is the most beautiful woman I know. And I'm not just saying that to score husband brownie points. Ash has luxurious blond hair and a magnificent figure that I could contemplate for hours, and frequently have.

Ash pulled Becky Birthday Cake from a box, smoothed some stray strands of russet fur between the costumed bear's eyes, and set it carefully on the table. The stuffed animal was one of the newest members of Ash's "Confection Collection," a line of twenty-inch mohair bears dressed as decadent desserts. I'm partial to all of my wife's creations, but Becky is a work of art. Ash had spent several hours twisting sturdy wires into a drum-shaped framework around the bear's upper body. Then she'd upholstered the cylindrical frame in an ivory-colored satin that looked exactly like vanilla frosting, and painstakingly hand-stitched five pink faux-icing rosettes to the top of the cake. A sixth oversized rosette, sporting a birthday cake candle, doubled as a hat for Becky. And if that wasn't impressive enough, nestled inside of Becky was a small potpourri bag containing cinnamon sticks and cloves, which made her smell just like a spice cake.

I thought the bear was a masterpiece, and tangible proof that Ash had elevated her skills as both a designer and artist to a new plane of excellence. Of course, the fact that

I have an informed opinion about artisan teddy bears at all *does* permanently demolish whatever street cred I used to have as a tough guy.

My name is Brad Lyon, and before a .357-magnum hollow-point destroyed my left shin and I was medically retired from the force, I was an SFPD homicide inspector. Now I'm an apprentice teddy bear artist and avid collector, having moved from grisly crime scenes to grizzly bears made out of mohair. Governor Arnold would probably call me a "girly man," but not in Ash's presence, unless he wanted a roundhouse left to the jaw. My wife of twenty-seven years is a sweet-tempered and beautiful woman, but if she thinks my manhood is under attack, she's as ruthless as an Israeli army border guard.

In the aftermath of my forced retirement, Ash and I realized that we were weary of the hamster-on-an-exercise-wheel pace of city life. Our two children, Christopher and Heather, were grown and there was nothing to keep us in San Francisco, so we relocated to Ash's childhood home of Remmelkemp Mill, a tiny village in Virginia's Shenandoah Valley that was simultaneously three hours ahead and fifty years behind the "Golden" State. Surprisingly, the only thing we really missed about California was our daughter, Heather, who'd carried on the family tradition and was a San Francisco cop. We were thrilled at the prospect of spending all of Sunday with Heather, and our only regret was that Chris, who was in Missouri, pursuing his career as a vintner, couldn't be here, too.

The Teddy Bear Flag Republic was the first and probably the only West Coast show we'd be attending, however. Shipping the bears was a hassle, air travel is one of the few forms of torture yet to be addressed by Amnesty International, and this time, as always, I ended up seated next to someone who was "just getting over" the flu, yet coughing so badly I suspected it was actually bubonic plague. Then there were the costs of renting a minivan, staying at a nice-enough motel to

ensure that our morning wakeup call wasn't the cops serving
an arrest warrant next door, and restaurant dining—which is
never cheap in wine country.

The bottom line was that we were going to have to sell
beaucoup bruins to break even with the expenses. Indeed,
the only reason we'd been able to afford the trip at all was
that a prominent San Francisco attorney had actually paid
for my airline tickets and two days' worth of meals and lodg-
ing. Big surprise: This wasn't an act of altruism, but so that
the attorney could grill me at a deposition, which I deliberately scheduled so that Ash and I could both come to the
Teddy Bear Flag Republic and visit Heather the following
day. Unethical? Maybe, but given the circumstances, I didn't
feel too broken up about it.

Five years earlier I'd been shot and crippled for life while
chasing a lowlife who'd stabbed and killed his former girlfriend. As I'd crashed to the pavement in front of a crowd of
stunned witnesses in Ghirardelli Square, my old partner,
Gregg Mauel, had demonstrated why he'd once won a gold
medal in marksmanship at the police athletic championships
by double-tapping the shooter and killing him instantly. The
unbelievable postscript to this tale was that the criminal's
mother had now filed a $17 million civil rights lawsuit
against Gregg and the San Francisco Police Department,
claiming police brutality. There are plenty of occasions
when suing the cops is appropriate, but this wasn't one of
them. So, long story short: As one of the most crucial witnesses to the suspect's death, I'd been brought back to San
Francisco to testify at a lengthy and contentious deposition
in advance of the civil trial. It was an infuriating experience,
but I'd resolved not to let the encounter ruin the rest of my
and Ash's weekend.

I'd have been perfectly content to sit hypnotized by the
sight of my wife bending over in her snug denim shorts for
another half hour, but I finally remembered that I had to do
some shopping. Ash's birthday was less than three weeks

away, and while I'd already bought her a gold and blue topaz bracelet, I'd deliberately held off on getting anything else, since I knew that some of our favorite bear artists would be at this show.

Pushing myself to my feet, I said, "I think I'll hit the bathroom before the show starts."

"Uh-huh." Ash was lost in thought and I wasn't quite certain she'd actually heard me.

She was holding one of my newest bears, utterly focused on what, to her, was the crucial decision of where it belonged on our table. Me? I'd have hidden Steve Mc-Bear-ett behind Ash's creations. Mc-Bear-ett was my mohair tribute to actor Jack Lord and the old television show *Hawaii Five-0*, but most collectors and potential customers just wouldn't be too excited over a black teddy bear dressed in a charcoal gray business suit, wearing half a shoulder holster. (The half shoulder holster wasn't a design error on my part—it was a commitment to authenticity. Check out an old episode of the program and you may notice that Steve McGarrett's shoulder rig lacks support straps. In real life, such a holster would fall off, yet on TV it remains miraculously attached to his shirt.) Another touch of realism that I was proud of was the fur on top of Mc-Bear-ett's head. I'd stiffened it with repeated coats of lacquer to recreate Lord's famously glossy and petrified hair.

"Be back in a minute, love." I kissed Ash on the temple.

"The map says that Penny is over on aisle three. Tell her I said hi and that I'll stop by a little later." Ash still sounded distracted, but it was plain she knew the real reason I was leaving was to visit bear artist Penny French's booth.

"Aisle three, huh?" I asked, secretly glad for the information. "What makes you think I'm going there?"

"Because you're a sweet man . . ." Ash paused to set Mc-Bear-ett down on an empty spot on the table as gently as she would a soufflé fresh from the oven. When she turned to look at me, her Delft China–blue eyes were merry. "And you're a terrible liar when it comes to fibbing to me. Oh, and also because you always get me the best birthday presents."

"Well, I hate to disappoint you, but I'm *not* going to Penny's booth, because I've already got your present."

"Oh, really?"

"Yes, and I'm certain you're going to love the latest season of *South Park* on DVD."

"Brad honey, you've done more insanely dangerous things than I want to remember, but even *you* wouldn't take that sort of risk."

"I know, so at least allow me to pretend that you don't know where I'm going. I'll be back in a little while."

Cane in hand, I slowly limped up the sidewalk toward the city hall, where all seven of the exhibitor's aisles intersected like the spokes of an old wagon wheel. It was still about ten minutes from the formal opening of the show, yet the collectors were already beginning to hover around their favorite artists' tables, hoping to discover that one special bear before someone else did. Not that there weren't hundreds of amazing stuffed animals made by popular artists, which guaranteed that no one would go home unhappy. On our aisle alone, there was a stellar assemblage of bear makers, including the award-winning Donna Griffin, Karen DiNicola from Australia, and Rosalie Frischmann, who'd made the sweet teddy bear wearing an old-fashioned sailor suit that sat on one of our shelves back home.

Working my way through the growing crowd, I spotted a middle-aged couple closely inspecting one of Mac Pohlen's mohair creations. These weren't your garden-variety bear collectors, however. Susan and Terry Quinlan owned and operated the finest teddy bear museum in the United States and they were obviously looking to add to their fabled collection. Located in Santa Barbara, the museum had opened after we'd moved to Virginia, but we'd heard about what an amazing place it was and regretted that we couldn't fit in a trip down the coast to see it. Bear artists dream of having their work on display at the museum, and I felt a tiny spark of excitement at the idea of the Quinlans discovering Ash's creations. That is, if they weren't scared away from our table by my bears.

Then I saw someone else I recognized: Lauren Vandenbosch, a native San Franciscan and one of the influential bear artists who'd helped foster the teddy bear renaissance back in the early 1980s. Pick up any teddy bear encyclopedia— believe it or not, there are such books, and we actually own a couple—and the odds are good that you'll find listings and photos of Lauren's Barbeary Coast Bears, a collection of stuffed animals dressed in authentic Gold Rush–era costumes. Ash and I used to see Lauren regularly at the West Coast bear shows and we owned Black Beart, one of her creations, who wore a black frock coat and was modeled after the celebrated California stagecoach robber.

It was the first time I'd seen Lauren since we'd left California and, unlike me, the years hadn't changed her. With her pink, smooth complexion, athletic figure, and curly brunette hair, she didn't look her age, which had to be at least mid-fifties. As a matter of fact, she didn't look much older than her picture in one of our teddy bear books, published fifteen years ago; it made me wonder if she had a *Dorian Gray*–esque portrait hidden in her attic. As I walked past, a sudden gust of warm wind blew her foam-backed "Barbeary Bears" poster from its wooden easel. It fell to the sidewalk in front of me, badly bending one of the upper corners, and by the time she came rushing around from the other side of the table, I'd already picked up the ruined sign.

Handing it to her, I said, "Don't you just hate it when that happens? We had a nice poster like that and someone knocked it off its stand at the Niagara show. Eighty-five bucks right down the drain."

Her jaw tightened when she saw how badly the poster was damaged. Leaning it against the table, she said, "Darn it, and I just put it up. Between the wind and the skateboarders, I really don't know why I continue to do this event."

"Probably because you're one of the people who put this show on the map, Lauren. And a lot of these folks came here to get one of your bears."

"I suppose." She squinted at me. "I don't mean to be rude, but do we know each other?"

"We met several times, back when my wife and I were just collectors. But it was years ago, and with the crowds that are always around your table, I wouldn't expect you to remember me." I extended my hand. "I'm Brad Lyon."

Lauren released my hand and waggled a finger at me. "Wait, I remember. Your wife was interested in making teddy bears and you bought Black Beart."

"What a memory," I said. "I'm impressed."

"But . . ." She looked down at my cane. "You . . ."

"I was hurt on the job when I was with the SFPD. Now Ashleigh and I are making teddy bears. In fact, we're almost neighbors." I hooked a thumb over my shoulder. "Our table is back there."

"Congratulations, but I hope that doesn't mean you've stopped collecting."

"Oh no, we always bring one or two bears back from shows. We're addicted."

"Good, because if you've got a second, I'd love to show you my new Age of A-bear-ius collection." She pointed to the table where there stood a protest march's worth of hippie-attired bears with long hair made from distressed yarn. "And you're in luck; I give other artists a ten-percent discount."

"Thanks for thinking of me, but I was just on my way somewhere. Maybe I'll come back in a little while," I said, hoping my tone didn't betray my slight annoyance over her clumsy segue into trying to sell me a bear. "And about the sign; do you have some packing tape and—I don't know—maybe a couple of pencils or something?"

"I think so. Why?"

"You might be able to jury-rig a splint to keep that corner relatively flat. It's possible you could fix it enough to use the poster for the show."

"That's a great idea. Thanks." Her eyes flicked in the direction of a woman who'd stopped to examine the Barbeary Coast Bears and I knew she was concerned about missing a potential customer.

"Well, I know you're busy, so I'll let you get back to work. It was a pleasure seeing you again. And thank you for being one of the people who infected us with the teddy bear–collecting virus."

"My pleasure, and if I get the chance, I'll try to come down and see your bears." Lauren gave me a wan smile as she darted toward the table.

"Ash would be thrilled. Our sign says 'Lyon's Tigers and Bears,' " I said, suspecting that she hadn't heard me.

I started toward city hall, but hadn't gone much farther than ten yards when the guy in the bear costume reappeared from around a corner, tramping in my direction. Since I was still in Boy Scout mode, I decided to do another good deed and offer him an encouraging word or two. I stepped into his path as we approached each other and gave him a casual, friendly wave to indicate I wanted to speak to him. The guy obviously didn't want to stop, but there wasn't much room for him to maneuver with the crowds and he was obliged to slow down.

As he tried to sidestep around me, I put my hand on his arm and said, "I know you probably didn't volunteer for this job, but we all appreciate what you're doing. So, thank you and try to have a little fun. It might make the time go more quickly."

The bear jerked his arm free from my grasp, and as he stomped past, a muffled male voice from behind the smiling bear's face snapped, "Hey, bite me, you old fart."

Although I'd turned forty-eight back in July, the fact is

that I *do* look old enough to remember when Ronald Reagan was best known as Bonzo the Chimpanzee's costar. Still, you don't expect spite from a teddy bear. My surprise gave way to complete shock as the costumed man then barreled up to the Barbeary Bears space, shoved Lauren's customer aside, grabbed one side of the aluminum folding-table and threw it into the air, sending the hippie and Gold Rush bears flying. Lauren fell backwards onto the grass and rolled to avoid the falling table, which slammed to the ground only inches from her legs. There were cries of alarm as the teddy bear fans tried to distance themselves from the rampaging mascot.

Meanwhile, the costumed attacker snatched up Lauren's metal cashbox from the ground and tucked it under his left arm, which I supposed now made him a *rob-bear*. But there wasn't time to dream up any more wretched puns, because the guy pivoted and began running back the way he'd come from—in my direction. That was when I made my first mistake: I decided that I was too hemmed in by innocent folks to risk clobbering the robber with my cane, so instead I tried to make an open-field tackle, which would have been a challenge even if I'd possessed two good legs. I dove for his fuzzy midsection, but as he rumbled past, the bear gave me a crushing straight-arm to the face, worthy of legendary NFL running back Jim Brown. The blow knocked me backwards and my cane went flying as I crashed onto the grass. By the time I rolled over and shook the stars from my vision, I could only watch as the bear ran toward West Napa Street and disappeared from sight.

The shouting and atmosphere of panic didn't diminish much, even after the crook was gone. There were repeated shouts for someone to call 911, strident voices demanding to know what had happened, and several kids sobbing with terror. Meanwhile, I was helped to my feet and someone handed me my cane as I assured everyone that I was fine and didn't need medical attention.

Suddenly, Ash was there. She hugged me tightly while saying in a frightened and slightly annoyed voice, "I *knew* I'd find you here. Are you all right?"

"Fine but pissed. I had a shot at tackling the guy, but he got away."

"What guy?"

"The dude in the bear suit. He just trashed Lauren Vandenbosch's display table and then Two-Elevened her," I replied, using the California penal code section for robbery. "I wonder how she's doing."

We wove our way through the milling crowd and I received yet another disagreeable surprise. A visibly trembling Lauren stood next to the wrecked table, clutching a teddy bear to her chest and listening in fearful silence to one of my least favorite people in the world.

Two

Ash saw my jaw tighten. "What's wrong?"

"Scumbag at twelve o'clock . . . or any other time of day or night for that matter," I said quietly.

"You know him?"

"Yep. That's Merv the Perv Bronsey, the vice squad's king of kinks. I thought I smelled manure."

"That creepy detective you reported to Internal Affairs?"

"Several times. And in what alternate universe would you expect to find *him* at a teddy bear show?"

"Lauren doesn't exactly look thrilled to be talking to him."

"No woman ever is."

"Let's go a little closer." Ash pulled on my hand.

The most charitable thing I could say about Bronsey was that he was too lazy to pursue the more arduous forms of police corruption. He might not accept bribes, but he would spend hours conducting "business inspections" of nude bars, and often seized hardcore porn magazines from adult bookshops under the pretext of examining them for pictures of runaway girls. Having someone like Bronsey in the SFPD vice enforcement bureau was sort of like putting Michael Vick in charge of a dog shelter. But the sad fact is cop work is like any other profession. There are two roads to career advancement: One is to work hard and the other is to become a human remora and attach yourself to the back of a shark-like boss, which—big surprise, considering he was a natural born suck-up—was the path Bronsey had chosen.

As we neared, we could hear that Bronsey sounded tickled as he said, "Like I said, it's a damn shame about this . . . random destruction. I'd really hate to see it happen again, but you never can tell."

"I told you, I don't know where Kyle is," Lauren sniffled.

"Not that it's in any way connected with this tragedy . . ." He flashed a toothy smile. Tall and beefy with long salt-and-pepper hair worn in a ponytail, Bronsey was dressed in a shabby pastel-colored suit and T-shirt ensemble that had gone out of style with *Miami Vice*. "But, wrong answer, lady. And maybe you'd better think about how terrible it would be if some crazy bear came to your house tonight."

"You know, that sounds an awful lot like a threat, Merv." I probably should have kept my mouth shut, but I've always hated bullies, especially if they're backing their play with a cop's badge.

Surprised, Bronsey pivoted, pulled his mirrored sunglasses down to look at me, and chuckled. "Well, if it ain't limpy Lyon, my favorite snitch. How's life as a cripple?"

"Not bad, since, unlike yours, my disability is just physical."

He ignored me to focus on Ashleigh. "And this must be your wife. Always wanted to meet her." He leered at Ash and said, "Seems to me that a fine-looking woman like you could do better than this gimp."

My hand tightened around my cane, but before I could

do anything Ash gave him a contemptuous smile and said, "Stick to smut books, Merv. I've heard you wouldn't know what to do with a real woman."

Bronsey's cheeks flushed and his eyes narrowed with anger. "Someone needs to teach you some respect."

"My mama always said that respect is earned, and you never give it to gutter trash," said Ash, anger causing her usually dormant Virginia mountain accent to emerge.

"Your mama—"

I stepped between Ash and Bronsey. "Don't go there, Merv. Not unless you want to fight both of us. And do you really want to make things any worse for yourself?"

"What are you talking about?"

"This woman was just the victim of a robbery and the only thing you can think to do is threaten her? That's egregious misconduct, even for you. I want your supervisor out here right now."

Bronsey squared his shoulders and sneered, "I don't work for the PD anymore. I've got my own private investigation agency." He glared at me, then his gaze shifted to something in the distance behind us. He turned to Lauren and snapped, "We aren't done. I'll see you very soon."

Bronsey turned, paused briefly to kick one of the fallen teddy bears from his path, and then walked quickly across the grass toward First Street. I looked over to see the reason for his unexpected retreat: Two Sonoma cops were threading their way through the crowds toward us. By the time they arrived, Bronsey was lost to sight.

I turned to Lauren. "I saw you fall. Are you okay?"

"I wasn't hurt. I'm okay."

"Yeah, but you *were* robbed."

"It was just a little money and none of my bears were stolen." Lauren brushed a stray ringlet of brunette hair from her eyes. "Still, thanks for your help with Bronsey."

"Oh, I think seeing the other cops scared him off more

than anything I did. What was he harassing you about, anyway?"

"It's all a huge misunderstanding, but thanks for asking." Lauren stooped to pick up the table. It was obvious she didn't want to talk about it.

Once the Sonoma officers learned that a robbery had occurred, the younger one began looking for witnesses while the senior cop spoke to Lauren. I waited, knowing they'd also want to interview me. Realizing it might be a few minutes before I was free, I suggested to Ash that she return to our unguarded table. You don't usually worry about theft at a bear show, but considering what had just happened, there was no point in tempting fate. Ash grudgingly agreed, but even though I promised to join her the moment I was finished, she looked worried.

"What's wrong?" I asked.

She took my hand. "Brad, honey, you've got your homicide inspector face on, which almost always means trouble."

"That obvious, huh?" I hung my head for a second. "Sorry, but it just infuriates me that Bronsey seemed connected to the robbery, and then just stood there smirking at us."

"He probably was, but that's for the local police to prove."

"And she's hiding something." I inclined my head in Lauren's direction.

"That may be true, but she's probably uncomfortable talking about her problem with an almost total stranger."

"Oh, as if *that's* a valid reason for not sharing a potentially embarrassing secret," I said in mock exasperation, and then sighed. "You're right, honey, and I'm sorry for sliding into cop mode. I promise that all I'm going to do is give a statement and then I'll come right back to our table."

"Thank you, sweetheart." She kissed me on the cheek and headed back down the grassy walkway.

Meanwhile, I moved a little closer to Lauren, who was

telling the cop about the robbery. I couldn't really blame the officer for trying to suppress a smile when she learned that the robbery suspect was a guy dressed in a furry brown bear suit. Even for California, that was pretty surreal.

What was even stranger, though, was that Lauren never said a word about her subsequent menacing encounter with Bronsey. That just didn't make any sense, since the ex–vice cop had clearly implied he knew something about the robbery. Probably, Bronsey had threatened to ratchet up the abuse if Lauren reported him to the police. But remembering how she'd rebuffed my earlier question, I also had to wonder if Lauren was trying to avoid saying anything that would lead to questions about Kyle—whoever *he* was— and why Bronsey was after him.

When it came time for me to talk to the officer, Lauren gazed at me with what I was uncomfortably aware were imploring hazel eyes. Obviously, she was hoping I'd corroborate her abridged version of how the robbery went down; an unreasonable expectation, however, considering that I was not only a retired detective, but I'd been knocked on my butt by someone who was presumably Bronsey's coconspirator. Lauren's head drooped as I began talking about Merv the Perv.

The cop frowned. "How do you know this guy is ex-SFPD?"

"I used to work there."

"You Eight-Thirty-Two?"

No, she wasn't asking my age or how many glazed doughnut holes I had for breakfast. Few people know that section 832 of the California penal code is the definition for a peace officer, so Golden State cops use the numbers as a verbal secret handshake. I nodded and said, "I worked homicide, but now I'm retired."

She squinted at my event nametag, hanging from a lanyard around my neck. "And you're a teddy bear artist? There's a major career change."

"Yeah, I've gone from stiffs to Steiffs."

"Huh?"

"Twisted teddy bear humor. Steiff is a world-famous teddy bear manufacturer."

"I'll take your word for it." The cop then turned to Lauren and said, "Any particular reason you didn't tell me about this guy Bronsey?"

"I didn't think there was any connection."

"Yeah, I'll bet. So, who's Kyle?"

There was a long pause before Lauren answered, "My son."

"And why is this PI targeting you to get to your son?"

Lauren looked away. "I don't know."

The cop sighed. "Look, lady, there's no point in me writing a crime report if you're gonna lie to us. You *do* want this investigated, don't you?"

"No . . . I'd just like to forget it ever happened. There wasn't much money in the box, so . . . no . . . I don't want to make a report." Lauren knelt to pick up several teddy bears from the grass.

"Fine. And how about you? You want me to cut paper for the Two-Forty-Two?" the cop asked me, using the penal code section for battery.

"I won't waste your time either. We both know that even if you did ID the guy in the bear suit, your DA's office would never file the case because it's a lightweight misdemeanor and I live out of state. Besides which, what's the worst that could happen to the suspect? Six months of unsupervised probation concurrent with whatever else he's currently serving?"

"Yeah, you were a cop all right." The officer called to her partner. "C'mon, we're Ten-Eight. No report."

As I watched the cops walk toward city hall, I noticed a young and pretty Hispanic woman leaning against one of the building's stone pillars. She was looking in our direction and I had the impression she was watching us, but the instant I made eye contact with her, she looked away. Obviously, word of the robbery had already spread through the teddy bear show and we were objects of curiosity. After a moment or two, I saw the woman pull a brochure from her rear pants pocket. She glanced at the booklet and then sauntered around the side of the structure.

Meanwhile, there was an uncomfortable silence between Lauren and me. She kept her gaze averted as she dragged the table over to its original spot, banged a small dent from one of the aluminum legs, and then retrieved the tablecloth from the ground. It was irrational, but I felt as if I'd let her down.

Finally, I said, "Look, I'm sorry if mentioning Bronsey upset you, but the police needed to know about him."

She spread the white cloth over the table and then looked up at me. "It's not your fault. I'm just so frightened and I don't know what to do."

"Understandable. You obviously need to talk to someone about this situation. Why not me?"

"Because you're an ex-cop. You might . . ."

"Tell someone? Lauren, I've already pretty much figured out that the police must be looking for your son, too. I could have suggested to the officer that she run Kyle for wants and warrants, but I didn't, did I?"

"You knew?" Lauren's eyes widened with alarm.

"Yep. So, doesn't that show you can trust me? Besides, the other thing you've got in your favor is that I'm automatically suspicious of anyone who'd hire a slimy character like Bronsey as a private investigator."

There was a long pause before Lauren said, "Have you ever heard of Lycaon Software and Entertainment?"

"The company that put out that pet shop slaughter computer game last year?" I asked sourly.

Although I don't play computer games, I knew that the Silicon Valley software behemoth, Lycaon, had made a fortune marketing evil and savagery as amusement. Their products were an obscene celebration of psychopathic behavior with heartwarming titles such as "High School AK-47 Massacre," "Arson Carson: Torching the Mall," and the aforementioned "Slay Day: Pet Shop." They were games that could be played by the entire family—the Manson family.

Lauren saw the look on my face and sputtered, "Kyle didn't have anything to do with that game. He worked in another department altogether."

"Worked, as in past tense?"

"He quit on Wednesday. He just . . . didn't fit in with the corporation's culture. Then things got nasty."

"Big surprise coming from a company like that. What happened?"

"Lycaon sent a couple of their security people to Kyle's condo. Kyle wouldn't open the door, so they kicked it open."

"Because?"

"They claimed he'd stolen company property."

"No offense intended, but did he?"

"My son is not a thief, but he could see what was about to happen, so he ran."

"What do you mean?"

Lauren took a deep breath. "Lycaon was worried that Kyle was going to work for a competitor and they wanted to muddy the proprietary waters in advance."

"Still not following."

"Kyle was one of Lycaon's top software designers. They want to keep him from making another company successful."

Suddenly, I understood, and shook my head in reluctant admiration. "So, the best way to do that is to falsely accuse him of theft. It provides a platform for them to claim that anything he develops for some future employer was ripped off from his old one. It's evil, but inspired."

"And that was just the beginning. Not only did they hire that goon to harass me, they also made a report to the police and now there's a warrant for Kyle's arrest."

"How'd you find that out?"

"Two police detectives came to my house looking for Kyle early yesterday morning."

"A criminal complaint filed and an arrest warrant issued in less than two days? That sounds like they dropped everything to work the case against your son."

Lauren glowered. "Down in the Silicon Valley, if Lycaon says jump, the local government asks, 'How high?' "

"I'm afraid politicians are like that pretty much everywhere. I'm assuming Kyle is in hiding, but that isn't a permanent solution."

"I know. He meets with an attorney on Monday morning."

"That sounds like your best option. Can I make one suggestion, though?"

"What's that?"

"The next time you see Bronsey, call the police and have him arrested. He doesn't get a free pass to terrorize you, no matter what Lycaon is alleging against your son."

She gave me a weary smile. "I will, and thanks for being so understanding."

"It's one of the prerequisites for members of the teddy bear community." I patted her arm. "Take care. I know it started badly, but I hope you have a great show."

Although I'd promised Ash I'd come right back to our table, I figured she wouldn't object to me taking a brief detour to my original destination, Penny French's booth. Her table was packed with wonderful bears, but one in particular grabbed my attention. It was a bruin dressed in a bumblebee costume, complete with stubby antennae, climbing up an artificial tree bedecked with yellow flowers. I knew Ash would love it, but the piece was almost three feet tall, and I didn't see how we'd be able to take it home on the plane. Fortunately, Penny showed me that the tableau was easily disassembled, and would fit into a large suitcase. I bought the bear and told her I'd come back for it at the end of the day. As I limped toward our table, I was pleased to have found the perfect gift—and also curious what the TSA X-ray operator would make of it when he scanned our luggage.

Two women were leaving our booth as I approached, one of them hugging a paper bag containing one of Ash's most recent creations, Rhea Red Velvet Cake, a bear made from scarlet plush fur and wearing a fabric cake-wedge costume. Meanwhile, Ash was restocking our table with fresh bears, which meant there'd been lots of customers. I was also pleased to see that she'd apparently received my earlier psychic distress signals and had removed Mc-Bear-ett from the table. Hopefully, that had happened before the Quinlans were in the neighborhood. I still had high hopes that one of Ash's bears would end up in their museum.

"That was mostly a big waste of time," I said as I lowered myself onto one of our wood-and-canvas folding chairs.

"How do you mean?"

"Lauren declined to press charges."

"Why, for heaven's sake?"

"It's your basic can of worms. Her son has been accused of stealing from his former employer and Bronsey was hired to recover the Four-Ninety-Six stuff." I used the California penal code section for Receiving Stolen Property. "Fortunately, it's none of my business."

"Thank you, God," Ash said mock-reverently as she gazed skyward.

"And thank *you* for putting Mc-Bear-ett under the table."

"I didn't. He was the very first bear we sold this morning."

"You're kidding."

"No, and you'll never guess who bought it."

"Someone with very bad eyesight?"

"No, the Quinlans. They're delightful people and Steve

Mc-Bear-ett is going to be in the Teddy Bear Museum."
Ash's eyes were bright with joy. "Honey, I'm so proud of
you."

"I don't understand. I saw them shortly after I left our
table and they didn't look insane."

"Of course they aren't. I really wish you'd realize that
you're getting to be an accomplished bear artist. Susan said
that she'd never seen anything like Mc-Bear-ett."

"That isn't necessarily a compliment. Besides, why buy
Mc-Bear-ett when they could have had one of your Confection Collection bears?"

"That's the other piece of great news." Ash was grinning from ear to ear. "They bought Becky Birthday Cake,
and she'll be in the museum, too!"

Three

Not only were two of our bears selected for the Quinlan Museum, the Plaza was packed with fur fanatics and it was our most successful sales day ever. We sold all but one of the pieces we'd brought from Ash's Confection Collection, most of her more realistic-looking big cat soft sculptures, and a cop's girlfriend even bought Jon and Ponch, a pair of plush bears I'd dressed in California Highway Patrol motorcycle officer uniforms. The day flew by and before we knew it, it was five o'clock and time to start packing up.

Although we'd been busy since morning, the adrenaline of the day kept both of us from feeling tired. This was a good thing, since we had a dinner date with my old partner Gregg Mauel and his wife, Susie. We drove to our motel in Novato, took showers, and changed clothes, and then headed south on the 101 Freeway toward Sausalito. We were distressed to see how much new development had taken place along the freeway corridor since we'd moved away and were also taken aback by how oppressively brown and parched the hills looked. Even the clusters of eucalyptus trees dotting the slopes were more of an ashy gray than green and seemed shabby compared to the emerald forests of the Blue Ridge Mountains.

Although it tends to be a little too touristy, I like Sausalito. Built on the coastal hills above the north side of the bay—which provides one of the more panoramic views of the San Francisco skyline and the Golden Gate Bridge you'll ever find—it is a tidy and fashionable small town. I particularly appreciate the architecture in the commercial district. It's an eye-pleasing mixture of styles that were popular in the decades before the soulless stucco and glass box became the norm for California business buildings.

Our destination was Scoma's of Sausalito. The popular eatery was located right on the water in a restored Victorian-era building that had once housed a ferryboat service. It had been one of our favorite restaurants when we'd lived in San Francisco, where we'd often celebrated anniversaries, birthdays, and the occasional murder conviction.

The restaurant was crowded, but we'd reserved a table by the big plate glass windows overlooking the sailboat-dotted bay. Gregg and Susie were already waiting for us when we arrived. With his kind eyes, silvery-gray hair, and customary expression of gentle amusement with the world at large, Gregg looked more like a benevolent minister from some Protestant sect than the hard-nosed homicide cop he was. And Susie looked as if she could have been Ash's cousin. Both were blond, blue-eyed, and beautiful.

We began our reunion by ordering a bottle of Napa Chandon Brut, and when the sparkling wine arrived, we clinked glasses as I offered a toast to the ladies. Then we chatted as easily as if we'd only seen the Mauels the previous weekend, instead of nearly two years ago, which is the mark of a true and abiding friendship. Naturally, it wasn't long before the topic switched to cop work.

I asked Gregg, "So, who's your partner now?"

"Danny Aafedt. It's not the same as working with you . . ."

"You're lucky to be partnered with him. Danny's a damn good detective."

"With the added benefit that I know he's never going to sing the Monty Python 'Lumberjack Song' to a murder suspect . . . unlike someone else I could name."

"It was just a subtle way of letting the macho man know that we knew he was a cross-dresser." I chuckled at the memory. "And he did cop to the murder."

"One of many. We were one hell of a team." Gregg held the glass up to salute me.

My voice suddenly thick, I said, "Will someone please change the subject before I get all soggy with nostalgia?"

Susie asked Ash, "Are you guys going to get together with Heather?"

"We're having brunch with her tomorrow. She's on duty tonight," said Ash.

"Do you ever see her?" I asked Gregg.

"Not often. She's mostly working nights, but I hear she's doing a great job. How do you feel about her transfer to dope?"

I glanced out the window at the San Francisco skyline, which was now beginning to glitter with lights. "I'm proud she was promoted to an investigative job so quickly . . ."

"But he worries." Ash took my hand. "We both worry."

"Working street narcotics enforcement in plainclothes is dangerous. Why didn't she take that assignment in the property crime unit?" I asked, momentarily forgetting our dinner companions.

"Because the apple doesn't fall very far from the tree."

"It wasn't as crazy out on the streets when I worked dope."

Ash smiled in gentle amusement. "Brad honey, you can't even look me in the eye when you say that."

"Okay, it was dangerous and I should have faith that

Heather can handle herself." Fortunately, our waiter arrived at our table before I could say: *It's just that I get a little frightened thinking of our daughter out there rubbing elbows with predators and the dregs of humanity on a nightly basis.* Once the waiter had taken our orders and departed, I topped off everyone's champagne glass and said, "Okay, time for another change of topic. You'll never guess who we ran into earlier today at the teddy bear show."

"Princess Diana. No wait, she's been dead for over ten years, so I *hope* you didn't see Princess Diana," said Gregg, oblivious to the frowning folks at the adjoining table who apparently didn't appreciate the macabre humor of homicide detectives.

"It was Merv the Perv. I didn't know he'd left the department and was working as a PI."

Susie wrinkled her nose. "Eww. I only met him once, but he made my flesh crawl."

"No kidding," grumbled Ash.

"And from what I've heard, he's a none-too-successful PI," Gregg said with a contented chuckle. "Most of his business is collecting overdue bills for those loan-until-payday places. What the heck was he doing at a teddy bear show?"

"Intimidating one of the bear artists for his client, Lycaon Software."

"The computer game company?" Gregg gave a low and admiring whistle. "I guess things are looking up for him."

"No matter how much money he makes, he's still a loser."

"But why would Lycaon hire him to harass a teddy bear artist?" Susie asked.

I briefly recounted the circumstances of the robbery and what Lauren had told me afterwards. When I finished, Greg said pensively, "I can't say I like the idea of some big company sending out their mercenaries to push people around."

"Me, either, but it's as American as deep-fried Twinkies." Then our dinners arrived and I suddenly realized how hungry I was and how much I'd been looking forward to this particular meal. It had been three years since I'd had one of my favorite foods of all time: the San Francisco version of cioppino, a hearty Italian seafood stew, served with warm and crusty bread. Now, you can get fine seafood in Virginia restaurants and sometimes you'll even find a dish optimistically listed on the menu as cioppino, but it can't hold a candle to the genuine article. So I didn't waste any time digging in, as Ash ate her linguini with lobster sauce, and Gregg and Susie split a surf-and-turf platter of behemoth proportions.

We'd finished dinner and were fighting the temptation of the dessert menu when Gregg's phone rang. He squinted at the phone's tiny screen, frowned, and answered it. It was a short conversation. Gregg tried to tell the caller that he wasn't on the call-out roster for this evening, but he was cut off in midsentence. He listened, sighed, and concluded the call by saying he'd be en route once he'd taken his wife home.

Shoving the phone in his jacket pocket he said, "As if you hadn't already figured it out, that was the dispatch center and I'm being called into work."

"But you were gone all last weekend," said Susie.

"Sorry, love, but we just had our third One-Eighty-Seven of the evening and the night is still young. They're calling out half the homicide bureau."

It felt like the time when I was a kid and got sick the day my Cub Scout pack went to see Willie Mays and the Giants at Candlestick Park. Trying not to sound too disappointed, I asked, "So, where are you going?"

"One of your all-time favorite places." Then, in a gravelly baritone, Gregg sang the first line of the theme song from a TV western that had been off the air for over forty years, *"Have gun—will travel, says the card of a man."*

"The Paladin Motel? I can't believe that pesthole is still open."

"Yeah, and it's just as charming as ever. Hey, how'd you

like to come out to the scene for a little while? I'll bet the old-timers would love to see you."

"I'd like that, but . . ." I gave Ash an imploring look.

She took my hand. "Go ahead, honey. I'll drive Susie home."

"And we'll have a girl's night. Margaritas and chick flicks," Susie added.

"You're sure? I know this wasn't what you had in mind for tonight."

Ash leaned over to give me a slow kiss. "Yes, I'm sure. Go play with your friends. What I had in mind for tonight can wait until you get back."

My cheeks must have turned beet red, because Susie started giggling. Gregg corralled the waiter, asked for the bill, and threatened to beat me with my own cane if I so much as even thought about paying for dinner. A few minutes later, we kissed our wives good-bye and climbed into Gregg's unmarked cop car, a blue Chevrolet Impala.

He fired the engine up and then tossed me the car's radio microphone. "Put us in service and let's see if anyone recognizes your voice."

"The same call sign?"

"The same."

It was stupid, but I had to swallow hard before I could key the microphone and say, "Two-Henry-Sixteen is Ten-Eight en route to the Paladin Motel."

There were a few moments of dead air and then the scanner picked up a transmission from one of the ancillary police radio frequencies that cops use to talk car-to-car. An older male voice said, "Yo, Lyon, when you get done there, you can finish the shift with me. I'll put my rookie in the backseat so he can watch how two real cops work."

I don't regret my new life as a journeyman teddy bear artist, but it felt as if I'd come home.

It was dark now, and as we crossed the Golden Gate Bridge, I could see the lights of a big ship heading out into the Pacific. We passed the Presidio and wove through the parklands of the Golden Gate Recreational Area and then the road transitioned into Lombard Street.

When the travel magazines mention San Francisco's "old world" charm, you can take it to the bank that they're not talking about this portion of Lombard Street. Admittedly, the famous flower-bedecked and serpentine section of the road that ran down Russian Hill is pretty, but farther west it's your typical busy American commercial thoroughfare lined with neon-lit businesses, motels, and restaurants. It's also where Lombard Street merges with Highway 101, so the traffic is often bumper-to-bumper in both directions. Tonight the eastbound traffic was in absolute gridlock.

"Road's probably blocked with emergency vehicles at the Paladin," said Gregg as he flipped on the flashing red-and-blue emergency lights at the top of the Impala's windshield.

"I've turned into a coward in my old age. Please don't drive on the sidewalk."

"But there's less traffic there."

Gregg carefully rolled the vehicle's right side tires up onto the curb so that he could pass the stopped cars. A few turns later, we pulled up approximately thirty yards from the front of the Paladin Motel. We couldn't get any closer because a solid wall of emergency service vehicles blocked the roadway. There were fire trucks, a paramedic rig, police cars, and motorcycles, as well as a vehicle I always hated to see at a crime scene—the big, dark blue Freightliner van that bore the gold-lettered legend SFPD EXPLOSIVE ORDNANCE DISPOSAL UNIT.

I radioed dispatch to let them know we'd arrived and then joined Gregg on the sidewalk, which was crowded with tipsy bystanders eager to spice up their weekend festivities with a little secondhand tragedy. On the other side of the street, the driver of a news van from one of the local TV stations did a perfect job of parallel parking next to a fire hydrant. Meanwhile, some of the drivers stalled in the eastbound traffic began to honk their horns, while others cranked up the volume on their CD players so that there were five or six different varieties of music—heavy metal, golden oldies, reggae, hip-hop, and even the theme song to *Raiders of the Lost Ark*—all simultaneously blowing my eardrums out. It was a typical late-summer Saturday night in San Francisco.

Gregg pointed at the bomb squad vehicle. "Man, I hope we don't have a victim who's been turned into a jigsaw puzzle."

"Especially after you had that big chunk of rare and juicy New York steak."

"Like I needed to be reminded of that." He switched his gold seven-pointed badge from his belt to his sports jacket pocket and handed me his department ID card. "Clip that on, just in case we run into some rookie who doesn't know you."

We pushed our way through the crowd and headed toward the motel with its flickering pink neon sign featuring a knight chess piece. As we neared the yellow crime scene tape barrier, I noticed a tall young woman with metallic blue spiked hair, silver inverted pentacle earrings, and an ankle-length leather coat. It wasn't her appearance that attracted my attention. It's Halloween every night in San Francisco. The reason was that she seemed to be eyeballing me. That was very odd, because let's face facts: The only time I draw stares from strange women these days is when I'm knocked on my butt by a berserk teddy bear. Then again, I might have been mistaken about the young woman's interest. Her blue wraparound sunglasses made it hard to tell precisely what she was looking at.

A second later, the penny dropped and I stopped so fast I had to use my cane to maintain my balance. I think I can be forgiven for not immediately recognizing my daughter, considering she looked like an extra from some post-apocalyptic sci-fi film.

Pointing an accusing finger at her, I said with mock severity, "Young lady, I thought we both understood that you were grounded."

Heather's face broke into a huge grin. "Daddy!"

She rushed into my arms and as I hugged her I was glad to feel that she was wearing a ballistic vest. I said, "Heather, honey, I'm so proud of you, but your mother is going to have a freaking coronary when she sees how you look."

"She already knows. We were worried about *you*. Where is Mama?"

"Staying with Susie while I take a limp down memory lane." I released her from the hug but held on to her hand. "So, what are you doing here?"

"We were working a buy-bust operation a couple blocks up when we heard the gunfire. My partner and I ran over, but by the time we got here, everyone except the WMA vic was GOA," she replied, using the cop acronyms for White Male Adult and Gone On Arrival.

It was both strange and profoundly satisfying to hear the little girl I'd dressed in pink bunny pajamas talking like the street cop she was.

Gregg asked, "Just so we're clear on this, our victim was shot, right?"

It was another very gratifying moment. Although Heather had known "Uncle Gregg" most of her life, she automatically slipped into report mode, saying, "The victim was shot once in the back and sustained an apparent coup de grace to the head. He was dead when we got to the room. There's an auto-pistol on the floor next to him."

"So, why is the bomb squad here?"

Heather shrugged. "I don't know for sure. Someone said that one of the responding uniforms found a possible IED in the motel parking lot."

As anyone who follows the news from the Middle East knows, an IED is an Improvised Explosive Device.

"Recognize the victim?" Gregg shouted to be heard over the warning beeps sounding from a fire truck that was backing up.

"He's laying facedown, so I didn't get a look at him."

"Any street buzz as to what happened?"

"No, sir, but if we hear anything I'll include it in our report."

"Call me first. Oh, and Detective Lyon . . . good job."

As Gregg and Heather conversed, I spotted a tall muscular guy with a shaved skull, a grizzly Karl Marx beard, and kitted out in the outlaw biker's standard uniform of denim and leather. He was patiently waiting to be noticed. I nodded in his direction and Heather gave me a shy smile before waving him over.

Oh-oh, I thought, hoping I'd imagined the sudden warm luster in my daughter's eyes.

"Daddy, I want you to meet my partner, Detective Colin Sinclair."

He stepped forward, and as we shook hands, he gravely said, "It's a great honor to meet you, sir. You're a department legend."

"I think you could probably find some brass who'd disagree with that assessment, but thanks."

Gregg said, "Sorry to interrupt, but it looks like the bomb squad is about to clear the scene. We need to touch base with the lieutenant and get to work."

As I gave Heather a farewell hug, she whispered, "I'll see you tomorrow. If it's all right, I'd like to bring Colin to brunch tomorrow."

"Does your mom know about . . . ?"

She realized I knew. "No, not yet."

I looked at those same bright blue eyes that had peered up at me from the baby crib and I suddenly realized that I was about to lose my daughter to another man. I nodded and told her not to worry and that we'd see them both tomorrow. As Heather and Colin moved back into the crowd,

I found myself wondering how I was going to break the news to Ash and whether the fact that we were going to be in a chichi restaurant would prevent her from continuing an old Remmelkemp Family tradition. The first time I'd met Ash's mother, Irene, she'd waited until we were alone, pointed to a butcher knife, and then threatened to skin me alive if I ever hurt her daughter. I took Irene at her word and knew that if Ash passed a similar message along to Colin, he'd believe it, too.

Four

Gregg and I headed toward a cluster of detectives and uniformed cops who were using a bus stop kiosk as an impromptu command post. I didn't recognize as many people as I thought I would; however, I knew Gregg's boss, Lieutenant Bobbie Jo Garza. I'd been her first training officer when she'd graduated from the police academy back in 1987. Looking up from her iPhone, she saw me approaching and smiled.

Garza said, "Coming out to check on me?"

"No need to. My rookies all either mastered the job or quit and I never had any doubts about how you'd do. How are you, Bobbie?" I shook her hand.

"Great, but a little busy trying to make some sense out of this chaos."

"Then I'll stay out of your way. I hope there isn't any problem with me tagging along out here with Gregg."

"None whatsoever. It's wonderful to see you." Her portable radio squawked her call sign as a cop trotted up to tell Garza that the medical examiner had arrived. She gave me an apologetic look that said we'd talk later.

Meanwhile, Danny Aafedt had arrived and was exchanging information with Gregg. Although he had a Norwegian name, Aafedt wasn't your archetypal blond Scandinavian. He had black hair, a dark full moustache, and a perpetual five o'clock shadow. We exchanged waves of greeting, but I didn't move closer to join the conversation, knowing that I was only there as an observer. Suddenly, I felt as out of place as . . . well . . . a handicapped teddy bear artist at a homicide investigation. I wondered if I'd made a huge mistake by coming.

I looked toward the Paladin, which was a classic early 1960s small motel: single-storied and flat-roofed, L-shaped, with pale green stucco walls. The soda machine looked to be as old as the structure and I wondered if it contained bottles of Royal Crown Cola for a dime. My guess was that the only modifications made to the building since it was built were the wrought-iron security bars on the windows.

There were a few vehicles in the small parking lot and I saw a figure in a bulky bomb-protection suit kneeling beside an older midsized sedan that could have been any color from gray to salmon under the saffron glare of the overhead sodium lights. Then the bomb tech stood up, pulled his padded helmet off, and trudged toward the command post. Everyone gathered around to listen as the gray-haired Emergency Ordnance Disposal Unit sergeant made his report to Lieutenant Garza.

Tossing the heavy helmet onto the bus bench, the bomb guy said, "The scene is safe. It's not a bomb, but whoever found it made the right decision to call us."

"Why?" asked Garza

"The FBI has been worried about terrorists disguising bombs as toys, and what we've got here is a big teddy bear packed with electronic equipment and circuitry, hooked up to some sort of battery I've never seen before."

"They called out the bomb squad for a Teddy Ruxpin?" someone on the periphery of the group said with a scornful laugh.

He was referring to a primitive robotic teddy bear with a built-in audiocassette tape player that had been briefly yet insanely popular back in the mid-1980s, and which had recently made a tepid comeback.

"That isn't a Teddy Ruxpin and here's a news flash, smart guy: A bomb isn't black and round with a hissing fuse. But hey, if you're set on having a closed-coffin funeral, feel free to assume that things like that are safe to handle." The EOD sergeant grabbed his helmet and then addressed Garza. "We're gonna head back to headquarters and you'll have my report by Monday."

Once the bomb squad man was gone, Garza said, "Okay, everyone, before we go in, gather round and I'll tell you what we know. At twenty-twenty-two hours, dispatch received the first of several nine-one-one calls reporting multiple shots fired at the motel. Patrol and vice units arrived on-scene and found our victim in Room Four. He's an unidentified WMA and, big shock, there's a gun on the floor next to him. Considering this is the Paladin, we all know what that might mean."

"A dope rip," said Aafedt. "Any suspect description?"

Garza shook her head. "Again, since this is the Paladin, the other room occupants naturally didn't see or hear anything. The only bit of information we have, and even that's iffy, is of a dark-colored sedan fleeing the scene southbound on Pierce Street."

"Hey, I know," said Gregg. "Let's put that info into one of those cool computers like they have on *CSI: Miami*. I'll bet it'll tell us the license plate, make, model, the suspect's name, his mom's address, and even when he last changed the car's oil."

Everyone chuckled bitterly. The only reason real cops watch supposedly authentic TV shows such as *CSI: Miami* is to poke merciless fun at them for their largely bogus portrayals of forensic technology. The programs take place in a magical land where DNA test results are available in minutes instead of the customary weeks; where there are machines that not only analyze and identify chemical compounds but can also tell you amazingly arcane things such as where a certain rare tree can be found; and where the investigators carry every imaginable piece of ultramodern crime fighting gear, except handcuffs. Real life is very different.

Garza gave out job assignments next. Gregg and Aafedt were named case agents and the techs were assigned specific functions. The medical examiner arrived and I got ready to cool my heels while everyone went to work.

Gregg cleared his throat. "LT, I wonder if Brad could come in with us."

"I'm sorry, but I don't see how. The defense could claim we compromised the integrity of the crime scene by letting a sightseer in."

Although I knew that Garza hadn't intended it as an insult, it stung that she'd called me a sightseer—even if it was essentially true. Suddenly I wanted to go beyond that yellow crime scene tape more than almost anything in the world. My mind racing, I said, "But you wouldn't be compromising the scene if you let an expert in."

Garza looked doubtful. "An expert in what?"

"Teddy bears. You've got a teddy bear that might be connected to the crime and I'm the closest thing you've got to an expert on stuffed animals. I make them for a living now and know an awful lot about the major manufacturers and artists. Hell, I'm even kind of a teddy bear history buff."

"I don't know . . ."

"And as part of my duties as a civilian investigative consultant for the Massanutten County Sheriff's Office, I worked a couple of major felony cases that—believe it or not—involved the theft of teddy bears." I hoped my voice didn't betray how close I was to shameless begging.

"A teddy bear expert," Garza said musingly and then grinned. "I love it. Have Inspector Lyon sign the entry log, get him some gloves, and let's get to work."

Even though my shin was beginning to ache a little, I felt like dancing a victory jig. A moment later, we passed beneath the yellow plastic tape and approached the motel. We paused as one of the crime scene photographers took some orientation photos of the exterior of the building. Then, accompanied by an evidence tech, I went over to check out the teddy bear next to the car while the rest of the investigators went to Room Four.

The sedan was a mid-eighties Chevrolet Celebrity with expired California plates. As it turned out, the car was actually beige, which just goes to show how sodium lights can alter a witness's perception of colors. The tech took some overview pictures of the car and then of the teddy bear, which was lying on the pavement halfway beneath the Celebrity and near the right rear tire. Once he finished, I borrowed the tech's flashlight and slowly knelt down on the still-warm asphalt to take a better look. The EOD sergeant was correct. This was no Teddy Ruxpin.

The toy bear lay facedown, and I could see why the bomb squad had been called. There was a hinged door on the bear's back and it was open, revealing a mass of the sort of electronic circuitry and wiring you'd expect to find inside a computer. The hardware wouldn't have looked so menacing if it hadn't been for the tiny red LED light on a circuit board. It was flashing on and off rhythmically as if signaling some sort of countdown. This was a visual clue you'd have to be felony stupid to ignore, since the toy was large enough to contain several sticks of dynamite.

The bear was about twenty-four inches tall and made from ivory-colored plush fur tipped with a hint of silver. It also seemed to have an awfully inflexible posture. This suggested a substantial framework beneath the fur. Another peculiar thing caught my eye. Ordinarily, a teddy bear's footpads are made of fabric or leather, but this bear's feet were oblong-shaped, with what looked like hard brown plastic soles, which had inset horizontal treads.

I was puzzled. The only reason you'd build a bear with strong sturdy legs and soles designed for traction was if you expected it to be able to walk. I was aware that robotic teddy bears were in use as experimental patient monitors at some hospitals, but so far as I knew, they weren't ambulatory. If this thing could actually walk, it belonged to the next generation of interactive toys and was worth a potential fortune. Which naturally led me to the question, what the hell was it doing here?

I had the tech take some close-up photos of the bear and then I picked it up. It was a lot heavier than I'd expected. I scrutinized the hardware for any sign of the manufacturer, but came up empty. Then I turned the bear around to examine its face. I couldn't be absolutely certain, but I didn't think the facial design was similar to any of the mechanized bears I'd seen pictured in a recent magazine article. This bear's visage was evocative of Knut, the famous polar bear cub from the Berlin Zoo who had stolen the world's heart back in 2006. The toy bear had friendly blue eyes and a hinged open-mouth apparatus.

"He's got power, so I wonder how you turn him on?" I asked meditatively.

Without warning, the bear's eyes lit up and it cheerfully replied in a young man's voice, "Hi, my name is Patrick Polar Bear and I'm your friend."

"Whoa. That look is so real, it's downright spooky," said the tech.

"Yeah, and the power source must be voice-activated by certain words."

It was irrational, but I had the uncanny feeling the bear was looking at me. It said, "What's *your* name?"

"Um, Brad."

"Hi Brad! Do you want to sing a song?"

"How about 'Driving That Train' by the Grateful Dead?"

"I'm sorry, I don't know that song. Would you like to teach it to me?"

It would have been interesting to see just how interactive the bear was, but this wasn't the time or place for experiments. Uncertain of how to deactivate the toy, I decided to inquire of the one source that might know. "Patrick, how do I turn you off?"

"Just say 'good night' and we can play when I wake up." I knew it was merely a product of its programming, but the bear genuinely sounded sad.

"Good night, Patrick."

"Good night, Brad. I'll see you in my dreams," said the bear as the light slowly died in its eyes.

I handed the bear to the evidence tech. "You need to bag this. It's definitely evidence."

"How can you tell?"

"For starters, this thing was dropped and abandoned, which doesn't make any sense. This bear is probably worth at least several grand."

"You're kidding."

"Nope. It's a cutting-edge robot."

"So, how'd it end up here?"

I glanced in the direction of the motel room where the body was. "I don't know, but we have to assume that the bear is somehow connected with the homicide."

"So, this is a *grizzly* murder," the tech deadpanned.

"Hey, you're stealing my material." I picked up the flashlight. "Secure Patrick in the evidence van while I check to make sure that nothing broke off the bear when it hit the pavement."

The secret to conducting a successful crime scene search is to take your time and avoid preconceived notions about what might be important. Think of a homicide in terms of a crossword puzzle. The clues are often obscure and misleading. Although I couldn't locate any debris from the bear, there was no mistaking the importance of what I soon found: a smear of fresh blood and some dark blue-colored fiber transfers on the asphalt, about five feet away from where the bear had fallen. It wasn't difficult to reconstruct what had happened. Whoever had run away had tripped, fallen, and skinned some clothed part of their body on the pavement. When the evidence tech returned, I showed him the blood stain, which he photographed, measured for the crime scene diagram, and then collected.

Using my cane as a brace, I stood up and looked at the license plate of the car. "Did you run this yet?"

"I'm about to do it now," said the tech.

I shined the flashlight's beam into the Chevy. There was a crumpled fast-food bag and empty soda cup with a protruding straw on the passenger-side floorboard and an improperly folded road map of the Bay Area on the front seat. Shifting the light to the backseat, I found something else that unquestionably qualified as evidence. It was the furry brown bear head and the rest of the costume worn by the guy who'd leveled me at the teddy bear show earlier this morning.

Glancing toward the motel room where the dead man lay, I suddenly had a bad feeling that maybe Merv Bronsey and his costumed partner had found Kyle Vandenbosch.

Five

I scanned the car's interior again, looking for Lauren's cashbox, but didn't see it. However, that didn't mean anything. It might have been under the wadded-up costume or in the trunk or, more likely, the suspect had gotten rid of it after taking the money. Meanwhile, I was trying to figure out the connection between the costume and the mechanized bear.

One possibility was that the crook had stolen the robot from one of the exhibitors at the bear show. However, I had to toss that theory out almost immediately. Ash and I kept up with the teddy bear community news and there wasn't even a whisper of an artist unveiling a mechanized bear at the Sonoma show. But even if such an amazing bear had been on display in the Plaza, it meant that the guy in the costume had somehow stolen it without anyone noticing—which I couldn't believe—and then elected to run the risk of discovery and capture by also robbing Lauren of some small amount of cash. Crooks don't behave that way. They make fast tracks after stealing something.

Furthermore, if Bronsey really did have Lycaon as a client, he'd want to make them repeat customers. That meant impressing them with a clean operation and quick results. Merv's mission was to terrorize Lauren so that she'd rat out her son, so it didn't make sense that he'd risk the success of the operation by allowing his furry accomplice to steal from someone else at the show.

The evidence tech said, "The vehicle comes back no wants and registered to a Darryl Wu out of San Leandro, with a release of liability."

"So, we still don't know who owns it, because whoever bought this car from Mr. Wu never took it to the DMV to reregister it."

"Do you think the Chevy is connected to the murder?"

"There's a good chance. You see that?" I pointed to the wadded-up costume. "Believe it or not, a suspect wore that thing to commit a robbery in Sonoma this morning."

"And then it shows up outside a motel room where a One-Eighty-Seven went down? The violence is escalating, so the guy must be—"

"*Furry-ous.* And if you try to work *fur-ensic* in, he won't be the only one demonstrating a proclivity for violence."

The tech smiled placidly. "I'll get some photos."

"Of all the cars in the lot."

"Yes, sir."

Speculating that shots might have also been fired outside the room, I checked the front of the Chevy for bullet holes, but couldn't find any. Glancing to my left, I saw the door to Room Seven opened a crack and the silhouette of someone's head peeking around the edge of the door.

Then a woman half-whispered, "Detective Lyon, is that you?"

"In the flesh. Who's there?"

"It's Kimberly." She poked her head out a little. "You remember me, don't you?"

In Victorian-era parlance, Kimberly Fleming was a

"soiled dove." However, being a hooker didn't make her a bad person. Indeed, one of the things I'd always liked about most prostitutes was that they were usually bluntly honest about the fact that they sold themselves to strangers, unlike so-called respectable people, such as politicians. In contrast to most of the other cops she'd met, I'd treated her as a lady and she'd proved a valuable street informant. Once upon a time Kim had been a pretty girl. But the combination of meth, poor nutrition, and the nightly anxiety of wondering if her next customer was going to be Norman Bates had quickly taken its toll.

"Of course, I remember you, Ms. Fleming." Realizing that she wasn't going to leave the room, I walked over to her. "How are you tonight?"

"Okay, I guess. I saw you through the window and couldn't decide if it was you or not."

"Understandable. I look a lot older than I did."

"And the cane. I heard you got shot."

"That's true, but I'm back now." I decided I wouldn't complicate matters by adding that I wasn't a homicide inspector anymore. "Would you feel safer if I came in there to talk?"

She glanced at one of the uniformed cops standing near the crime scene tape. "Yes, please."

Kim held the door open for me. The shabby motel room smelled of marijuana, Mexican food, and a cinnamon-based perfume so strong I could almost taste it. Once we were in better light, I could see that she'd aged even more than I had in the past few years. Her features were haggard and her eyes as dull as a John Tesh album.

Pushing the door shut, I asked, "Has anyone talked to you?"

"No, sir. I mean, the cops knocked on my door . . ."

"And you didn't answer because you have an arrest warrant for prostitution, right?"

She nodded glumly.

"Don't worry about that. I'm just interested in knowing what happened tonight. Where were you when the shooting started?"

"Here."

"That must have been scary."

"Tell me about it. We're talking and suddenly—*boom, boom, boom*—it's like a war movie. I hid in the bathtub."

"So, you were with a customer?"

"Yeah. We were still discussing price."

"And I imagine he bailed when the gunfire stopped."

"Him and half the other people in the motel." Kim shook her head in disbelief. "Man, I never thought she actually meant it."

"She?" I tried to keep my voice casual.

"Some chick. I think she was the wife of the guy in the room."

"Do me a favor, Ms. Fleming. Back up and start at the beginning."

"I was on the stroll out on the sidewalk." She pointed toward Lombard Street. "On the stroll" was a euphemism for standing by a roadway to solicit johns.

"And how long was that before the shooting began?"

"I don't know. Maybe ten minutes. It wasn't a long time."

"Did you see where the woman came from?"

"No. In fact, I didn't even notice her until she started banging the hell out of the door."

"What did she look like?"

"White, I think. She sounded white. Nice figure, from what I could see." Kim thought for a second. "Kind of long dark hair, jeans, and maybe a brown jacket."

"Young? Old?"

"Youngish. Maybe in her twenties. I didn't want to get that close, Mr. Lyon. She was really pissed off and crying—not that I blame her. There's too many married guys out here screwing around when they should be home."

I nodded in sad agreement. "Could you identify this woman if you saw her again?"

"I don't think so."

"What happened next?"

"Like I said, she was banging on the door and yelling about how she knew he was in there, and that she couldn't believe how he'd betrayed her," Kim said.

"Did she ever mention the guy's name?"

"Not that I remember."

"And the guy never answered the door?"

"No. I felt so bad for her."

"Did she say anything else?"

"Oh, yeah. Right before she took off, she shouted that he was going pay for what he'd done to her. Pay with blood. She was screaming that at the top of her lungs." Kim looked away from me and I suspected she was suddenly sorry she'd implicated the other woman.

"Which way did she go when she left?"

She pointed eastward. "She walked away."

"Did you see if she had a car?"

"No."

"Did you ever see or hear the woman again?"

"No."

Kim's answers were becoming monosyllabic and I knew she was anxious to end the interview. She was on the clock, and also frightened that her pimp would find out she'd been talking to a cop. Unfortunately for her, I wanted some more answers. I asked, "Was anyone arguing or shouting right before the shooting began?"

Kim shook her head.

"Look, I know you want to wrap this up, but I have just a few more questions and I want you to think very carefully about this next one. You said she was pounding on the door. Did she do anything else, like try to push it open?"

Her eyes became slightly unfocused as she recalled the

scene. "Yeah. Yeah, there was a point when she had both hands pressed against the door while she was crying."

"Like this?" I held both my hands up, palms outward and fingers spread.

"Uh-huh."

"And was that car we were looking at already parked there when the woman was pounding on the door?"

She went over to the window and pulled the curtains aside to take another look at the Chevrolet. "No. It must have pulled in after I came inside."

"Any idea whose car it is?"

"No, sir."

"I promise this is the last question. I'm assuming you know Mervin Bronsey, who used to work the vice squad. Have you seen him around here tonight?"

Kim's eye's widened with alarm. "No, thank God He's a sicko."

"Yeah, I got that memo a while ago. Thank you, Ms. Fleming. You've been very helpful and I just wonder if you could you do me one more favor?"

"What's that?" she asked with a slightly resentful sigh.

"If you can't get out of this line of work . . ." I gestured toward the unmade bed, "promise me that you'll be very careful. I'd hate to see something bad happen to you."

Sometimes an unexpected word of compassion can be as surprising and painful as a sudden slap to the face. Kim looked as if she was going to cry. "See you around, Detective Lyon."

"I hope so. You take care, Kim." I gently shut the door behind me.

The tech did a double take when he saw me come from the motel room. "So, that's where you went. One minute you were here and the next, I turn around and you're gone."

"One of my old informants wanted to talk to me. Did

you find anything in any of the other cars that's worth following up on?"

"Nothing."

"Then keep an eye on that Chevy while I get down to Room Four. I've got some important information for the detectives."

A few moments later, I stood outside the murder scene and noted that there were no signs of forced entry on the door or its frame. Inside, a man was lying faceup in a small pool of blood on the stained industrial carpeting, which meant the medical examiner must have turned the victim over. I didn't recognize the dead guy, whose peroxide blond hair looked as if it had been styled with a weed-whacker. He wore a baggy pair of arctic camouflage military fatigue pants and a black T-shirt that bore the charming message: *I MAY NOT BE MISTER RIGHT, BUT I'LL SCREW YOU UNTIL HE GETS HERE.*

Whoever had rented the grim little room was traveling light. There was nothing in the tiny closet, and the only toiletries visible on the bathroom sink were a toothbrush and a travel-sized tube of Colgate toothpaste. A glance at the unmade bed, strewn with prepackaged food, told me the room's occupant must have been having dinner when things went south. There was a half-full plastic container of sushi on the nightstand along with an open bottle of that rascal of the vineyard, Boone's Farm Blackberry Ridge wine.

Next, I quickly scanned the room and counted the bullet holes. There were three in the far wall, two in the wall where the door was located, one in the ceiling, and another two in the victim. That made eight, which was a lot of ammo expended in a room that wasn't much bigger than a walk-in closet.

Gregg, Aafedt, and Garza were huddled in quiet conversation as the ME completed his preliminary inspection of the corpse.

I waved to signal I had news and the three cops came out. I asked, "Have any witnesses said anything about a woman having a screaming fit outside this door about ten minutes before the One-Eighty-Seven went down?"

"First we've heard about that," said Gregg.

I recounted how I'd met Kim and quickly outlined what she'd told me.

When I finished, Aafedt said, "I'll get a tech started on processing the door. With any luck we'll get both latent prints and biological evidence from the tears."

As Aafedt left, Garza glanced back at the corpse. "She said she was going to make him 'pay in blood'? That's a pretty definite statement of intent. So is our victim a philandering husband?"

"I'm assuming you still haven't IDed him yet," I said.

Gregg shook his head. "No. He didn't have a wallet and nobody recognized him, so it looks like we're going to have to submit his fingerprints for analysis."

"Which could take hours. I'm suddenly concerned our victim might be the son of a teddy bear artist that Ash and I know," I said.

Garza gave me a sharp look. "Why would you think that?"

I pointed toward the Chevy. "There's a bear costume inside that car. It's the same one a guy wore during a Two-Eleven I witnessed at a teddy bear show in Sonoma earlier today."

Garza watched my face and waited for the punch line, but when it didn't come, she said, "A robber dressed as Winnie the Pooh. You're kidding."

"Nope, and I've got a bruise on my butt to prove it happened—not that I think you want to see it. The suspect flat ran over me."

"But how does this relate to our murder?"

"I believe the thug in the costume was connected with Merv the Perv Bronsey, who was also there."

Garza reacted as if she'd just caught a faint whiff of raw sewage. "I couldn't believe the state gave Bronsey a PI license."

"And apparently, now Merv has a client with very deep pockets. Lycaon Software." I went on to describe the robbery, how Bronsey had threatened Lauren Vandenbosch, and the tale she told afterwards.

"And you think our vic might be Kyle Vandenbosch?" asked Gregg.

"I hope not, but maybe Kyle wasn't telling his mom the truth about how he left his job. What if he actually stole that robotic bear from Lycaon?"

Six

"It's an interesting theory, but aren't you jumping to some major conclusions?" said Garza. "For starters, how do you know that Lycaon even made that thing?"

"I don't. But Lycaon—a Silicon Valley powerhouse—hired Bronsey to recover *something*, and that teddy bear robot represents cutting-edge computer technology. It can talk and looks like it's designed to walk," I said.

"It talks?" Garza lifted an eyebrow.

"Whether it's clever programming or genuine artificial intelligence, Patrick talks."

"Patrick?" Gregg gave me a quizzical look.

"Patrick the Polar Bear. He told me his name."

"O . . . kaaay," said Garza, who was obviously a little creeped out that I'd been chatting with a teddy bear.

"But why would Bronsey or whoever it was kill this Kyle to recover the bear?" Gregg sounded doubtful.

"Toys are a multibillion-dollar industry. What if Lycaon developed a teddy bear that could walk and talk? What if it could actually play with a child and maybe also double as an electronic watchdog? You think it might be worth a few shekels?" I asked.

Gregg's eyes widened. "It could be Tickle Me Elmo squared."

"Give that man a cigar."

"Let's get a photo of Kyle Vandenbosch to compare against our dead guy." Gregg turned to an evidence tech. "Get on the computer in your van and print me a copy of his driver's license photo."

As the tech left, Garza said, "In the meantime, we found car keys on the victim. We might as well find out if they go with the Chevy."

Gregg took a small manila evidence envelope from his pocket and removed a key ring. He unlocked the car with the first key he tried.

"So, the car is definitely connected to our dead guy," said Garza.

"I think we'd better run this guy Vandenbosch for warrants," said Gregg. He spoke into the radio and a moment later emitted a low whistle.

"Ten-Thirty-Seven-Frank?" I asked, using the radio code for a felony arrest warrant.

"Yep," replied Gregg. "Santa Clara SO has charged him with multiple counts of grand theft, computer fraud, and felony vandalism. His bail is one million dollars."

"Man, that seems like a pretty high bail for nothing more than hibernating," I said, keeping a poker face.

"What are you talking about?" asked Garza.

"If Patrick belongs to Lycaon, the only thing Kyle's really done is . . . *bear-napping*."

"Drop the pun or I'll shoot," said Gregg.

"Both of you are brain-damaged." Garza reached up to massage her left shoulder. "So, how did the robo-bear end up out in the parking lot?"

I was about to apologize for *bruin-ing* Garza's night, but

decided against it. Instead, I said, "Because whoever ran from Room Four dropped the bear when they tripped and fell. I found a small amount of blood and blue fibers on the pavement near the Chevy. Your tech collected the evidence."

"But why didn't the shooter pick up the bear afterwards?" Garza asked.

"He or she may not have even seen that it was dropped. You know what it's like when you're in a firefight. You develop tunnel vision."

"Yeah, and they were probably running for their life, and in a hurry to get the hell out of here," said Garza.

A man called out "Inspector Mauel!" and I turned and saw my daughter Heather and her partner Colin Sinclair striding toward us across the motel parking lot. It was obvious they had news.

Gregg asked, "What's up?"

"We got some pretty interesting info at the liquor store down the block." Colin pointed eastward.

"The Jolly Jug. They've been Two-Elevened twice in the past four months," said Gregg.

"Yeah, and the owner just installed a security TV camera that covers the parking lot. That's how the clerk could see there was an occupied car backed into a parking space near the rear of the lot."

Heather took up the narrative. "The clerk thought they were scoping the store out in advance of robbing it. Then he heard gunfire coming from this direction."

"A few seconds after that, someone ran up to the car and got into the front passenger seat. Then it took off like a bat out of hell." Colin pulled out his notebook. "The vehicle is an oh-seven Dodge Avenger with Cal plates of seven-ocean-charles-ocean-zero-two-six."

"The clerk saw all that over a tiny TV monitor?" Gregg didn't try to hide his skepticism. Like me, he knew that witnesses were often notoriously inaccurate.

Colin grinned. "No, *we* did. The camera is hooked to a digital recorder and we replayed it. One of the store's overhead lights lit up the front plate enough to read it. The Avenger is registered to a Burgess Fleet Leasing out of San Jose."

"Which probably means they lease cars to companies all over the Bay Area," said Gregg. "Any chance we can make an ID on the person in the video?"

"I'm no expert, but I don't think so," said Heather. "It's shot from a funny angle and takes place so fast that you can't even really tell whether it's a man or a woman. It's just someone in dark clothes."

"Did you notice anything else from the video?"

"We think the vehicle is black in color. But it's a black-and-white video, so it just shows up as dark," Colin replied.

Heather added, "The clerk got a quick look at it out the window and he was pretty certain it was black."

"But he didn't get a look at the occupants?" asked Gregg.

"No, the only thing we can tell is there were a minimum of two people in the vehicle," said Colin.

"The clerk said the Avenger took off eastbound on Lombard Street—not that that means anything as far as where they were going. With this traffic, it would have been all but impossible to make a left turn out of the lot," said Heather.

Gregg glanced at the gridlocked highway and nodded slightly. "So, this probably isn't the dark-colored sedan that someone reported fleeing southbound on Pierce."

"We need that digital recording," said Garza.

"We already seized the recording machine and monitor and gave it to one of the techs." Colin pointed toward one of the white CSI vans outside the crime scene tape barrier.

"Good work," said Gregg.

"Thanks. We'll get back to our witness canvass," said Heather, giving me a look that said she'd see Ash and me tomorrow.

As the vice cops departed, the evidence tech returned

from the van and handed Gregg a sheet of white paper. "Here's Vandenbosch's DL photo."

Gregg held the sheet so that Garza and I could look at it, too. It was obvious to all of us that the man pictured in the photo looked nothing like the murder victim. Still, we'd double-check to make sure we were right. The ME was packing up as we came back into Room Four. Gregg held the photograph, close to the dead man's face and the ME agreed with us. The victim wasn't Kyle Vandenbosch.

"Any preliminary findings?" Gregg asked the ME.

The ME pushed his glasses up. "I think there's a strong possibility he was shot with two different guns. Neither of the projectiles that hit him was through-and-through, so we'll know for certain after the postmortem."

"I thought the entry wound in the head looked smaller than the one in his back. Which one was the primary killing wound?"

"If you're asking me to speculate," the ME said in a voice that suggested he didn't like the idea of being rushed to any sort of judgment, "it was the head shot. I don't think the round he took to the back hit anything that would have killed him immediately. And the gun was fired at fairly close proximity to the victim. There are powder burns in the T-shirt fabric."

"Any guess as to the caliber of the round used for the coup de grace?"

"Unofficially, a twenty-two."

"The gun preferred by professional assassins," I said, without thinking. "It isn't very noisy, the bullet bounces around inside the head, and often the projectile is so damaged and splintered that you can't match it to a gun."

The ME gave me a quizzical look. "I'm sorry, but do I know you?"

"Brad Lyon. I'm the department's teddy bear expert."

"Oh, the suspected bomb. Teddy bears . . . that's an interesting field of specialization." The ME made *interesting* sound exactly like *pathetic*. He gave me a feeble, chilly smile and turned to Gregg. "The post is tomorrow morning. I'll call you when I know the time."

Once the ME was gone, Garza said, "Since this isn't Kyle Vandenbosch, we need a different theory as to what happened here."

"Not necessarily. That bear costume is pretty strong evidence linking the robbery in Sonoma with our murder." Hooking a thumb at the victim, I said, "The costume was in his car, so there's a good chance he could've been the one wearing it at the teddy bear show."

"Even it that's true, that doesn't mean Bronsey was here," Garza reminded.

"Or Vandenbosch," I admitted. "Still, I think it would be a good idea to talk to Vandenbosch's mother, tonight."

"You think she was lying earlier when she told Bronsey that she didn't know where Kyle was?" Gregg asked.

"There's no way of telling. But I think it's safe to assume that if Kyle *was* here, he would have called his mom to warn her that a gunfight had just gone down in his room and . . ." A sudden and ugly thought occurred to me and I slapped my forehead. "Oh, Lord, I am so stupid for not thinking of this sooner."

"What?"

"What if our shooter went to Lauren's house?"

Gregg snatched his portable radio from his pocket. "I'll run her driver's license and get her residence address."

"If it's in the city, have dispatch expedite a unit to check her welfare," Garza said.

Gregg nodded as he began talking into the radio.

"And if she's all right, I really think I should help whoever's going to question Lauren," I said. "Otherwise, I don't think there'll be an interview."

"How do mean?"

"She'll tell you to pound sand and not say a word. However, things might work out a little better if I'm there. I'm not a stranger, and if I really worked the limp, Lauren might even feel a slight sense of obligation, considering I got knocked on my butt this morning trying to rescue her cashbox."

"God, you are a manipulative SOB," Garza said admiringly.

I waved my hand dismissively at the compliment. "Furthermore, I know all the questions to ask Lauren and I'm plugged into the teddy bear industry. Most importantly, I might be able to convince her that the smartest thing Kyle can do is turn himself in. That way, you can interview him and find out what happened here."

Gregg looked up from the radio. "She lives in the Sunset District and we've got a patrol car en route. You want me to grab Danny and head south?"

"No, I'll stay and finish processing the scene with Detective Aafedt," said Garza. "You take Rasputin here and interview Ms. Vandenbosch."

Seven

As I limped across the parking lot, I suggested to Gregg that he could reduce our response time if he got the car and picked me up. A couple of minutes later, we were driving east.

"I'm going to call dispatch and have them run a DMV check of vehicles registered to Bronsey," I said as Gregg swerved to avoid a city bus that had just pulled away from the curb.

"Good idea. So, tell me, are you having a good time?"

Before I could answer, the Impala went airborne for a split second and then bounced off the pavement as it rocketed over a dip at an intersection. Afterwards, I said, "Gregg, make sure you enjoy this now, because you're going to miss the hell out of it when you've pulled the pin."

I radioed in the information request and a half minute later the dispatcher told me that Bronsey had only one vehicle currently registered in his name. It was a 2004 GMC Sierra 1500 pickup truck, the sort of big vehicle that the farmers back home drove. It had California personalized plates of SYDWYNDR, and an unpaid parking citation on file told us the truck was white in color.

Gregg laughed scornfully when I passed along the information about the truck. " 'Sidewinder'? Why do the losers always have macho personalized plates?"

"Actually, his isn't that far off the mark. Bronsey *is* a rattlesnake."

"That's true. The huge pickup truck is priceless, too. How do you work an undercover op in a vehicle like that?"

"Hey, nobody ever noticed Magnum in that red Ferrari."

Gregg turned right onto Fell Street and we headed westward. The road took us through the southwest corner of Golden Gate Park and past Kezar Stadium, the old home of football's San Francisco 49ers. Off to the left and in the distance I could see Mount Sutro with its enormous television-broadcasting tower silhouetted against a night sky that was now almost pearly from the coastal clouds.

An SFPD police cruiser was double-parked on Lauren Vandenbosch's street in front of what I assumed was her house. The patrol cops were standing by the black-and-white and they came over to meet us as we got out of the car. Their names were Hong and Siliotti and they weren't happy campers.

"Everything Code Four?" Gregg asked the cops.

Hong made a sound of disgust as he motioned toward a two-storied townhouse. "We got the call and blasted over here. We knock on the door, telling her we're there to check on her safety and she won't let us in."

"She's all frantic and we figure the guy is in the house holding her against her will, so we Eight-Forty-Foured the door," said Siliotti, using a California cop argot term to describe kicking a door open. "The door frame got all messed up."

Hong hooked his thumbs in his gun belt. "Good news: no bad guy. Bad news: she went ballistic, screaming about how she's not going to take any more police harassment."

"And then she throws us out, yelling that she's going to file a complaint against us for trespassing and vandalism," Siliotti said morosely.

"You did the right thing. If she actually files a complaint, tell the IA investigator to talk to me," said Gregg. "You guys can go Ten-Eight."

"Thanks, Inspector," said Hong as the cops returned to the patrol car and took off.

I sighed. "I'd have kicked that door in, too, but it's going to make it that much more tough to get Lauren to talk to us."

"Yeah, and I don't think she'll be any friendlier if she sees you wearing *this*." Gregg reached over to pluck his police department ID card from my jacket pocket.

"So, how do you want to work the interview?"

"Considering I don't know anything about teddy bears and you're familiar with the woman, I'll let you run with the ball."

"Great, but you do realize the DA's office is going to have a meltdown when they read your report and find out you let a civilian play such a pivotal role in a murder investigation?"

"They can learn to deal with it. Besides, I figure the more you help with this case, the greater the likelihood you'll be subpoenaed and get another subsidized trip to the West Coast."

"I've always liked the way you think. Let's go talk to Lauren."

I wasn't completely certain which of the 1950s-era townhouses was Lauren's residence, but it became easy to figure out once we got to the sidewalk. All of the tiny front yards were lush with greenery, yet only one featured a three-foot-tall, brown resin statue of a grinning teddy bear wearing a straw hat and leaning on a shovel.

There was a dark green Subaru Outback parked in Lauren's driveway and the back of the car was decorated with a bumper-sticker that read: WHEN ALL ELSE FAILS, HUG YOUR TEDDY BEAR. Out of old habit, I put my hand on the Outback's hood as I walked past. The metal was still slightly warm.

Gregg noticed my interest and also felt the metal. "Somebody's been out driving tonight."

I said, "Yeah, she should have been back from the teddy bear show hours ago."

"Maybe she was down on Lombard Street."

"Or she ran some errands and stopped for dinner on the way home. Still, this thing could look like a dark-colored sedan if the light was bad."

We mounted the narrow brick steps of the porch and I gently tapped on the fractured front door with my cane. "Lauren?"

"WHAT PART OF 'LEAVE ME THE HELL ALONE' DON'T YOU UNDERSTAND?" Lauren screamed from inside the house.

"Lauren, it's Brad Lyon. I was there today when you got robbed."

"You lied! You're still a detective! Go away!"

"No, I didn't lie to you and I'm sorry the officers had to kick your door open. But we had reason to believe that Bronsey had come over here to hurt you."

"Why?" She sounded more frightened than angry now.

"Because it's possible the guy who robbed you at the teddy bear show was murdered less than two hours ago. Since we know he was helping Bronsey look for your son, we got worried for your safety."

Lauren yanked the door open and a piece of the door frame snapped off. It looked as if the patrol officers had arrived just as she was preparing to go to bed. She wore a lime green ankle-length bathrobe and fuzzy slippers with teddy bear heads on the toes.

In a panicked voice she said, "Oh, my God. Is Kyle all right?"

"The truth is, we don't know. That's why we really need to talk."

She squinted past me at Gregg and suspiciously asked, "Who's he?"

"Gregg Mauel. He's my old partner from the homicide bureau and I've told him all about how Kyle is being railroaded," I replied, electing to stick with Lauren's perception of events for now.

"But if you aren't with the police, what are you doing here?"

"We were having dinner when Gregg got called out to investigate a murder. I went along to say hi to some old friends and ended up seeing some things that made me think the guy who robbed you was killed. Long story short: I'm just helping the police."

"I don't see how this has anything to do with Kyle or me." Lauren got ready to push the door shut.

"What if I told you that we found an amazing robotic teddy bear at the murder scene? We think someone dropped it while he was running away."

Despite the poor illumination, I could see her complexion go pale. "A robot teddy bear?"

"Yeah, I know it sounds strange, but I believe it's a very valuable prototype for a new computerized toy." The porch light of the house to the left came on and I added, "And I hope I'm not jumping to a wrong conclusion, but Kyle may have lied to you when he said he didn't steal anything from Lycaon. We might want to go inside to discuss this."

She stepped aside to let us in. Gregg took up a position near the door while I went into the snug living room. A candle burning on the coffee table gave off the aroma of freshly baked apple pie. There was a fireplace on the far wall and some framed photos on the wooden mantel. I went over to look at the pictures. One showed a much younger Lauren hugging a boy with piney woodlands in the background. Another featured her standing next to an older Kyle, who was dressed in a cap and gown.

Not wanting her to know that I'd already recognized Kyle from his driver's license photo, I pointed to the pictures and asked, "Kyle?"

Lauren joined me by the fireplace. "That was when he was little . . . before his dad died. We owned a little cabin up near Volcano."

"In the Gold Country. Was that what inspired your Barbeary Coast bears?"

"I guess."

"What college did he graduate from?"

"Stanford. Brad, what happened tonight?"

"The police responded to reports of a gunfight at a flophouse on Lombard Street. When they arrived, they found a man dead in one of the rooms." I glanced toward a rocking chair in the corner. "You mind if I sit down? My leg is killing me."

"No, go ahead."

I settled into the rocker. "So, was your son staying at the Paladin Motel?"

"I really don't know."

"But you have been in contact with him."

"Not since late this afternoon," Lauren whispered as she sat down on the couch. "He called to say he was all right. I haven't spoken to him since."

"Why don't you call him now?"

Lauren glanced toward the kitchen where a telephone stood on the white tile counter. "I can't. He calls me from pay phones. He didn't have the chance to grab his cell phone before he ran from his apartment."

"Still, what is Kyle's cell number?" I noticed Gregg pull his notebook from his jacket pocket as Lauren recited the number.

I asked, "When Kyle called, did he mention where he was?"

"No, because he knew I'd come and help him. He's trying to keep me safe."

"That must be upsetting for you."

"Terrifying, actually." Lauren sighed. "Can you tell me why you're so sure that Kyle was there? Did anybody see him at that motel?"

"We don't have any witnesses to the shooting, so we can't be absolutely certain he *was* there. It's a long story, but there's a good chance the murder victim was the man in the bear costume who robbed you. That also means it's possible Bronsey was there."

"And?"

"You told me Bronsey was hired to recover property stolen from Lycaon by your son. You said it was a frame job, but we found a very sophisticated teddy bear robot near the murder scene." I paused and then sighed. "It was produced in a computer lab."

"So you think Kyle stole it from Lycaon?" Lauren asked angrily.

"I can't say for certain, but it would explain why they've pulled out all the stops to find your son . . . and why there's a million-dollar warrant for his arrest."

"A million dollars?"

I sat forward in the chair. "Yep, and no judge—not even one receiving generous campaign donations from Lycaon— would issue a bail amount that high unless there was compelling evidence that the property taken was of extraordinary value, and that Kyle was viewed as a flight risk."

"Oh, God."

"Did Kyle ever mention working on anything like that bear?"

Lauren looked at the flickering candle flame and I had the sense that she was just beginning to realize the full scope of her son's treachery. "No."

"I'm really sorry you had to learn about it this way. I just have a few more questions and then we'll go."

She nodded listlessly.

"What kind of car does Kyle drive?"

"A Toyota Prius. I don't know the license plate."

"That's okay. What color is it?"

"Like a mint green."

"Does he have any friends he'd be staying with?"

"No."

"A girlfriend?"

"As far as I know, he isn't seeing anyone regularly."

"Did you go anyplace in your car this evening?"

She looked up. "Why?"

"Because when we got here the hood was still warm."

"I went to the store because I was out of coffee. Is that against the law?"

"Not at all. Does Kyle own a gun?"

Her nostrils flared and she gave me a stern look. "My son did not kill that man."

"I'm sorry, but we have to look at it as a possibility. It could have been that he was acting in self-defense and—"

"My son did not kill that man!"

"Yes, but does he own a gun?"

"Not to my knowledge."

"How about you? Do you own a gun?" I asked quietly.

Lauren stood up. "No, and get out. I thought you were here to help me, but I can see that you're just trying to frame my son, too. He didn't kill anybody."

I pushed myself out of the rocker. "If that's true, then the best thing Kyle can do is surrender himself to Inspector Mauel. The shooter is still out there and he doesn't know that we have the robot. The next time he sees your son he might decide to shoot first and look for the bear later. Tell Kyle that when you talk to him."

Eight

Gregg put one of his business cards on an old-fashioned treadle sewing machine that was next to the door. I followed him from the house, feeling troubled. Not only had I failed to get the information I'd all but promised Garza I'd deliver, I also had the niggling suspicion that I'd overlooked something important.

"There's a greater chance that I'm going to be a freaking contestant on *Dancing with the Stars* than that Kyle left his cell phone behind," I murmured as we walked back to the unmarked police car.

"Dude, this constant thinking the worst about people is going to give you some really bad karma," Gregg drawled, sounding exactly like one of San Francisco's many refugees from the Age of Aquarius.

"I'll be sure to work on that in my next life. Did you notice the way Lauren stared at her house phone when we were talking about Kyle's cell phone?"

"Like she was praying it wouldn't ring."

"But I don't think she knew about the shooting. She seemed genuinely shocked and frightened."

"Agreed."

"So, she'll be on the phone to him the second she's certain we're gone." I opened the car door and got inside.

Gregg fired up the Impala. "We need to run a GPS search for the cell phone."

"Good idea . . . if it's his cell phone he's using," I pondered aloud.

"What do you mean?"

"Maybe I was wrong. Maybe he *did* leave his phone behind. Kyle is tech savvy, so he'd have to know that he'd give his location away if he used his phone. He probably has a new one by now."

Shortly after, Gregg's phone rang and he pulled over to talk. As he spoke to Lieutenant Garza, I mentally reviewed my conversation with Lauren, but still couldn't figure out what I'd missed. However, I wasn't so lost in thought that I didn't hear Gregg tell Garza that he'd meet her at police headquarters once he'd dropped me off. The field trip was over.

Gregg slipped the phone into his jacket pocket. "We're coming up dry pretty much everywhere."

"How so?" I asked.

"There are no new witnesses and the car leasing company is insisting on a search warrant before they release any information about who has the Dodge. But here's an interesting tidbit," said Gregg. "Either Lauren was lying or Kyle doesn't tell his mommy everything. Aafedt ran a records check and ascertained that Kyle bought a Sig-Sauer P two twenty-three months ago, from a shop in Santa Clara."

"Forty-five auto. That's some serious firepower."

"And it just adds to the confusion, since the only cartridges we recovered from the scene were from a nine-mil."

"You'll figure it out and I know you've got hours of

work ahead of you, so I think I ought to call it a night. Thanks for letting me come out to play."

"My pleasure. It was great working with you again," Gregg said sadly as he steered the Impala back onto the roadway.

Ash was waiting for me at Gregg's house in suburban Corte Madera, on the north side of the Golden Gate Bridge, so we headed in that direction as I listened to the strangely comforting sound of the police radio.

As we passed the Golden Gate Bridge toll plaza, I said, "It occurs to me that even if you ID the victim from his fingerprints tomorrow, that's only half the job. You're going to need to positively link him to Bronsey."

"I know. Any ideas?" Gregg asked

"That bear costume is a good lead. There can't be that many costume shops in the city and I imagine they'd want to swipe your credit card to bill you, just in case the suit isn't returned."

"You think Bronsey might have rented the costume?"

"More likely him than your victim. Would you have accepted a credit card from the dead guy?"

"No way. I'd have automatically assumed it was stolen."

"And assuming that Merv was the brains of the operation—which is a scary thought—it would have been up to him to get the costume."

"We'll follow up on that," said Gregg. After a moment, he slapped the steering wheel. "Damn, I miss working with you. Look, can I call you if we come up with any other weird teddy bear angles?"

"Depend on it."

Gregg stopped long enough to drop me off and tell Susie not to wait up, because he wouldn't be back until much later. Ash and I said good night and as we drove back to our motel, I started to tell her about my evening.

"You saw Heather? How did she look?" Ash did her best to sound innocent.

"Great, other than the fact her hair is blue," I said with a chuckle. "Were you going to mention that to me before we met them for brunch?"

"I—What do you mean, *them*?"

"Blue hair was apparently going to be the least of the surprises tomorrow morning. Heather is bringing her partner, Detective Colin Sinclair. I like him, but obviously not as much or in the same way as our daughter does."

"Oh, Lord. She's . . . ?"

"Yep, I have the feeling you're going to meet your future son-in-law."

Ash slumped in the car seat. "That's impossible. In my mind, she's still playing with her My Little Ponies in the sandbox."

"I know exactly how you feel." I patted her hand.

"He'd better not break her heart."

"He seemed like a good man. However, if you want to give young Colin the traditional Remmelkemp warning, we can stop at a department store tomorrow morning so you can pick up a carving knife."

"There's a Macy's at Northgate Mall in San Rafael. I wonder what time they open on Sundays," Ash said pensively.

A change of topic was clearly in order, so I started to tell her about the murder and the robotic teddy bear I'd found. We'd arrived at the motel and were walking to our room by the time I finished the story.

"A walking, talking teddy bear?" Ash asked incredulously. "What did it look like?"

"He's a polar bear with a really cute face and his name is Patrick. That teddy bear is going to make someone a big mountain of money."

I unlocked the door and we both went into the hotel room.

"It's strange that Lauren didn't know anything about the bear," said Ash.

Sitting down on the bed, I replied, "I know, but she looked completely poleaxed when I told her about it."

"I can understand why. She's a wonderful teddy bear designer, and it must have been heartbreaking to find out that her son had excluded her from a project like that."

Ash's words caused me to suddenly realize what had been bothering me about my conversation with Lauren. I said, "If, in fact, he did exclude her."

"What do you mean?"

"What was the very first thing you asked me about the bear?"

After a second or two of thought, Ash replied, "What did it look like?"

"Which is exactly the question I'd expect from a teddy bear artist. But Lauren never asked me to tell her about the bear. Maybe that's because she already knew what it looked like."

"Sweetheart, I think you may be jumping to conclusions."

"Me?" I pretended to be shocked.

"Yes, you. You'd just told her that her son might have been involved in a murder. Lauren was probably so worried about Kyle that she couldn't have cared less about the bear."

"I suppose you're right. But I'm almost certain she's lying about not being able to contact Kyle."

Ash began slowly unbuttoning her blouse. "Maybe she has a good reason. Is it possible that *Lycaon* actually tried to steal the bear from Kyle?"

"I'm not following." Actually, I was following something, but it was with my eyes.

"What if Kyle developed Patrick on his own time and with his own money?" Ash slid her blouse off and gave me a tiny smile.

"And Lycaon decided to grab the project and claim it as their own?"

"It wouldn't be the first time a big company pulled a vicious stunt like that." Ash was now undoing the buttons of her skirt.

"And it . . . they . . . I just forgot what I was going to say." I sounded dazed. It was impossible to focus on the Byzantine investigation while watching my wife perform a chaste yet incendiary striptease. "You're doing that on purpose, aren't you?"

"Of course." She leaned over to give me one of those patented long slow kisses that make me light-headed.

When I caught my breath, I whispered, "You Remmelkemp girls are lethal. God help Colin Sinclair."

Our bodies were still on East Coast time, so we woke up early. The morning was foggy, but I knew from experience that the sky would be blue and clear by lunchtime. There was no way I was going to last until noon without eating, so we partook of the motel's free continental breakfast. I was good, resisting the gut bombs—doughnuts—in favor of a bowl of blueberry yogurt mixed with low-fat granola. Then we returned to our room to shower and dress for brunch.

Being a guy, I was ready in less than forty-five minutes. Ash took much longer but, as always, it was worth the wait. I gave her an appreciative stare when she emerged from the bathroom in her tweed skirt and jacket ensemble with a crimson top and black suede boots.

"How do I look?" she asked, while slowly pirouetting.

"Beautiful enough to be worried that Colin might hit on *you*."

Ash smiled shyly and handed me her gold bracelet, which I put on her wrist. Then she adjusted my tie and we were out the door. We drove south toward the city and our destination of the luxurious Mark Hopkins Hotel on Nob Hill. Sunday brunch in the hotel's famous penthouse lounge, the Top of the Mark, was going to cost a king's ransom, but

I couldn't think of a more romantic place to formally meet the man our daughter loved. I was also relieved when Ash didn't insist on stopping at the Macy's to look at the cutlery.

As we crossed the bridge, I realized that we'd be early and I began contemplating a brief detour. I knew I had no business even considering chasing down leads in a murder investigation, but I felt a need to redeem myself after the previous night's failures. Besides, I wasn't planning anything more than a quick rolling recon of Merv's old stomping grounds.

We took the same route along Lombard Street that Gregg had driven last night and passed the Paladin Motel. The Chevrolet Celebrity had been towed away and the doorway to Room Four was blocked off with an oversized sheet of plywood. A few minutes later, I turned right onto Van Ness Avenue.

Ash noticed when I continued south. "Weren't we supposed to turn there?"

"Yeah, but we're way early and I just want to take a second and check something out."

"Where?"

"In the Tenderloin District," I mumbled.

"Where all the prostitutes, drug dealers, and crazy street people are, right?"

"It's Sunday morning. Maybe they're in church."

Ash rolled her eyes. "That would be my guess, too. Brad, honey, what are we looking for?"

"Merv the Perv's pickup truck."

"Aren't the police searching for it?"

"Probably not. There's nothing solid to put Bronsey at the murder scene. So there'd be no reasonable suspicion to issue a 'stop and detain' on Merv."

"Why do you expect to find him in the Tenderloin?"

"You look for a hyena on the savannah. This is his natural environment."

"And what are we going to do if we find his truck?"

"Call Gregg. Nothing more. We won't even get out of the car." We stopped for a red light and I looked at her. "Or we can turn around and go back to the Mark Hopkins."

"This is absolutely crazy, you know." Ash fixed me with her deep blue eyes. However, when she spoke again, there was no mistaking the faint trace of eagerness in her voice. "What's the description and license on the truck?"

I leaned over and kissed her nose. "I knew you'd be interested, Deputy Lyon."

The Tenderloin District of San Francisco earned its name almost a century ago from the crooked policemen who worked its streets. With its houses of prostitution, gambling dens, and saloons, the graft was so abundant that the old-time cops bragged that they could afford the finest cuts of beef, such as tenderloin. I knew the cops were more honest in the Tenderloin District these days and there was some creeping gentrification, but little else had changed. The streets were dirty and the atmosphere tinged with despair. Fortunately, it was still early, so there weren't many street people out.

We'd been searching the neighborhood for about ten minutes when Ash spotted a big Sierra pickup truck parked in a narrow lot across the street from a topless bar. I pulled into the lot and we confirmed it was Merv's license plate. It didn't look as if the truck was occupied, but Ash jumped out to check before I could object.

Climbing back into our van, she said, "Empty."

"Then Merv must be in there." I pointed toward the bar.

"The Cask and Cleavage?" Ash's voice was equal parts astonishment and revulsion.

"Hey, it says it's a gentleman's club, so it must be a classy place."

I pulled the cell phone from my jacket pocket and hit the speed-dial code for Gregg's home phone. Susie answered and told me that her husband had already returned to work and was likely at the murder victim's autopsy.

Next, I called Gregg's work cell, but it immediately rolled over to voice mail. That meant he'd turned his phone off during the postmortem. I left a message about "accidentally" finding Merv's truck on our way to brunch.

Disconnecting from the call, I said, "I sure hope Gregg gets that message before Merv takes off."

"Just how important is it that somebody talks to him?"

"Very. But hey, I promised that all we'd do is check the area and call Gregg if we found anything."

Ash glanced at the dashboard clock and casually said, "We've got forty minutes before we're supposed to be at the Mark and it's only a few minutes away. So . . ."

"So, you want to go in and try to talk to Merv? I don't think that's such a great idea, my love. That place is a freaking dive and there's the possibility that Merv will behave like any other cornered animal."

"But there's no way he could know that you were at the Paladin last night. And we could call Heather and her partner to back us up, if you're worried about it being dangerous."

"Which I am. Tell me, why are you so set on me talking to Bronsey?"

"Because you were the very best interviewer in the SFPD and you can get the information from that creep. Tell me I'm wrong." Ash jutted her jaw out defiantly.

"Okay." I handed her the phone. "But I'll let you call our daughter and explain why we need backup."

Nine

Ash called Heather and I was a little surprised that our daughter didn't demand so much as a word of explanation as to why her parents were conducting their own private homicide investigation in one of the most vile and crime-ridden parts of the city.

Then Ash handed me the phone, saying, "She wants to talk to you."

I said, "Hi, Heather honey. Thanks for humoring your strange folks."

"Are you kidding, Daddy? I've always dreamed of working a One-Eighty-Seven with you."

"I know, but this is strictly unofficial and I don't want you running afoul of your supervisors."

"*You* never worried about that," Heather said sassily.

"Which might explain why your dad never made lieutenant."

"That's because you never tested for lieutenant, Daddy. You told me that all you ever wanted to be was a detective and you passed those genes on to me."

I felt both humbled and proud, but this wasn't the time for a Kodak moment, so I said, "Okay, I just don't want to get you in trouble."

"Don't worry. Now, what do you want us to do when we get there?"

"Does Bronsey know either of you?"

"I don't think so."

"How about the bar? Will the employees make you as cops?"

"I've never been in there. Let me ask Colin if he's ever worked the place." There was a pause and then Heather came back on the line. "Colin says he's never been there either."

"Good. Then pretend to be customers and just keep an eye on us. And unless I signal you, don't try to stop him if he leaves," I said. "There's no probable cause to arrest him. Keep one other thing in mind: Merv is probably armed and a wee bit stressed."

"I'd never do anything to put you or Mama in danger."

"I know . . . and you'd better have your ballistic vest on, little girl."

"*Yes*, Daddy," she replied in exactly the same half-exasperated tone she'd used years ago when I told her that curfew was eleven P.M. "We'll be en route."

Heather lived in an apartment in Burlingame, which was about fifteen miles south of our location. Even if she drove like her Uncle Gregg, it would still take a minimum of twenty minutes for Heather and Colin to arrive.

I hung up and Ash said, "It's a good thing Colin was already there."

"Yeah, we caught a break," I replied, when what I wanted to say was: *Honey, I'll bet they're living together.*

Ash watched as I fiddled with the phone's menu buttons. "What are you doing?"

"Turning the ringer off. If we get a call while we're in

there, Merv might figure it's a bust signal and that we've set him up."

We got out of the van and I scanned the street while tightening my grip on my cane. Dressed as we were for a fancy Sunday brunch, we might as well have been wearing signs that read, PLEASE ROB US. But our luck seemed to be holding. The only street person visible was a leaping fellow down the block who seemed to be performing *Rite of Spring*, sans orchestra. I took both of Ash's hands before we headed for the bar.

Looking into her eyes, I said, "Okay, here are the rules of engagement. Like I told Heather, Bronsey is probably armed. So, if for some reason this thing goes south, you are to find cover and stay there."

"What about you?"

"I'll be doing the same thing," I lied. She didn't bother to call me on it. We both knew that if someone began busting caps, I'd shield her body with mine. I continued, "Finally, please keep that jacket buttoned."

"Why?"

"That top is a little low-cut. Ordinarily, I like that. A lot. But if Bronsey begins staring there—and he will—I'm going to have this uncontrollable urge to throttle him instead of chat."

Ash smiled as she buttoned up the jacket. "I love you, Inspector Lyon."

"I love you, too, Deputy Lyon."

We started across the street. With each step, I tried to summon forth the ghost of my old homicide inspector swagger. Guns and badges don't impress many people. It's that intangible thing called "command presence"—the mixture of quiet confidence, courage, and decisiveness—that gives a cop dominion over the sort of folks that you'll routinely find in a topless bar.

At the same time, I was trying to figure out just how I

was going to induce Bronsey to talk to us. From past experience, I knew his credo was "Deny everything and demand proof," and there was no hard evidence linking him to the murder scene. In the end, I could only see one option. I had to pretend that Lauren had asked us to find her son and that I wouldn't call the cops if Bronsey gave us the straight scoop.

The Cask and Cleavage was located on the ground floor of a narrow three-story brick building. There was a virtual carpet of cigarette butts on the sidewalk near the front door and the broken Cobra Malt Liquor bottle was a nice decorative accent. Ordinarily, I hold doors open for Ash and let her go through first, but this wasn't the sort of place for chivalry. I entered first, just in case things went to hell immediately.

Inside, the lighting was dim and the old Bob Seger song was deafening. I waited a moment for my eyes to adjust to the gloom and then scanned the interior of the lounge. There was a bar on the left, upholstered booths on the right, and a narrow elevated stage in the center of the room against the back wall. Fortunately, the stage was empty.

I was relieved to observe that there were only two other people in the shabby saloon. Standing behind the bar was a sour-looking older guy with a shaggy white moustache-and-goatee combo that gave him the appearance of a dyspeptic West Highland terrier. Bronsey sat in a corner booth, slouched over, as if in deep contemplation of his drink. As we got closer, I could see that he was wearing a brown leather bomber jacket decorated with patches from what I suspected were imaginary fighter squadrons. However, the intervening table and poor light prevented me from seeing whether he had jeans on and, more importantly, if one of the knees was torn.

I gave Ash a look that said, *Here goes nothing*, and tapped lightly on the table. "Merv, I think we need to talk."

Bronsey slowly lifted his head and regarded us with

bleary, bloodshot eyes. It took a second or two for his brain to decipher our images. Then he said in a weary and hopeless voice, "I don't know what you're doing here, Lyon, but go away before I kick your ass."

"I'll let you get back to your rum-and-coke journey to Nirvana, once you tell me about Kyle Vandenbosch and what happened at the Paladin Motel last night."

He stiffened slightly and his eyes darted toward the door and I couldn't tell whether he wanted to run or whether he was worried about whoever might come into the bar next. Recovering slightly, he said in a dismissive tone, "I don't know what you're talking about. And even if I did, why would I tell you?"

I said, "Look, Merv, you don't like me. I don't like you, but with all your faults I find it hard to believe that you're pulling armed Two-Elevens and killing people."

"What are you talking about?" The statement wasn't as much a denial as it was a feeler to find out how much I knew.

"We talked to Lauren Vandenbosch last night and she told us an interesting story."

"Really? Why would she call you?"

"The teddy bear artist community is very tight. It's a fur thing—you wouldn't understand. Anyway, Lauren says that her son called to tell her that you and your partner robbed him at gunpoint last night."

"That's a freaking lie!"

"But you were there. Unfortunately for you, your partner was thoughtful enough to leave the bear costume in his car before being murdered," I said, expanding on my bluff and offering supposition as fact.

"I'd like to see you prove I was there."

Noting that Bronsey had never actually denied being at the Paladin, I continued with my disinformation campaign. "Dude, don't worry about *me* proving anything. You need to be concerned with Kyle Vandenbosch. His mom called

us to ask whether we thought the cops would go light on
Kyle for the theft charges if he came forward to be a helpful homicide witness."

"Against me?"

"That's what it sounded like."

"That double-dealing little son of a bitch." Bronsey
didn't sound angry now, so much as scared. "And he's still
got his mommy fooled, too."

"How do you mean?"

"Before I say anything else, what do I get for cooperating?"

"Time," I lied. "I promise to give you twenty-four hours
from the end of the interview before contacting the police.
You can either get a good lawyer or, if you've got a pass-
port, you might consider flying someplace that doesn't
have an extradition treaty with the U.S."

"Jesus. It's that bad, huh?" Bronsey emptied his glass
with two gulps.

"Yep. Kyle's version of the story is that you gunned
your partner down during the commission of a robbery.
That's first degree with special circs." Since Bronsey was a
former cop, there was no need to add that the district attorney could ask for the death penalty in such a case.

There are times when silence is the most effective interrogation tool, so I kept quiet and waited for Bronsey to say
something.

Finally, Bronsey said, "Sit down."

Ash and I slid onto the bench on the opposite side of the
table while Bronsey signaled the bartender for a refill. Once
the drink was delivered, I said, "Okay Merv, why don't we
start with how Lycaon picked you to do their dirty work."

"I'm not working for Lycaon."

"That's not what Kyle told his mom."

"That's because that little backstabber has been lying to
her from the very beginning."

"Interesting. So, who is your client?"

"I don't know and that's the truth."

"Did they contact you?"

"Yeah. On Thursday afternoon I get a call from a number with a blocked ID. It's a guy asking if I want to make two grand for a couple days' work."

"And you said?"

"I didn't get a chance to say anything. The guy tells me that if I'm interested I should go up to the old Nike place on Bunker Road at six o'clock and look for a car with one of those Jack-in-the-Box heads on the antenna. Then he hangs up."

Bronsey was referring to the decommissioned 1960s-era Nike missile base on the hilly Marin headlands north of the city. Once upon a time, it existed as an antiaircraft battery to protect San Francisco from Soviet bombers. But now the facility was a museum dedicated to the Cold War, which made it an ideal place to stage an apparent chance meeting.

I said, "Sounds pretty cloak-and-dagger. Obviously, you went."

"Yeah. I got there early, but the car was already there. Two guys inside."

"Make? Model?"

"A new Saturn Aura. It had Nevada plates. I found out later that the plates were reported stolen from Las Vegas back in June."

"Somebody at the PD still runs license numbers for you, huh?"

"I have friends," Bronsey said petulantly. "Anyway, the guys in the Saturn knew what kind of truck I drove, because the minute I pull up, the passenger comes over carrying a gym bag."

"What did this guy look like?"

"White, in his forties, clean-shaven, kind of going bald in front. Eyes as cold as a freaking lizard's."

"You get his name?"

"Rule number one was 'no names.' He told me to stay in the truck and then he got inside." Bronsey took a sip of his drink. "I knew right then I was in over my head, because the first thing the guy does is whip out this little device and waves it around the inside of the truck. He tells me that our conversation is confidential and he wants to make sure that we're not going to be overheard or recorded."

"There's usually a good or, more likely, really bad reason why someone would worry about listening devices. That should've made warning bells go off in your head."

Bronsey held up his hand to forestall me from making any further judgmental observations. "I know. I know. But two thousand dollars for a few hours' work? The finance company is looking to repo my truck, so I couldn't pass it up."

Ash folded her arms and you didn't need to be an expert in body language to know what she thought of Bronsey's rationalizations.

I asked, "And just what was the job, Merv?"

"Lizard Eyes knows all about me. He knows my PI business is in the crapper. He knows I need the money. He says that all I have to do is contact a guy, deliver the bag, and pick up some merchandise."

"When were you supposed to deliver the goods to Lizard Eyes?"

"Tomorrow. The guy is supposed to call to set up another meeting."

I chuckled in disbelief. "My God. Weren't you at least a little worried that you were being asked to work as a dope mule?"

"I'm not an idiot, Lyon." Bronsey glowered at me. "I told the guy that if this was a dope deal, he could go straight to hell. Look, I may not have been a recruiting poster cop, but I've never been in the narc trade."

"So, I guess it must have come as a shock when the guy told you that you were buying a stolen robotic teddy bear."

"He never said it was hot."

"And I'll bet you never asked."

There was a long pause and then Bronsey said, "Just for once, come down from your freaking high horse and try to look at it from my point of view. I was drowning, Lyon. The guy told me that there was nothing illegal in what they were doing. They just wanted to keep their company's name out of a potential lawsuit."

"Okay, Merv, I'll assume you didn't believe you were breaking any laws." I glanced at Ash, whose look of annoyance clearly said that she didn't like being lied to. "Even if my wife doesn't buy a word of it. What else did this guy tell you?"

"He says that Kyle Vandenbosch is getting a royal screwing from some company I never heard of, called Lycaon. The story was that Kyle developed some whiz-bang new toy on his own dime and wanted to sell it to the guy's company, but that Lycaon is claiming it's theirs."

"And you were supposed to conduct the actual transaction, so that the buying company's hands would stay as clean as Pontius Pilate's."

"I guess."

"So, you accepted the job. What happened next?"

"The guy gave me Vandenbosch's phone number and told me that he didn't care where I set up the meet, so long as it was done quickly and the location had a telephone landline." Bronsey took another swallow of his drink and crunched an ice cube between his teeth. "If I had it to do all over again, I'd have taken that number and flushed it down the toilet."

Ten

"But you still have Kyle's number?" I asked.

Bronsey nodded. "Yeah."

"Could we have it?"

"Why not? I sure as hell ain't gonna call him."

He reached into his back pocket to retrieve his wallet and as he did his jacket flapped open, revealing a black auto-pistol in a brown leather shoulder holster. He opened the wallet and handed me a dog-eared business card. It read MERVIN J. BRONSEY, CONFIDENTIAL INVESTIGATIONS, and his phone number was printed beneath the name. There was another number handwritten in pencil on the back of the card. It was completely different from the phone number that Lauren had told us was Kyle's cell. I slipped the business card into my shirt pocket.

The front door swung open and I pretended to give the newcomer a disinterested glance. I didn't want to provide Merv with even the slightest hint that we were waiting for someone to arrive. However, I was beginning to get nervous. More than twenty minutes had passed and there was still no sign of Heather and Colin.

A groggy-looking, bearded tramp stumbled into the bar and I could smell the booze emanating from his person all the way across the room. Back when I started in cop work, I'd have referred to him as a "drunken bum" or "wino," but I suspected that modern-day San Francisco cops were encouraged to call such people more politically correct names, such as "sobriety-challenged victims of societal oppression." The rummy shuffled up to the bartender and diffidently offered to sweep the sidewalk in front of the bar for five bucks. I turned my attention back to Bronsey as the bartender nodded and went to go get the broom.

I asked, "Did your original contact tell you what the merchandise was?"

"Yeah, a robot that looked like a teddy bear," said Bronsey.

"I think it's safe to assume you know as much about real robots as I do, which is nothing. Given that, what was to prevent Kyle from selling you a mock-up of the genuine article?"

"Him and Lizard Eyes had already worked that out. I had to talk to the bear and watch it walk. Sounds weird, I know."

Actually, it didn't, but I couldn't say anything and I hoped Ash could keep her poker face.

Bronsey continued, "The buyer said that if I wasn't freaking amazed, then abort the deal and walk away."

"But if you *were* amazed?" I asked, while watching the wino leave the bar.

"I was supposed to call a number on a landline phone and then plug one end of a data cord into the phone jack and the other into the back of the bear. I'd get a call on my cell when they were done with whatever they were doing."

"Which was probably interacting with the bear's computer system to ensure it could do everything that Kyle promised the buyer."

"That's what I thought, too."

"And this guy gave you a data cord?"

"Yeah, but I left it in the room." Bronsey sounded a little sheepish. "I guess the thing stayed connected to the phone jack, when I grabbed the bear to run."

As far as I knew, the detectives never found a data cord in the motel room, which meant that unless Merv was lying, someone had tidied up the room before the cops arrived. I asked, "Do you remember the contact number the buyer gave you?"

"He made me write it down. But I left the card on the nightstand near the phone. I was just getting ready to make the call when everything turned to crap."

I remembered the detectives hadn't found a business card either, so it must have vanished with the data cord. I said, "Even the area code would be helpful."

"No area code. It was a local number. Started with a six . . . I think."

"But you can't remember. Were you told how much money there was in the gym bag?"

"Four hundred thousand dollars. It was the most cash I've ever seen. The guy made me count the bill bundles and told me that I'd end up as one of the ingredients of gourmet sausage if I didn't give it all to Vandenbosch."

"That must have gotten your attention."

"You got *that* right. You know how some guys talk big smack and you know it's all just BS? Not this guy." Bronsey rubbed his unshaven throat. "He meant exactly what he said."

"But you went ahead with the deal."

"Like I told you, I didn't really have a choice."

Ash couldn't hold her tongue any longer, not that I could blame her. Bronsey's self-pitying view of events was nauseating. She said, "You had a choice. You could have told him no and gotten another job. There are all sorts of jobs in the security field."

"I'm not going to be some freaking department store rent-a-cop, honey." Bronsey's hand tightened around the glass and he continued in a goofy yet sarcastic voice, "Excuse me sir, have you paid for that leather jacket?"

"Merv, relax," I said.

Bronsey pointed at Ash. "You don't understand. You think your old man was the only one who liked being a cop? I was king of the freaking streets out here. You don't just walk away from that and then be satisfied with a job keeping teenagers from ripping off the earring display."

It came as a mild epiphany to realize that, in his own way, Bronsey had been proud of being a cop, even if it was for all the wrong reasons. I gently pressed my leg against Ash's to signal that I wanted to get the interview back on track and said, "I understand what you're saying, Merv. Now let's get back to Kyle. When did you call him?"

He exhaled sharply, took a drink, and said, "That night. Thursday."

"Tell me about the phone call."

"I called him and gave him the code word."

"What are you talking about?"

"The guy with the money gave me a code word so that Vandenbosch would know that I was the courier. Didn't I tell you that?"

"No, but you've got a lot on your mind. What was the code word?"

"Talus. First time Lizard Eyes told me, I thought he said, 'Dallas,' but he spelled it for me."

"The buyer likes playing word games," Ash murmured. "Talus is the name of a mechanical bronze warrior from Greek mythology."

I've known my wife for almost three decades, yet she still has the capacity to surprise me. I asked, "How the heck do you know that?"

"I grew up reading *Bulfinch's Mythology*."

"And I grew up watching Bullwinkle. It's a good thing I fell in love with a smart girl." I turned back to Bronsey, "Okay, so you give this guy the secret password. What happened after that?"

He took a swallow from his drink and then heaved a big sigh. "This guy Vandenbosch sounds like a little geek. But he's copping this monster attitude, like he thinks he's some bad-ass criminal genius."

"Understandable. We both know that it's the cowards who always act like the movie tough guys," I said, hoping Bronsey didn't realize I was including him in that description.

He nodded in vigorous agreement. "I tell him I want an immediate meet, but he says he can't, because he thinks he's being watched. Then he asks if I want to make an extra thousand on the deal."

"And you said . . . ?"

"I wanted to know what I had to do. He tells me that he wants to make it harder for Lycaon to file a lawsuit claiming they own the toy."

"Did he have some ideas as to how to accomplish that?"

"Lyon, this kid is an utter weasel. He says he wants me to pretend I work for Lycaon and mess with his mom bigtime."

I sat back and interlaced my fingers across my chest. "Define *mess with*."

"Call her and threaten her. Follow her when she's going someplace. Scare her so that she complains about Lycaon harassing her."

"Rob her at a teddy bear show?"

"Yeah, that was all Vandenbosch's idea." Bronsey wagged his finger at me. "The kid says that the worse we can make Lycaon look, the better for him. And I didn't hurt her. There was never any plan to hurt her."

"Physically. So, let me get this straight. You agreed to

terrorize an innocent woman and run the risk of going to state prison for stalking and robbery for a measly thousand dollars?"

He looked down at the table and muttered, "No. I wouldn't agree to do it until he doubled his offer."

"Well, I'm relieved to hear that you stood up for your principles." I glanced at Ash, who was gaping at Bronsey as if he were an enormous cockroach.

Outside, I heard the unmistakable throaty rumble of a big Harley-Davidson motorcycle coming to a stop in front of the bar. Whoever was riding it revved the engine loudly a couple of times before shutting the hog off. The overwhelming majority of Harley owners are decent folks, but I also knew that decent folks would never leave their prized bikes unattended outside a bar in a demilitarized zone like the Tenderloin. There's only one kind of Harley owner who feels safe doing that: the kind who wear motorcycle gang colors and absolutely hate cops, whether they're still on the job or retired. I shot a wary glance at the door and was suddenly a little relieved that Bronsey was armed.

Bronsey had also turned in his seat to watch the entrance. The door flew open and it took every ounce of self-control I possessed not to shout, *Young lady, just where do you think you are going dressed like that?* It was our blue-haired daughter, Heather, who was marginally attired in denim cutoff shorts that were way too short and tight, black boots, and a skimpy black tank top. Merv was staring like he'd just seen paradise and I wanted to slap him. Meanwhile, Ash was slack-jawed with amazement.

Heather sauntered over to the bar, followed by Colin, who looked every inch the grimy outlaw biker, right down to the tattoo of a laughing Satan on his right bicep. He had a smoldering cigarette in the corner of his mouth, and when the bartender meekly said there was no smoking in the bar, Colin gave a brutal laugh and told the guy to shut up unless he wanted his ass beat. This seemed to settle the issue of whether he could smoke in the bar. Heather and Colin sat down on bar stools, ordered beers, and demanded that the bartender turn the music up. A few seconds later, the place was vibrating to the sounds of Eric Clapton's "Cocaine."

I cleared my throat. "Getting back to Vandenbosch's diversionary operation. Merv? Can I have your attention, please?"

Bronsey finally tore his gaze from our daughter's derriere. "Yeah, Vandenbosch."

"Merv, focus on me and don't look back over there again. Motorcycle Man will squash you like a bug if he sees you looking at her like that," I said quietly, while resisting the urge to clobber him myself. "Was the man killed at the Paladin the same guy who was dressed in the bear suit in Sonoma?"

"Yeah. His name was Joey Uhlander. He used to be one of my street snitches when I was still on the PD and he did odd jobs for me." Bronsey held up his empty glass to signal the bartender that he needed another refill, which also gave him another opportunity to devour Heather with his eyes.

Ash gave me a brief and icy sidelong glance that unmistakably said: *I don't know how much more of this I can take before going postal.*

Once the drink had been delivered and Bronsey had paid for it, I asked, "So, why did you bring Uhlander in on the deal?"

"I couldn't pull off the robbery and then hang around to pin it on Lycaon, could I?" Bronsey sounded annoyed that I was so obtuse.

"But why dress him in a bear costume?"

"Joey grew up in Sonoma. He was afraid somebody would recognize him."

"And if he looked like most street snitches, you probably wanted him in disguise anyway. Especially at a teddy bear show. He'd have stuck out like a sore thumb."

"That, too."

"Not that it's important, but how much did your associate get for his work?"

"A hundred plus whatever was in the cashbox."

"Did he get anything extra for going to the Paladin with you?"

"No." He took a big swallow of rum and coke and then continued in a small voice, "I feel bad for Joey. I had no idea that crap was going to go down."

"You must have had *some* idea that there could be trouble."

"What do you mean?"

"Kyle told his mom that Uhlander pulled a gun," I lied and reminded myself to be damn careful. If I said anything to give away the fact I'd been at the Paladin with the detectives, the best-case scenario was that Bronsey would bail before we could find out what had happened in the motel room. And I didn't even want to think about the worst-case scenario.

Bronsey grimaced. "Look, you've got to believe me. I didn't know Joey was carrying. But even so, he was acting in self-defense."

"Were you armed?"

"I'm a PI. I have a Concealed Carry permit."

"I guess that's a big *yes*. What kind of a gun?"

"Glock nine-mil."

"So, who picked the meeting site at the Paladin?"

"Vandenbosch. He called me just after seven to tell me that he'd slipped whoever was tailing him. He said to come over to the Paladin, Room Four, at eight o'clock."

"So, you and Joey went. Did anybody else go with you?"

"No. Why?"

"Because Kyle's mom also says that some woman tried to force her way into the room just before you got there. Kyle apparently thought you sent her as a distraction."

"Then that was geek boy's first time staying at the Paladin. You know what kind of place it is, Lyon. It'd be suspicious if a chick *wasn't* trying to get into your room."

"Agreed. But just so that we're clear on this, you don't know who the woman was?"

"Not a clue." Bronsey sounded like he was telling the truth.

I asked, "Did you and Joey go there in different vehicles?"

"Yeah. I took my truck. Joey had some beater car."

"And there's no delicate way to phrase this, so I'm just going to come right out and ask. Were you and Joey going to rob Kyle of the bear and keep the purchase money?"

Bronsey had the glass to his lips and managed to catch himself before spraying us with his drink. "You've got to be kidding. I wouldn't cross Lizard Eyes for a million bucks. That dude is poison."

"So, you just went there to make the deal."

"And get out ASAP."

I noticed that Ash was trying not to stare in the direction of the bar and I had a powerful premonition that I probably shouldn't look to see what she'd found so fascinating. Still, I turned and saw Heather and Colin entwined in an amorous embrace. I knew it was crucial that nobody made them as cops, but their performance seemed to be above and beyond the call of duty. I had to wave my hand in front of Bronsey's face to get his attention. "Getting back to the Paladin . . ."

Bronsey took a noisy sip of booze. "We show up and knock on the door and the little doofus lets us in."

"Was he worried that Joey was there?"

"Nah, he knew Joey was coming along. I'd told Vandenbosch that I wasn't going to carry four hundred grand around this freaking town without some extra security."

"What happened next?"

"We're in the room and Vandenbosch tells me to give him the bag. I say to him, 'Whoa, cowboy, let's see the goods first.' That's when he pulls this big teddy bear from like a blue nylon equipment bag."

Ash seemed to have temporarily forgotten about what was still happening at the bar. She leaned forward a little, now utterly focused on Bronsey's narrative. Unfortunately, that meant Bronsey felt obligated to study her décolletage in what he erroneously imagined was a discreet manner. It was frustrating. Despite his age and macho man bluster, the guy was like a sex-crazed eleven-year-old boy.

"Merv, stop gawking at my wife's chest and tell me about the bear."

Bronsey looked up. "At first I wanted to laugh. Lizard Eyes had paid four hundred grand for *that*? Then Vandenbosch told the bear to turn on."

"And?"

"The freaking thing comes to life. The eyes light up and the mouth is moving and Vandenbosch is talking back and forth with it."

If I wanted to continue to pretend I knew nothing about the bear, I had to feign naked skepticism. I said, "Come on, Merv. Don't yank my chain."

"I'm not lying. The thing could walk *and* talk. I put the bear on the floor and it walked around a freaking corner and over to Vandenbosch."

"Yeah, and I suppose it talked to you, too. What did it say? Howdy, Merv, only *you* can prevent forest fires?"

Bronsey was becoming irked. "Look, wise-ass, for starters it was a polar bear, not Smokey, and I talked to it like I would another person. The thing remembered my name. Suddenly, I'm thinking maybe Lizard Eyes is getting a bargain."

I held up my hands in supplication. "Okay, I believe you. But you've got to admit, it sounds pretty implausible."

Ash patted my knee to surreptitiously thank me for not saying the idea was *fur-fetched*.

"You had to see this thing to believe it, Lyon," he replied, sounding a little mollified.

"I wish I had. So, obviously you were amazed and

moved on to step two: your secret client's online confirmation test. Is that when things went bad?"

He nodded. "I take the bear over to the phone and get ready to call. Then we all hear someone try to open the motel room's door. Vandenbosch and I look at each other and I can see he's thinking that I've brought someone else along."

"But you hadn't."

"No. Like I said, it was just me and Joey. I start to tell the geek that I don't know who's at the door when, all of a sudden, this other guy jumps out of the bathroom with a gun." Bronsey mimed a two-handed grip on a handgun. "He'd been hiding there all the time and it turned out that *we* were the suckers. It was a robbery."

"Tell me about this other guy."

"Not much I can say. He was wearing a black ski mask and like an old Navy peacoat. He had a big freaking revolver. Maybe a forty-five Long Colt with a six-inch barrel."

As I knew, it was far more likely that the robber's gun was a .22 caliber revolver, a much smaller gun. But Bronsey's misidentification was consistent with the observations made by most other victims of violent crimes. They frequently perceive their assailants and weapons as being much larger than they actually are.

I asked, "What was Kyle doing when this happened?"

"He whips out an auto-pistol, but you can tell he's so scared that he's about to crap his pants."

"What did the gunman say?"

"He never said a word. Vandenbosch did all the talking. He told us to throw our guns on the floor and put the gym bag on the bed."

"Did you?"

"Joey had the bag and he tossed it on the bed. The guy in the ski mask has the drop on us, so I don't have a choice." There was an importuning note in Bronsey's voice.

"I understand."

"I start to give my gun up, but then Joey yanks his out and suddenly, I'm in the middle of a freaking firefight. I grabbed the bear and ran."

"When you bailed, did you see whoever was at the door?"

"No, but I was kind of busy running for my life."

"So, Joey gets the dirt nap and you escape with the bear. Messy, but still *mission accomplished*. Where is the bear now?"

Bronsey swallowed nervously. "I-I dropped it in the parking lot. There was still gunfire coming from the room. I was so scared. I didn't have time to pick it up. I just got the hell out of there."

"And now you're a lot more than just scared, aren't you?" I said. "Because you have to find some way to explain to Lizard Eyes that he not only isn't going to get his amazing robo-bear, but that you also lost his money and potentially got his company connected with a murder." I tried to keep the sardonic amusement from my voice. "I have a feeling that he isn't going to be real happy."

"I know."

"How did you find out for sure that Joey had been killed?"

"I heard about it on the news radio station later last night," said Bronsey. "They didn't give Jocy's name, but they were talking about the police investigating a shootout and murder at the Paladin."

"I know this is going to sound silly, but did you ever consider coming forward and telling the cops what happened?"

Bronsey gave me a scowling look. "And set myself up for a nice long stay at San Quentin? You know what they do to cops in prison."

"But all they could charge you with was one count of

receiving stolen property. You and I both know that nobody goes to prison for that. So, what are—oh! I get it, now."

"Get what?" Ash asked.

"He's worried about going to prison for the murder of Joey Uhlander. Right, Merv?"

Bronsey drained his glass and said nothing.

I rested my chin on my hand. "You lied when you told us that you never fired your gun at the Paladin. How did Joey get shot?"

Perhaps four seconds of silence passed, but it seemed longer. Finally, Bronsey looked down at the tabletop and said, "It was an accident. The dumb son of a bitch thought he was Wyatt Earp or something. He jumped in front of me as I tried to get a round off at the guy in the ski mask."

"Friendly fire. It happens. Where'd it hit him?"

"In the back, I think. Joey screamed and went down."

"Then you panicked and ran."

"Yeah."

"And when they do Joey's autopsy, they're going to find a nine-mil projectile in his back that can be matched to your gun."

"It was an accident!"

"I believe you. Actually, I have some relatively good news for you."

Bronsey squinted at me suspiciously. "What are you talking about?"

I realized I was taking a big chance by revealing our involvement in the investigation, but we couldn't afford to let Bronsey vanish. We needed his cooperation as a witness to the murder.

I said, "The medical examiner doesn't think the bullet to the back is what killed Joey. He was executed with a round to the head that was probably fired by the guy wearing the ski mask."

"How the hell do you know that?"

"Sorry, Merv, but you aren't the only one who's been a little economical with the truth during this conversation. I was at the Paladin last night with Inspector Mauel."

Bronsey's eyes lit up like balefires. "You set me up, you lying, crippled bastard."

"No, the original deal still stands." I tried to keep my voice calm. "We came here by ourselves, so you can walk out and no one will stop you."

"If that's so, then I'm sure you won't mind having your wife keep me company until I'm very far away from San Francisco," said Bronsey as he reached for his pistol.

"Merv, don't dig yourself in any deeper," I said, trying to jerk my cane free. Bronsey wasn't going to take my wife without a fight.

"I'm not going anywhere with you, you creep!" said Ash.

Bronsey flashed a cruel smile. "Oh, we're gonna have some fun, you little . . ."

Then Merv froze in midsentence and his eyes bulged with fear. He had a pretty good reason. Heather and Colin were standing beside the table and both of them were pressing the barrels of their semiautomatic pistols against Bronsey's left temple. For once, he didn't seem interested in ogling Ash or my daughter.

Colin said, "SFPD, Bronsey. And that's my fiancée's mother you were planning on taking hostage. You want to tell me what you were about to call her?"

"Oh, my God, please don't hurt me."

"Yeah, that's what I thought you'd say."

Bronsey withdrew his empty hand from his coat and sagged against the seat. Heather and Colin yanked him from the booth. They disarmed him and a couple of seconds later had Merv in handcuffs and sitting on the floor. Heather got on her cell phone to request a patrol car as

Colin had a quiet chat with Merv. Meanwhile, Ash just sat there looking stunned.

I took her hand. "Sweetheart, you're safe. They've got Bronsey in custody."

"I don't care about Bronsey," said Ash in a dazed voice. "Brad honey, our little girl is getting married!"

Eleven

We went outside to await the arrival of the black-and-white that would transport Bronsey to police headquarters. The overcast had burned off while we were inside the bar and now the sky was bright blue, signaling another perfect late summer's day. There were more people out on the streets now, but they gave us a wide berth when they saw the silver seven-pointed stars that Heather and Colin had clipped to their belts. They sat Bronsey down on the curb and I saw that his jeans had both knees intact.

Bronsey gave me a look of sheer loathing. "Once a snitch, always a snitch. Not that I've got anything to worry about. You got nothing on me."

"Are you kidding?" I asked. "Some mysterious joker gave you four hundred grand to make a quick buy of something he says is being claimed by a competing company. That sounds like at least one count of Four-Ninety-Six to me."

"Receiving Stolen Property? Big deal. Even if the DA files, the worst I'll get is probation."

"And then there's the shooting of your partner. I'm gullible. I actually believe it was an accident, but other people might not feel the same way. After all, we only have your version of how you shot Uhlander in the back."

Bronsey snickered. "You don't even have that. It's my word against yours as to what I might have told you when I was real drunk and then later denied."

I nodded sagely. "Very creative. A jury might be fooled by that argument. But you've still got problems, because the crime lab will be able to confirm that your gun fired the bullet the ME recovers from Joey's back."

"So? I loaned my piece to somebody last night and then he returned it and, gee, I don't remember his name. Face it, Lyon. You got no independent witnesses, so you can't prove that I was at the Paladin."

"Bet I can. Colin, do me a favor and pull up Merv's pant legs so I can see his knees."

"You ain't touching my legs!"

Bronsey tried to shove himself to his feet, but Heather forced him back down onto his butt. Then Bronsey tried to kick Colin.

I said, "Why the panic, Merv? You get to leer at legs all day and you're suddenly shy when someone wants to look at yours."

"Bite me, Lyon."

Heather pushed down on Bronsey's shoulders and I hung onto one leg while Ash held the other down. Bronsey continued to struggle as Colin pushed up both pant legs. There was a gauze pad taped to his left knee and dried blood showed through the white fabric. The blood was still red instead of rusty brown, indicating a recent injury.

Using my cane to help stand up, I said in a chiding voice, "Or is it because you fell and scraped your knee in the parking lot of the Paladin and you didn't want us to see that you might have left a blood transfer at the scene?"

Bronsey tried to deliver a vicious kick at my bad leg, but

missed. Heather shoved hard on his shoulders while Colin sat on his legs and suggested that unless Merv was really keen on the idea of being lit up like the White House Christmas tree with an electronic stun gun, he'd better chill out, *muy pronto*. Bronsey settled down and I was pleased to observe that our future son-in-law seemed to have excellent communication skills.

I said, "And just for the record, Merv. We did find blood and fiber traces in the parking lot. So once they test it against your blood and the torn jeans they'll find in your apartment, they *will* be able to put you at the Paladin. Have a nice life."

Bronsey started to say something, thought better of it, and then turned his head away. Ash and I moved down the sidewalk a small distance. A few seconds later, Colin came over to talk to us, while Heather continued to monitor Bronsey.

The tall bearded cop lowered his head almost penitently and said, "Sir, it's a pleasure to see you again. Mrs. Lyon, my name is Colin Sinclair. I'm in love with your daughter and I've asked her to marry me. We were going to tell you at brunch this morning, but . . ."

I shook his hand. "But instead you came to our rescue. Thank you for protecting my wife in there."

Colin scrunched down a little so that he was almost at eye level with Ash. "Mrs. Lyon, I'm sorry you had to learn about the engagement this way, but I got so mad that a maggot like Bronsey was threatening you, I just kind of lost it."

Ash's suppressed smile told me she liked Colin, but wasn't ready to let him know it yet. She said, "That's all right. The important thing is that you love my daughter."

"Enough to run the risk of being skinned with a carving knife, ma'am. But Remmelkemp girls are worth it."

"Truer words were never spoken," I murmured.

Ash looked like she was going to cry and then she suddenly reached up to give Colin a big hug. I glanced over at Heather, who looked as if she was also clouding up. It was a Hallmark Channel made-for-television movie moment, if you could overlook the suspect in custody, the zombie-like drug addicts, litter-strewn street, and sirens yelping in the distance.

Ash finally released Colin and wiped her eyes. "Okay, before we talk about anything else, I have to know. Is that a real tattoo?"

Colin looked down at Satan's face on his bicep and sighed. "Unfortunately, yes, ma'am. A couple of years ago I went really deep undercover on a dope operation. I had to have at least a few tats or they would have figured out I was a cop."

"Mom, ask him where the other one is!" Heather called.

Colin's cheeks turned pink above his beard and he said in a confidential tone, "Mrs. Lyon, I love your daughter more than life, but sometimes she can be a bit of a brat."

Ash glanced at me. "She comes by it honestly."

My jacket pocket began to vibrate and my first thought was that maybe a rat had climbed into my pocket while we were in the Cask and Cleavage. Then I remembered that I'd turned off the ringer to my cell phone. The phone's screen said the call was coming in from a number with a blocked ID.

I knew it was Gregg returning my call. I thought I'd make his day half as surreal as mine had been thus far and answered the phone with my best Raymond Burr impression. "Hello, this is Chief Robert Ironside."

Colin gave Ash a quizzical look and I overheard her explain, "It's from a TV program that was on before you were born. I hope you weren't expecting normal in-laws."

However, Gregg *was* old enough to remember *Ironside*, the old cop show set in San Francisco, and he even one-upped me by dropping the name of a secondary character, "Hi Chief, this is Sergeant Ed Brown and please don't tell me that you're down in a Tenderloin strip club interviewing Bronsey."

"Now, don't burst a blood vessel, partner. We didn't know when you were going to be clear of the autopsy and all we intended to do was talk to Merv."

"Whenever you use a word like *intended*, I'm always scared to hear the rest of the story."

"Well, there's no reason to be scared this time. Heather and her fiancé managed to overpower Merv before he could actually take Ash hostage."

"Your wife was taken hostage?" Gregg sounded unnaturally calm.

"Only for a second. You see, Merv kind of panicked after admitting he'd accidentally shot your victim in the back. The dead guy's name is Joey Uhlander, by the way."

"Where are you now?"

"Still at the Cask and Cleavage, but we'll be heading over to the Hall of Justice once our transport unit arrives. I haven't even told you half of this sordid story."

"Okay, then, we'll meet you there at the office. And since you seem to be the one with all the answers this morning, would you care to offer any suggestions as to how I'm supposed to explain all this to Lieutenant Garza?"

"Leave that to me. I'll just tell her that I have some mental health issues."

"Yeah, it's always best to stick with the truth."

"After all, it's a murder investigation involving a white teddy bear, so I can claim that I'm *bi-polar*."

"Good-bye, Brad."

A black-and-white came around the corner and Heather flagged it down. As the cops shoved Bronsey into the backseat of the patrol car, Heather told them to take the prisoner to the Homicide Bureau offices in the Hall of Justice. The police cruiser left and Heather told Colin that, if he didn't mind, she was going to ride over to HOJ with us. Colin shot Ash a wary glance before kissing Heather good-bye. Then he climbed onto the Harley and started the bike. However, he didn't ride away from the curb until we'd pulled out of the parking lot. We followed him out of the Tenderloin.

Ash turned in her seat to ask, "Engaged? Really engaged? Not just talking about it?"

"Really engaged," said Heather from the backseat.

"So, that means there's an engagement ring."

"Yes, there is, Mama."

Heather reached into the front pocket of her jeans and pulled out a ring. She slipped it onto her left ring finger and held her hand out for Ash to inspect it more closely. I don't know that much about jewelry, but even I could tell that Colin had spent a small fortune on the ring. It was yellow gold with a big fiery solitaire diamond surrounded by a ring of tiny emeralds. From the satisfied look on Ash's face, Colin's stock, which was already bullish, had just gone up again.

As we drove, Heather gave us a brief biography of her betrothed. Colin was twenty-nine and had grown up across the bay in Concord, where his parents still lived. He'd served as a paratrooper in the army's elite 82nd Airborne Division before becoming a cop. Along with his duties as a vice detective, he was also a member of the department's SWAT team. Colin's passions, aside from our daughter, were collecting antique firearms, rugby, and honing his considerable skills as an amateur pastry chef. Heather began to describe a decadent baklava that Colin had made last week and my stomach began to rumble.

The Hall of Justice was on Bryant Street. When we arrived, Colin turned and drove down a driveway marked "Police Vehicles Only." I continued around the complex and parked in the lot for the general public. We walked toward the large building that had been my professional home during the fifteen years I'd worked homicide. I was relieved to see that, at least outside, things still looked pretty much the same. The one sad exception was the new names engraved on the granite shrine dedicated to SFPD officers slain in the line of duty. I paused to read the fresh entries, acutely aware that if the guy who'd shot me had taken a second to really aim, my name might have been included on that roster of death. Ash knew what I was thinking. She took my hand and squeezed it.

Envisioning another name carved on the wall, I glanced at Heather. "You didn't wear your vest, like I asked."

"I couldn't. Not dressed like this," said Heather.

"Should I tell the department to put that as an epitaph under your name?"

She took my hand. "Daddy, a man I admire very much told me that cops are paid to take risks."

"He wasn't talking about his daughter . . . even if she is a damn good cop."

We left the shrine and approached the entrance to the Hall of Justice. Near the doors, we passed a sign that told you in five different languages that you had to go through a metal detector and that it was a bad idea to try and bring a gun inside. We went into the building and Heather got Ash and me visitor ID tags. Then we rode the elevator up to the fifth floor, where Gregg, Aafedt, and Colin were waiting for us in the Homicide Bureau.

The office was pretty much as I remembered it—right down to the buzzing overhead fluorescent lights and the ghostly scent of the thousands of cigarettes that had been smoked there before the building was declared smoke-free. That's what made it so weird. Gregg's work area was still decorated with racing memorabilia and photos of him and Susie at the Indianapolis Speedway. My work space hadn't changed much either. Aafedt had replaced the photos of Ash and me with pictures of him and his wife, but the police shoulder patch collection I'd started and later abandoned was still on the wall behind my desk. It became even more déjà vu–ish when Ash took a seat in the same chair she used to sit in when she'd occasionally came to the office to join me for lunch.

Going to my old desk, I asked Aafedt, "You don't mind?"

"Make yourself at home. You broke that chair in."

"Who says you can't go home again?" I asked, sitting down.

"Yeah, and it's nice to see you managed to get here without having to request the SWAT Team," said Gregg. He turned to Colin and Heather. "And if I heard correctly over the phone, congratulations are in order. When's the date?"

Heather looked uncomfortable. "Thanks, but no offense, Uncle Gregg; we're trying to keep our relationship quiet for now."

Heather and Colin had a good reason for wanting to keep their relationship secret for the time being. Like most police agencies across the country, SFPD strongly discouraged married and cohabitating couples from working as street partners.

I said, "My bust. I should have kept my mouth shut . . . not that I've ever had to say that before."

Gregg gave me a look of bug-eyed astonishment. "You took the words right out of my mouth. Don't worry, Heather, I never heard anything."

Aafedt said, "Me, either. But you'll have to excuse Colin and me for a second. We've got Bronsey in an interview room and we may have to hold him down so that a tech can collect DNA samples from him."

"Need some help?" asked Heather.

"The more the merrier," said Aafedt.

"Hang on," said Gregg as he pulled an eight-by-ten sheet of photo paper from a folder. "If he's cooperative, show him the photo lineup and see if he can pick Vandenbosch out."

As the three detectives went down the hall, Gregg said, "You'll be pleased to learn that your information on the victim was correct. Latent prints called us just before you got here to confirm they matched our dead guy's prints to Uhlander's knowns."

"Here's something else that might help." I pulled Bronsey's business card from my shirt pocket and gave it to Gregg. "The number on the back is what Bronsey called to contact Kyle."

"Good, because it was an utter waste of time getting the warrant to activate the GPS on Kyle's cell phone. It hasn't been turned on since Wednesday."

"And Bronsey was given that number on Thursday."

"We'll call this one from the cold line in a little while and see if someone is interested in going on a trip."

He was referring to a special phone line in the Homicide Bureau. Crooks and reluctant witnesses tend not to answer the phone if the screen says the call is coming from a blocked ID or, even worse, SFPD. However, they do respond at least once to calls from H&B Tours Inc. The initials stood for Homicide Bureau and the investigators *are* in the travel business, after a fashion. Over the years they've sent thousands of folks to places all over California, such as Folsom, Pelican Bay, and San Quentin.

"What about Kyle's Toyota?" I asked.

"We got the license plate from DMV and put out a BOL to patrol, telling them about the million-dollar warrant. We haven't heard anything back yet."

"You might want to contact dispatch right now to let them know he should be considered armed and dangerous."

Gregg grabbed the phone and called the dispatch center with the new information. When he was done, he tossed me a manila evidence envelope and said, "Okay, so what did Bronsey tell you?"

I looked down at the envelope. "What's this for?"

"Is your wrist broken? If you're so committed to helping us investigate this murder, you can also fill out the evidence paperwork for the business card."

"But I only want to do the fun stuff."

"Just like at home," Ash said sotto voce.

As I filled in the boxes on the evidence envelope, I brought Gregg up to date on what Bronsey had told us.

I hadn't gotten very far into the story when Gregg held up his hand for me to halt. "Some guy from a *toy* company threatened to kill Bronsey?"

"We're not dealing with elves in Santa's workshop. Like I said before, toys are a multibillion-dollar international industry."

"Any chance we can find out which company?"

"Not unless the phone at the Paladin records local outgoing calls. Even then, I'll bet the phone company's records will show that the number was issued to an imaginary person—"

"—who paid for his installation and first month's service with a forged check."

"You've heard this story before."

Later, Gregg interrupted again. "Kyle paid Bronsey to rob and terrorize his own *mother*? What is this guy? The brother of *The Bad Seed*?"

"You're making him sound like such a monster," I said, my voice laced with sarcasm. "Kyle made it clear that he didn't want Merv to actually *injure* her."

"Well, then I guess that makes it all okay."

By the time I'd gotten to Bronsey's version of the robbery, Heather and the other detectives had returned to the office. They looked unflustered, so I supposed that meant Bronsey had surrendered to the inevitable and provided the DNA samples.

Returning the photo lineup to Gregg, Aafedt said, "Bronsey made a positive ID on Vandenbosch."

I resumed my story, and when I got to the part about Bronsey accidentally shooting Uhlander in the back, Gregg muttered, "Nice shooting, Tex."

"His story explains the scene," Aafedt said. "Uhlander gets hit in the back, goes down, and our unidentified guy wearing the mask finishes him off with the twenty-two."

"You recovered a projectile from his head?" I asked.

"Yeah. It wasn't too dinged up, so we'll probably be able to match it to a gun . . . if we ever find the weapon."

"And there were no forty-five slugs recovered from the scene."

"Nope. Just nine-mils and twenty-twos."

"So, Kyle never fired a round. That may give us some leverage."

Gregg shook his head in amusement. "Uh oh. He's got that look on his face again."

"Brad, honey, we are done for the day. We are going to brunch with Heather and Colin." Ash sounded like a judge handing down a stiff jail sentence.

Heather gave Ash an embarrassed smile. "Actually, we can't, Mom. Colin and I have to cut paper on Merv's arrest. We're going to be here for hours."

After twenty-seven years of marriage, Ash and I can carry on whole conversations without saying a word. Her expression clearly said: *This is your fault.* I replied with a tranquil look that asked: *And whose idea was it to go into that freaking dive and interview Bronsey?* She responded with a puckish smile that said: *I've quite forgotten.* I closed our little telepathic chat with: *Funny how that famous steel-trap memory of yours has conveniently failed.*

Turning to Gregg, I asked, "So, what are you going to charge Bronsey with?"

He replied, "Until we have some other version of the shooting, I think we're going to book him for attempted One-Eighty-Seven. For all we know, the shooting wasn't an accident. Bronsey and Uhlander might have gotten into an argument over the bear."

"Good thinking."

"We'll also charge him with receiving stolen property, conspiracy, and the attempted kidnapping of Ash. That ought to be enough to keep him in jail at least until he's arraigned."

"And the more you stack up the charges, the greater the chance that Bronsey will decide to cut a deal and become a helpful witness."

"I prefer to think of it as a way of encouraging Merv to do the right thing," Gregg said piously.

"Uh-huh." I said, "Okay, since we can't have brunch at the Mark Hopkins, who's up for *carne asada* burritos? I'll buy, if someone wants to fly."

Colin and Heather volunteered to make the food run and our daughter wrote down our orders. Since it would be difficult to transport the food on a motorcycle, Aafedt tossed Colin the keys to his unmarked car. I gave Heather the cash and the affianced couple headed for the elevator.

Gregg asked, "So, you were saying something about leverage."

I tilted the chair back and put my hands behind my head. "You and I both know that it's academic whether or not Vandenbosch pulled the trigger."

"He's still a principal in a murder committed during the commission of a robbery."

"Exactly. But Kyle's mom doesn't know that. If we talk to her again, we might be able to paint him as an accessory who's in a world of trouble because of his trigger-happy partner."

"Who's *we*?" Ash asked.

"You and me," I replied. "She's paranoid about the cops, but she might respond to us—or you. You're both teddy bear artists."

"And she might listen if I explain to her that Kyle was responsible for the harassment and robbery." Ash thought aloud.

"God help us. Now they've *both* got that look on their faces," said Gregg.

Twelve

Later, as we ate our burritos, I said to Gregg, "Hey, you never told me what Lieutenant Garza's reaction was to our little expedition."

Gregg swallowed and replied, "She said, and I quote: 'As long as we're going to have to bring him back for court anyway, make him an official consultant and work him like a dog.'"

"I can live with that, if it's *our* dog she's talking about. By the way, where is Garza?"

"On her way to Fresno."

"Now, there's a garden spot, especially in September." With its oppressive heat, smog, and humidity from agricultural irrigation, Fresno, in the Central Valley, is so close to Hell that you can see Lucifer's mailbox if you stand on a reasonably tall ladder.

Gregg nodded. "She isn't going there by choice. She's a POST instructor now and she's scheduled to teach a class tomorrow in critical incident management."

I wasn't surprised that, along with her duties as a police

lieutenant, Garza was also a lecturer for the California
Peace Officer's Commission on Standards and Training.
She was brilliant, hardworking, and self-motivated. More
importantly, she possessed the street credentials needed to
instruct other cops, who are always on the lookout to tor-
ment a back-office pogue teaching a subject he or she has
only read about. In fact, I expected that before another ten
years passed, I'd get a phone call from Gregg telling me
Bobbie Jo had been hired as the chief of police for a Bay
Area city. For that matter, someday she might even end up
as the chief of SFPD.

Ash said, "Gregg, as long as you're going to use us as
consultants, maybe I could examine the bear once we're
done with lunch."

"Sorry, but I've already logged it into evidence and
taken it to the crime lab. I want the cyber criminalist to take
a good long look at him first."

"Very wise," I said. "Bronsey told us that Kyle turned
Patrick on just before the robbery. The bear obviously has
some memory capacity. If we're lucky it might still have a
digital recording of Kyle's voice."

"When are you flying back to Virginia?" Gregg asked.

"Early Wednesday morning," said Ash.

"If the lab guys finish with Patrick before then, I'd be
happy for you to look at him and tell me whatever you can."

Gregg's desk phone trilled and he grabbed it. Apparently, he was expecting a call but this wasn't it, because he
began rolling his eyes. He concluded the call by thanking
"Deneb" and telling her that he'd be sure to run down the
lead right away. Meanwhile, Aafedt had begun to laugh.

"Not who you wanted it to be?" I asked.

"No, that was Lady Deneb. I think her real name is
Phyllis and she really wants to be a psychic detective like
on TV. Anyway, she was scrying and—"

"Scrying?"

"That's apparently the word you use to describe gazing

into a crystal ball and pretending you see something," said Gregg. "And I'm happy to announce that Lady Deneb has solved the case for us. She called to let me know that the shooting victim from the Paladin is actually a clone that escaped from the secret government labs in Fort Ord."

Ash stopped chewing and stared at Gregg.

"A clone. God, I miss this place," I said in a homesick voice.

"But there's more. The Tri-Lateral Commission and the Illuminati hired an assassin to kill the clone, because they don't want anyone to see how he was bioengineered by the aliens."

"Huh. His insides looked pretty normal to me," Aafedt said thoughtfully and then took a big bite of burrito.

I said, "And aliens? I thought the guy was produced at Fort Ord."

"He was, but the aliens and army are working together. And . . ." Gregg paused for dramatic effect. "She told me to look for a . . . silver car."

"Well, that's helpful. There are probably only a hundred thousand of them in this city alone."

"And we saw a silver car on the way back from lunch." Colin's voice was full of faux dread.

"Yeah, and I hope you're happy." Heather gave her fiancé a very realistic look of exasperation. Then she turned to us. "I *told* Colin we should stop that silver car, because it had a bumper sticker on it that read MY LITTLE ILLUMINATI ASSASSIN WAS AN HONOR STUDENT. But *no*, he just blew me off."

Colin hung his head, pretending to be ashamed. I joined in the laughter, trying not to let the sudden ache of loss affect me. There were so many things I missed about being a homicide detective. The investigative work was fascinating, intellectually demanding, and exciting. But this was something else I yearned for: the irreverent cop humor, greasy and delicious Mexican food eaten at desks, and the warm atmosphere of camaraderie.

I took a sip of *horchata*, the chilled Mexican cinnamon-and-rice milk drink, to make the tiny lump in my throat go away, before asking, "So, who were you hoping was actually on the phone?"

"Burgess Fleet Leasing. We faxed them a search warrant a little while ago to get the information on who has that Dodge Avenger."

"But they're taking their sweet time getting back to us," Aafedt added.

Gregg finished his burrito, picked up the phone receiver, and pressed for a different outside line than the one he ordinarily used. "As long as we've got a moment, I'll try that cell number you gave me."

We sat quietly as he pressed the number and waited for an answer. Then Gregg tilted his head and listened.

He hung up a second later and said, "It rolled right over to voice mail."

"So, Kyle's either on the phone or the thing has been turned off," said Aafedt.

"My money is on off, and probably in the bay." I glanced at my watch. "I guess we'd better be heading over to Vandenbosch's mom's house. What are you guys going to do while we're at Lauren's?"

Gregg pulled some legal paperwork from a file. "We're heading down to Redwood City to search his apartment. Maybe we'll find something that the Lycaon security guys missed."

I looked at Ash. "Considering how our last interview ended, it probably wouldn't be a good idea for me to just show up on Lauren's doorstep. How would you like to call her home number and test the waters?"

"I'd be happy to."

However, before we could call, Gregg's phone trilled. The conversation was succinct and culminated with Gregg telling the caller that he'd pick up the paperwork tomorrow morning.

Hanging up, he said, "Our investigation just got murkier. That was Burgess Leasing and they say that the Dodge Avenger is part of the car fleet they lease to Lycaon. Unfortunately, they can't tell us who it was assigned to."

"I don't need Lady Deneb's freaking crystal ball to tell you it's someone from their security department," I said.

"This was the car parked down the block from the motel?" Ash asked.

Heather said, "That's right, Mom. We recovered digital video that shows someone running to the car and jumping inside right after the shooting."

"And since it almost perfectly fits the time frame, we have to look at the possibility the person getting into the Avenger was our shooter in the ski mask," said Gregg.

"If it was someone from Lycaon, why were he and Kyle cooperating?" I asked.

"Maybe they weren't. Maybe Lycaon tracked Kyle down and one of their security guys went into the motel room just before Bronsey showed up."

"But why didn't he disarm Kyle?"

"He could've made a bad search. Hell, even experienced officers can miss a gun while frisking for weapons, and it sounds like this guy could've been a rent-a-cop."

"But why would a Lycaon guy have ever allowed Bronsey and Uhlander in the room?"

Aafedt said, "Maybe Kyle told him about the big bag 'o money and offered to set Bronsey up to be robbed."

"In return for getting to leave the room alive?"

Gregg nodded. "We've got to assume that Lycaon was up to no good. They knew where Kyle was and they knew he had a million-dollar warrant, yet they didn't call the police to have us make an arrest."

"Because Lycaon was going to get their property back and also FUBAR Kyle." Aafedt finished the thought for his partner, using an acronym that stood for Foul-Up Beyond All Recognition, although I suspected he had a more pungent word than *foul* in mind. "That way they would have also provided an object lesson to anyone else at their company who might be considering stealing from their employer."

"Then this golden opportunity arises," said Gregg. "Lycaon can recover their wonder bear and also rip their competitor off for four hundred K. That had to feel good."

"But they didn't recover the bear," I said.

"No, which means there are two bunches of corporate goons looking for Bronsey. Lycaon wants the bear, and Lizard Eyes and his posse are going to want their money back. Jail is the safest place for him right now."

"And Lycaon can't tell the police that they think Bronsey has the bear, because it would implicate them in a murder," said Aafedt.

"But why didn't the Lycaon guy just kill Kyle, too? I mean, why leave a witness who can come back to blackmail you?" Heather asked.

Gregg replied, "It was a bloody madhouse in that room. Kyle probably booked before the other guy could shoot."

"And for all we know, some of the bullet holes were caused by the guy shooting at Kyle and missing," Aafedt added.

"So, are we looking at Kyle as a victim now?" I asked in disbelief.

"Not a victim," said Gregg. "He's like so many of the freaking tinhorn desperadoes we've dealt with over the years. He stole that bear and thought he was a bad ass, up until he ran into the genuine articles."

"And now he's on the run, being chased by hired guns from two different corporations, both of whom probably want to make sure Kyle can't tell any embarrassing tales. After all, that would be bad for the quarterly dividend." Aafedt's voice oozed with contempt.

"Oh, I can't wait for tomorrow morning when we pay Lycaon a surprise visit," said Gregg.

Gregg's was the best theory we had thus far to explain

the cryptic elements of the murder, but I wasn't convinced. I still had unanswered questions: If Kyle was armed with a .45 automatic, why hadn't he used it on the Lycaon goon? And who was the woman who'd been pounding on the door minutes before the murder and screaming that Kyle would pay in blood?

Yet, I decided not to say anything. This was Gregg and Aafedt's case and they were extremely skilled detectives. Indeed, with their day-to-day work investigating murders, they probably had a better grasp of the situation than someone who'd been away from the game for over two years and whose most recent claim to fame was winning an "honorable mention" at a Baltimore teddy bear show.

"I still think we need to talk to Lauren again," I said.

"Agreed. You and Ash go there, we'll go toss Kyle's place, and then we'll Eighty-Seven back here," said Gregg, using the numeric code for a rendezvous.

I gave the cell phone to Ash. "Why don't you make the call? She probably won't answer if she thinks it's a telemarketer, and she'll freak out if she sees the call is coming from the PD."

Ash went into the office across the hall for some quiet and after a few seconds we heard her talking. That was a good sign. It meant that Lauren was home and at least willing to chat with Ash. However, when Ash returned to Gregg's office a few seconds later, I knew there was trouble. My wife looked agitated.

"What?" I asked.

"Lauren is a complete basket case. Kyle called her a little while ago. He wouldn't say where he was, but did tell her that his life was at risk. Oh, and he also said he was sorry for having put her in danger," said Ash.

"Gee, he only waited twelve hours to let his mom know there might be an armed thug after her. Maybe we've misjudged him," muttered Colin.

"What else did Lauren say?" I asked.

"Nothing else. She'll only talk in person. She says she thinks her phone is tapped."

"And it might be. Remember, we're dealing with computer wizards."

Gregg said, "Maybe we should go with you."

Ash shook her head firmly. "No. She won't talk to you, and I almost had to beg before she'd agree to let Brad come along."

"We'll be en route," I said, getting to my feet.

"This isn't fair," said Heather in a peevish tone that was only partly sham. "You guys are all going out in the field, while we have to stay here and write reports."

"You know the rules, Heather honey," I called out as we left the office. "Finish your homework before going outside to play."

Thirteen

As we pulled out of the Hall of Justice parking lot, Ash said, "This investigation is more complicated than one of my mama's diamond chain quilts. Any suggestions on how to handle this interview?"

"You'll do fine, Deputy Lyon. All those years spent being a good mother have made you an excellent interrogator."

"But you must have some ideas."

"The only advice I have is that you need to decide in advance what information you want to keep from Lauren, at least during the first part of the interview."

"We don't want her to know that Bronsey was arrested."

I nodded. "Good. Why?"

Ash thought for a second. "Because we want her to think that Bronsey might come after her again, which may make her frightened enough that she'll tell us the truth."

"You don't sound comfortable with that."

"Honey, you have to admit it's kind of cruel."

"No, it's *real* cruel," I said, turning onto Eighth Street.

"Look, I don't enjoy the idea of scaring the bejeezus out of Lauren either. But she hasn't told us the entire truth and fear is a wonderful tool for getting to the facts."

"I guess. I just wish there was some alternative."

Putting my hand on her knee, I said, "Maybe you'll find another option. Interviewing isn't a science. It's an art and you need to develop your own style."

"But I want your help." She took my hand.

"Yeah, but what works for me might not work for you. Your greatest assets are that you're wholesome, genuinely kind, and compassionate. It could be that Lauren will respond to that."

"We can hope."

"I'm convinced you can handle this. The important thing is for me to keep my mouth shut, until we come to a point when Lauren wants to include me in the conversation."

"Because we want to give her the illusion of control," Ash said contemplatively.

"You aren't as innocent as you look . . . thank goodness."

We cut over a few blocks to Oak Street and turned west. Soon, we were traveling through the Haight-Ashbury District, although most San Franciscans simply call it The Haight. The neighborhood became world famous during the hippie era and now—forty years later—a new generation of faux flower children had come to wander the streets in pursuit of the long lost psychedelic magic. It was a silly pilgrimage that reminded me of a dog chasing a car: He wouldn't know what to do with it if he caught it.

Another few blocks brought us to my favorite roadway in San Francisco: Lyon Street. Rock legend Janis Joplin's old house was near the intersection and I was pleased to see that the prayer in one of Janis's most famous old songs had finally been answered, even if it was almost forty years too late. There was a Mercedes Benz parked in front of the home.

We turned onto Lauren's street about ten minutes later

and I was relieved to see that her Subaru was parked in the driveway. It meant that she was home and hopefully still willing to talk to Ash. As we got out of the car and headed for the house, I noticed my wife looking covetously at the resin bear statue in the front yard.

The door opened before Ash could knock. Lauren looked tired and stressed and the flesh beneath her eyes was puffy, as if she'd been crying. She scanned the street nervously as she let us into the house. We went into the living room, which still faintly smelled of apple pie. We declined Lauren's offer to make coffee, and she listlessly asked us to sit down.

"I can't believe this is happening," Lauren said as she slumped into the rocking chair. She gave me a hangdog look of mortification, "And I'm sorry for not telling you the entire truth last night, Brad."

"That's okay. You had good reasons not to trust me," I replied. "You look worried. Did Bronsey call?"

"No. There was a hang-up earlier this morning, but I couldn't tell who it was from."

I gently pressed my knee against Ash's to signal that she should take over. She said, "You told me that Kyle is in danger. Did he say why?"

Lauren pressed her fingers to her mouth and then removed them. "They told Kyle they were going to kill him if they didn't get the bear."

"Who did? Lycaon?"

"No. The other company he was dealing with. I don't know its name."

Even though Ash knew all about Lizard Eyes and the competing corporation, she did an impeccable job feigning ignorance and surprise. "*Another* company? Lauren, what the heck is going on here?"

"It's a long story."

"And we're here to listen to every word of it because we want to help."

"Thank you." Lauren looked like she was going to cry. Then she took a deep breath. "It all started over a year ago. I told your husband that Kyle didn't have anything to do with those hideous games that Lycaon produces, but that was a lie. He helped design that pet shop massacre computer game, although he hated doing it."

"Then why didn't he leave the company?"

"I asked him to, but he told me that he couldn't just walk away from a job with that kind of salary and benefits. And where would he go? All the software companies are producing that depraved stuff," she said plaintively.

"But something happened a year ago," said Ash.

"Yes. Kyle went to a huge high-tech convention up in Seattle and saw an android that was invented by some Japanese scientist."

"An android?"

"Apparently the robot looked just like the scientist and even behaved like a human being. Kyle said it was the most incredible thing he'd ever seen."

"I can't even imagine. So, Kyle came back from Seattle with the idea to make Patrick the Polar Bear," said Ash.

Lauren's eyes widened. "How do you know his name?"

"Brad told me about him last night. He sounds fabulous." Ash glanced at me, obviously wanting me to explain further.

"I had no idea Patrick was voice-activated and I turned him on by accident. Your son is brilliant. You should be proud," I said.

"I am . . . At least, I was."

Ash asked, "Did Kyle tell his supervisor at Lycaon about his idea for the bear?"

"Absolutely. He wanted to keep everything aboveboard. But the management said they weren't interested."

"That sounds crazy. Did they say why?"

Lauren's lips compressed. "They weren't interested in something as sweet and kind as a teddy bear that could be a companion for the next generation of latchkey kids. No, what they wanted was for Kyle to develop a new computer game where the players get to be famous serial killers."

"Instructional software for predators? That's just evil." Although I'd resolved to remain mostly silent, the words just slipped out.

"Kyle felt the same way, but he had to have a safety net before jumping," said Lauren.

Ash said, "So, he began working on Patrick."

"Yes, while dragging his heels as much as possible on that abomination of a game."

"And he didn't create Patrick at the Lycaon plant?"

"No." Lauren shook her head adamantly. "He was being paid to develop game software, not tinker with a mechanical teddy bear that supposedly nobody wanted. They wouldn't have allowed him the time, resources, or workspace."

"So, where was Patrick made?"

"In Kyle's apartment. It's more of a computer lab than a home anyway. He spent almost every night and weekend either working on the robotic body or the software. It was like he was obsessed, which made me happy."

"Why?"

"Because it was good to see my son in high spirits again." Lauren glanced at the photo on the mantel of a beaming Kyle graduating from Stanford. "He was excited at the prospect of finally doing something . . . honorable . . . with his computer skills."

Ash nodded. "As a mother, I can understand that. I'm guessing you helped Kyle in whatever ways you could."

"Yes. Money became an issue. The machinery and equipment were so expensive, and since Kyle was basically experimenting, sometimes he bought stuff that he later found out just wouldn't work."

"So, as a supportive parent, you lent him a hand with the money."

"At first, I told him not to worry about groceries or meals. It was nice to cook for my son again." Lauren's smile was bittersweet. "Later, I dipped into my savings and cashed in a CD to help him pay for the equipment."

"And I'm assuming you also designed and created the actual teddy bear part of the project."

She nodded. "I wanted to make him out of kid mohair, but Kyle insisted on fur with a faint metallic tipping. That meant going with synthetic plush."

"I could tell the bear was made by a true artist," I said, hoping the flattery didn't come across as utterly blatant, because it wasn't.

"Thank you."

"What about Patrick's voice? Is it Kyle's?" Ash asked.

"Yes. He recorded over fifteen hundred individual words for the vocal files. He wanted Kyle to actually talk," Lauren said proudly.

"That's a bigger vocabulary than most people have," I said.

Ash said, "So, at some point Kyle finished the bear."

"Yes, right about the same time he met that scheming little bitch." Lauren's jaw tightened.

I almost said: *Last night, you told me that Kyle doesn't have a regular girlfriend.* Instead, I glanced at Ash, who said, "What's this woman's name?"

"Rhiannon Otero. She worked with Kyle at Lycaon. He never saw what hit him."

Meanwhile, my mind was racing. Otero was a Hispanic name and I wondered if Rhiannon was the woman I'd noticed watching us at the teddy bear show in Sonoma the previous morning. And if she was Kyle's girlfriend, it was even more likely that she was the mystery woman seen trying to batter her way into the room at the Paladin. Another unpleasant thought occurred to me: Had Rhiannon accompanied Bronsey to the bear show to point out Lauren as the woman to terrorize?

"Was she his girlfriend?" Ash asked.

"No. She's a parasite, and the reason why Kyle is in such a terrible situation now."

"How do you mean?"

Lauren glanced at the picture on the mantel again. "Kyle has always been very . . . shy . . . around women and as focused as he was on completing Patrick, he'd been living almost a hermit's life for a year. He and Rhiannon were talking one afternoon when he accidentally mentioned Patrick."

"Is Rhiannon pretty?" I asked.

"I suppose so, if you can overlook the makeup applied with a garden trowel."

"Take it from a guy. Him mentioning the bear wasn't an accident. He was boasting."

Ash said, "What happened after that?"

"Suddenly, my son had a very *affectionate* girlfriend." Lauren's tone was acidic and you didn't need to be an expert in semantics to know that *affectionate* was a euphemism for *slutty*.

"So, are you suggesting that she initiated a relationship in order to benefit from the sale of Patrick?"

"That's exactly what happened. Up until she found out about the robot, that little gold-digger couldn't have cared less about my son."

"But Kyle thought the attraction was genuine."

"And he wouldn't listen to me when I tried to warn him. Rhiannon changed my son. I started seeing less and less of him."

Although I really wanted to believe Lauren's unflattering assessment of Rhiannon, it also appeared as if much of her animosity toward Kyle's girlfriend was born of jealousy. What's more, Lauren hadn't explained *why* she believed Rhiannon's relationship with her son was based on a profit motive.

Ash was obviously thinking the same thing. "I'm certain Rhiannon was a bad influence on Kyle, but what did she do to make you call her a gold-digger?" she asked.

"I don't know all of the story, because Kyle wouldn't tell me. But it seems that little Rhiannon took it upon herself to contact some toy company and tell them that Patrick was for sale."

"When did this happen?"

"Sometime in late August."

"What did Kyle think of that?"

"He was thrilled," Lauren said incredulously. "He thought it was great. He told me that it would give him leverage when he offered Patrick to Lycaon again."

"So, he thought this was an opportunity to start a bidding war?"

"He wasn't thinking anything. Rhiannon was running the show."

I cleared my throat. "Before I forget, you wouldn't happen to have a picture of Rhiannon with Kyle, would you?"

"Why?" she asked suspiciously.

"I want to see what she looks like, because I have a feeling I saw her at the teddy bear show yesterday morning."

"That's impossible. She's with Kyle. She has been since this whole rotten thing began on Wednesday."

"Still, I'd like to look at a photo, if you have one."

Lauren got up from the rocking chair. "I could look upstairs on the computer. There might be a picture in an e-mail. If I find one, I'll print it."

"Thanks. I'd appreciate that."

Ash waited until she was certain Lauren was upstairs and out of earshot before whispering, "What are you talking about?"

"Right after the Sonoma officers left, I noticed a young, pretty Hispanic woman standing near the city hall. She seemed to be eyeballing Lauren. I didn't think it was important at the time, so I never said anything."

"Wow. You just *happened* to notice a pretty girl," Ash said teasingly.

"Who was young enough to be my daughter."

"Some men your age are attracted to that."

"Some men my age are pigs. What do you make of all this?" I quietly asked.

"It's hard to tell. It's possible that Rhiannon began a relationship with Kyle because she recognized that the robot might make him—and her—rich."

"But, if that's the case, why was she pounding on his door at the Paladin last night?"

"You think that was her?"

"We have to assume it was. The witness thought the woman was acting like a betrayed wife."

"But if it *was* her, it means they've broken up."

"Not necessarily. Remember, my witness was on the lookout for johns. She may not have noticed if Rhiannon came back to the room and finally convinced Kyle to open the door."

"Which means that Rhiannon *could* be our killer." There were footfalls overhead and Ash glanced toward the ceiling. "But if Lauren suspects that, why didn't she tell us right away? It's not as if she likes the girl."

"We don't know what Kyle's told her. Besides, she may realize that the story has to be told in a certain way to keep her darling boy out of prison."

"So what do we do?"

I squeezed her hand. "It's groundhog time, my love. You've been doing great, but now you have to start really digging."

Fourteen

We heard Lauren start back down the stairs and we stopped talking.

As she resumed her seat in the rocking chair, Lauren said, "Sorry, but I couldn't find any pictures of her. Kyle e-mailed me one of the two of them, but . . . well, I deleted it."

"Thanks for looking," said Ash.

Lauren tapped nervously on the chair's wooden armrest. "Can I ask you two some questions?"

"Sure."

"Where is Patrick right now?"

Ash glanced at me and I said, "At the Hall of Justice."

"Provided this all works out, when can we have him back?"

"Probably never. Patrick was collected as physical evidence in a murder and it's the law in California that police departments maintain homicide evidence forever."

Lauren sat forward in the chair. "Forever? That's insane."

"It may look that way, but it's a good rule. It doesn't happen often, but innocent people have been convicted of murder and other major crimes. We keep all the evidence, so that the defense attorney or even another detective can someday correct a horrible error."

"It's not a weapon. We're talking about a toy."

"A toy that appears to have been the motive for a brutal murder."

"But if we promised to bring him back to court . . . ?"

"I'm sorry, but that just isn't possible. The defense attorney is entitled to the same access to pristine evidence as the prosecution, so the detectives will have to keep Patrick."

"So, Kyle just loses out on something he spent tens of thousands of dollars on and slaved over for a year?"

"Lauren, I'm not trying to be a smart aleck, but Kyle has much bigger problems right now than losing Patrick."

Lauren's head sagged. "I know."

Pressing the issue with the cool stealth of a boa constrictor, Ash said gently, "And that's because he was in that motel room last night when the murder happened, wasn't he?"

There was a long pause before Lauren answered, "He was there . . . with Rhiannon."

"Did he tell you what happened?"

"No. The idiot is head-over-heels in love, so all he'll say is that a man was killed and that he and Rhiannon are in this situation together."

"But you're reading a message between the lines?"

Lauren looked up and her eyes were feverish. "He's covering for her! Kyle is going to throw his life away and end up in prison for some grasping little whore! It makes me so sick I could vomit!"

Ash nodded empathetically. "I understand you're upset, but I want to be clear about this. You think Rhiannon killed the man, right?"

"I *know* she did! My son couldn't kill anyone!"

Maybe, I thought, *but he clearly never had any problems dreaming up buckets of savagery for computer games.*

"I want to believe you, but in order to prove that, you need to calm down and tell us the whole story," said Ash. "You said a few minutes ago that everything began to go sour on Wednesday . . . ?"

Lauren took a deep breath and seemed to recover some of her composure. "That was the day that Kyle met with the vice president of his division. Even though they'd all but laughed him out of the office the first time, he wanted to give Lycaon a final chance at acquiring Patrick, before offering him to the other company."

"That was very loyal of Kyle."

"It *was* loyal . . . and as stupid as trying to hand-feed a Bengal tiger. Once my son finished making his earnest little pitch, the VP told him that Lycaon wasn't going to pay anything for Patrick. Under the terms of Kyle's employment, the company already owned the bear."

"How?"

From outside there came the sounds of a vehicle pulling into the cul-de-sac and then two car doors slamming. We all tensed and the room went silent. No doubt, Lauren was alarmed that the noise might herald the arrival of Bronsey or perhaps the police, while Ash and I were concerned that it was Lizard Eyes and his thugs. Lauren shot a furtive glance out the window and then relaxed, which allowed us to also. Obviously, she recognized the car and its occupants.

Looking back at Ash, Lauren said, "I'm sorry. Where were we?"

"You were going to explain why Lycaon claimed they owned Patrick."

Lauren leaned over to rest her chin on her hand. "Kyle was told that he'd signed some form when he first started work with them. The fine print apparently said that Lycaon retained all the rights to any freelance projects he might create."

"Did he?"

"Kyle didn't remember doing so, but a company like that wouldn't have any qualms about forging his signature on a document."

"I suppose not. Still, you said Kyle created Patrick at home. How could they claim ownership?" Ash sounded outraged.

"Big corporations like Lycaon don't explain things to the peasants. The VP simply told Kyle to go home and bring Patrick back."

"So, he hadn't brought Patrick to the presentation?"

"No. Sometimes my son is painfully naïve, but I think in the back of his mind, he thought there was at least a chance that they'd try to steal Patrick."

"Did the VP at least offer Kyle a bonus?"

Lauren gave a humorless laugh. "He wasn't offered so much as a dime in compensation. In fact, the VP told Kyle that if he didn't cooperate, he'd be out of a job, blackballed in the industry, and that Lycaon would still get Patrick."

I found myself muttering, "Which only goes to show that successful psychopaths don't go to prison. They end up running corporations."

Lauren nodded in agreement.

Ash said, "So, what did Kyle do?"

"God bless him, he surprised me." There was approval in her voice. "I thought he was going to collapse like a house of cards, but he decided they weren't going to push him around anymore."

I wondered if Kyle's relationship with Rhiannon might have sparked some of this backbone and newfound self-confidence, but kept quiet.

Lauren continued, "He figured if they could lie, so could he. He told the VP that he'd cooperate. Then he raced home, grabbed Patrick, and started looking for a place to hide."

"And the first place he came was here, right?" Ash asked.

"Yes, but he didn't stay for very long. He knew Lycaon

would send their security people out looking for him and they'd come here. He wanted to protect me."

Ash gave her a sympathetic look. I suddenly suspected what was going to happen next and wondered just how my wife was going to debunk Lauren's iconic view of Kyle without derailing the interview.

"Oh, Lauren, I'm so sorry to be the one to have to tell you this, but Kyle was never interested in protecting you," Ash said gravely.

"What are you talking about?" Lauren fixed her with an intense gaze.

"Brad and I were coming into the city this morning to meet our daughter. That's why we're all dressed up." She gestured at our clothing. "But we were so worried about you and your son that we ended up looking for Bronsey."

"For the police?"

"No, for you. You were one of my main inspirations for becoming a teddy bear artist and I just couldn't stand the idea of a bad man like Bronsey harassing you."

Lauren's eyes softened a little. "Did you find him?"

"Yes, and we talked to him. It turns out he's as scared as you are."

"Why?"

"Because he wasn't working for Lycaon. He'd been hired by another toy company—probably the one that Rhiannon contacted—to buy Patrick from your son."

"It that's the case, why was he hounding me to tell him where Kyle was?"

Ash sighed. "That was apparently your son's idea. Bronsey said that Kyle offered him two thousand dollars to harass you and make it look as if Lycaon was responsible."

"I don't believe you. Why would Kyle do that?"

"He thought that if you'd been victimized, it would make Lycaon look bad if it ever came down to a lawsuit over who actually owned Patrick."

"That's a lie!" Lauren slapped the chair's armrest.

"For your sake, I wish you were right. But why would Bronsey make something like that up?"

"That's obvious. To have an excuse for robbing me."

"But, that isn't an excuse. He implicated himself . . . and Kyle."

"And you'd take the word of that thug over my son's?"

"Right now we have to, because the police can verify an awful lot of things that Bronsey said. For instance, Bronsey and his partner didn't break into that room to rob Kyle. Your son knew they were coming. He'd called them. Bronsey went there to buy Patrick and he'd brought a lot of money."

"This is insane. I think you should—"

"Lauren, Kyle has been feeding you a bunch of big fat lies. And, as a mom, I know how much you don't want to believe your child could do that to you." Ash's voice was stern, yet empathetic. "Now, we'll leave right now if that's your decision, but I at least wanted to offer you the opportunity to hear the truth."

Lauren looked as if she'd just sucked on a lemon, and her knee was jiggling up and down like crazy. At last, she said, "What else did that filth say?"

It took every molecule of self-control I possessed not to raise both my arms and give my wife a series of worshiping bows. Ash had accomplished her mission of moving the interview into the informational Mother Lode and hadn't had to use fear or intimidation as an impetus. With a start, I realized that I could learn more than a thing or two from her.

Ash said, "Now, I suppose you're wondering why we believe Bronsey. Brad and I both know that he's a congenital liar. It would have been easy for him to point the finger at Kyle for the murder, yet he didn't."

"This is making no sense."

"It will. Bronsey told us that he was in the process of testing Patrick when a man with a gun jumped out of the bathroom to rob them. He was wearing a ski mask—"

"That wasn't a man! It was Rhiannon!" Lauren's voice was fierce and exultant.

Ash raised a finger to caution her. "We don't know who it was. Bronsey was pretty certain it was a man wearing a ski mask and a black coat."

"Take my word for it, the only one it could have been was Rhiannon. God, Kyle is lucky that she didn't rob him, too."

"Actually, Bronsey said that Kyle also pulled out a gun."

"That's impossible. He doesn't own a gun."

Ash glanced at me to respond and I said, "Unfortunately, that isn't true. The police have proof that Kyle purchased a forty-five semi-automatic pistol about a month and a half ago. That's a large caliber pistol. Not the kind you use to plunk at tin cans. Guns like that are intended for one purpose only—to kill people."

Lauren turned to Ash. "Kyle couldn't shoot anyone!"

Ash nodded. "I hope you're right. But Kyle *did* help whoever this person was in the ski mask to rob Bronsey and his partner of four hundred thousand dollars."

"Four hundred thousand dollars!" Lauren looked wild.

"I'm sorry, Lauren. I know this is hard, but you need to know the entire story. Kyle ordered Bronsey and his partner to throw down their guns and hand over the bag of cash."

"No." Lauren pointed accusingly at Ash. "That didn't happen. It couldn't have. Or if it did, it was because Rhiannon said she'd shoot Kyle if he didn't cooperate."

"I suppose that's possible. But didn't Kyle tell you that he and Rhiannon were *both* implicated?" Ash gently countered.

"Oh, my Lord, what has she gotten him into? How . . . how did the man get shot?"

I nudged Ash's knee with mine to let her know that I thought it was probably best if I replied to the question. There was no point in muddying the interview by telling Lauren that Bronsey had accidentally shot Uhlander.

I said, "Bronsey's partner pulled a gun and the person in

the ski mask immediately opened fire. Then it turned into a general gun battle. The detectives are still trying to figure out the sequence of events after that."

"Bronsey ran from the room with Patrick," said Ash. "He fell and dropped the bear in the motel parking lot. But he didn't stop to go back for Patrick, because there was still gunfire coming from the room."

"And it looks as if Kyle and the other suspect were in such a hurry to get out of there before the cops arrived that they didn't see Patrick on the ground," I added.

Lauren held up her hand for us to stop. "But you haven't answered my question. How was the man killed? Was it with this gun my son supposedly has?"

I said, "No. The victim was shot in the back of the head execution-style with a different caliber gun. The detectives think it was the person in the ski mask that did it and I'm inclined to agree."

"It was Rhiannon. Just like she must've been the one who convinced Kyle to pay Bronsey to rob me, the scheming little bitch."

I shrugged. "Even so, that still doesn't let Kyle off the hook."

"Why not?"

"I'll try to explain. Right now, it looks as if Kyle and someone else—Rhiannon if that will make you happy—engaged in a conspiracy to commit an armed robbery."

"But Kyle didn't shoot anybody!"

"It doesn't make a difference who pulled the trigger. As far as the law is concerned, both people committing the robbery are equally culpable of murder," I said somberly.

I declined to add that the district attorney could also allege that "special circumstances" existed in such a case, which potentially meant the death penalty. The poor woman had enough on her plate as it was.

There was an element of panic in Lauren's voice as she said, "But what if Rhiannon forced him to do it?"

"That's not what he told you, though. Not that I expect you'd testify in court to Kyle saying anything about assuming responsibility for the murder. After all, you are his mother."

Lauren's cheeks flushed.

I continued, "Kyle's problem is that it looks as if he's on the run with four hundred thousand dollars after committing a murder. He's the only one who can change that impression."

"By talking to the police," said Ash.

"But they'll arrest him."

I nodded. "Yeah, they probably will. But at least he can give his version of the shooting first and cut a deal with the prosecutor. And I can assure you that if Rhiannon is taken into custody first, she's going to dump a world of crap on your son."

"But—"

"Hang on, because I need to share one of the ugly realities of the criminal justice system: Juries don't like to convict women of violent felonies. It's just the way most people are. They'd rather believe that an evil man led the poor woman astray. Guess who the evil man will be this time?"

"So, Kyle should do the smart thing and surrender himself to Inspector Mauel," Ash quickly added.

"Can you call Kyle?" I asked.

Lauren looked as if she might be ill. "I would, if I thought he'd answer." She turned to face Ash and I could see the misery and hopelessness in her eyes. "But Kyle told me that he thought Lycaon had figured out the number he was using, so he was getting rid of the phone."

"So, you don't know when . . . or if . . . you're going to hear from him again. I'm so sorry," said Ash.

I said, "What can you tell us about Rhiannon? Do you know where she lives?"

"Saratoga, I think. Kyle said something about her having

a condo there," said Lauren, naming a city that was about fifty miles south.

"Do you know what kind of car she drives?"

"I only saw it once, at Kyle's apartment. It was a dark blue Acura, I think. A sedan. I don't know the license."

"That's all right. Just knowing what kind of car is helpful. And unless you think of anything else we need to know about Rhiannon, I think we're done," I said.

Lauren looked exhausted. "And I suppose the first thing I have to do is find my son a good defense attorney."

"At the risk of offering unwanted advice, can I make a final suggestion?"

She rubbed her eyes and nodded slightly.

"Kyle's a man now and maybe it'd be best if you let him clean up the huge mess he and Rhiannon have created . . . the mess that they sucked you into."

Lauren mulled my words for a few seconds and then frowned. Looking up at me, she said, "You might be right. Maybe I have babied him a little."

I bit my tongue to prevent myself from saying: *Oh, you think?* Instead, I asked, "And are you comfortable staying here alone?"

"Bronsey isn't going to come here, is he?" There was a fresh tremor of fear in her voice.

Now that we had the information we needed, there was no point in keeping the knowledge that Bronsey was in custody from her. I said, "No. He's in jail and not getting out anytime soon. But there's a possibility that the people from the other toy company might come here looking for their money."

"How likely is that?"

I had a sudden inspiration and replied, "Once this story hits the media—and it will if someone drops a discreet dime to an old reporter friend at the *Chronicle*—not very. The other company won't want to run the risk of bad publicity, so

I expect they'll write the money off as a bad investment and bring their goon squad home."

"Good. I'm not going to become a prisoner in my own home."

"That's an excellent attitude, but I'm also concerned about Kyle showing up here with Rhiannon."

"Obviously, my son has made some terrible mistakes, but I know that he'd never hurt me . . . or let someone else hurt me. Besides, I have the feeling I may never see him again," Lauren said sadly.

"Why?" Ash asked.

"He said 'good-bye' at the end of his last phone call. We never use that word. He always says, 'Love you, Mom, and see you soon.'"

"Where do you think he'll go?"

"I don't know and I'm going to try not to care." Lauren pulled a tissue from a box on the end table. Dabbing at her eyes, she said, "Well, he's a man now and he's got to live with his decisions. It's time for me to cut the apron strings."

Ash stood up. "It's a difficult decision, but I think you're doing the right thing."

"I hope so. Ashleigh, thank you for enduring my temper tantrum and telling me the truth."

"It wasn't that bad, but I'm not going to say 'my pleasure,'" said Ash with a sad smile.

"And Brad, I'm sorry . . ."

I used my cane to pull myself from the overstuffed couch. "There's nothing to apologize for. You believed you were looking out for the safety of your son, so there's no way I can fault you for that."

"So, what are you going to do now?" Ash asked.

Lauren looked toward the stairs. "I'm going to pour myself a big glass of wine, go up to my sewing room, and get as far away from the real world as I can by working on my teddy bears."

"They are kind of magical that way, aren't they?" Ash asked.

Lauren gave my wife a shy look. "Hey, what are you doing tomorrow?"

Ash glanced at me and I shrugged. She replied, "Nothing, I guess."

"Then how would you like to come over and work on teddy bears with me? There'll be no talk about Kyle or any of this other insanity. We'll just have a girls' day, playing with the mohair. I'd really like that."

"So would I," said Ash. "What time?"

"Make it early and you can stay for lunch."

"I'd be delighted."

As the women exchanged hugs, Lauren said in an envious tone, "Oh, and please bring one of your bears. I'm dying to get a closer look at how you do your lip-sculpting."

Fifteen

We drove out of the neighborhood and I pulled into a convenience store parking lot to call Gregg, who I assumed was in Redwood City by now. There were a couple of teenaged boys loitering in front of the store and you didn't need to be an expert on adolescent behavior to recognize they were waiting for an accommodating adult to buy them some beer. I guess I still look like a cop, because the kids took off when I turned my Ray·Ban aviator sunglasses on them and treated them to my best don't-make-me-get-out-of-my-police-car stare.

Ash watched the silent episode. "Having fun?"

"Just a little. It's nice to know I still look the part, even if I can't back it up physically anymore."

"I don't know . . . there are some physical things that you're still *really* good at."

"I love it when you bolster my fragile male ego."

She patted my knee. "Brad honey, I hate to break this to you, but your ego is anything but fragile."

I pressed the number for Gregg's phone and he answered on the first ring. "Inspector Mauel."

I said, "You owe Ash, big-time. I think she's broken the case."

"Really? What did Lauren say?"

"Her new version of the story is that Kyle was seduced to the dark side by his gold-digging girlfriend, Rhiannon Otero. He called his mommy this morning and seems to have half admitted that he and his lady love were responsible for the murder."

"So Rhiannon might be our person wearing the ski mask?"

"Lauren is convinced of it. However, I don't think we should jump to conclusions. I've got no doubts that Lauren also believes Rhiannon is responsible for the crash of the *Hindenburg* and the eruption of Krakatoa."

"But if his girlfriend was inside the motel room, who was the woman pounding on the door?"

"Maybe they made up before Bronsey arrived."

"Did Lauren say anything else about Rhiannon?" Gregg asked.

"Yeah. Supposedly, she worked with Kyle at Lycaon and lives in Saratoga. Also, she drives some sort of dark blue Acura sedan," I replied.

"Marvelous." Gregg's tone was vinegary. "That's another car that might have been the one observed fleeing the scene. We'll run vehicles registered to her through DMV to get the plate number."

"And there's a lot more background information to the story, but it can wait until we get down there."

"Which answers my question of whether you guys are done for the day."

"That's your call. But if you find Rhiannon at her condo, you might need our help with the interview, especially when it comes to questions about her relationship with Kyle."

"That's true. Head south and I'll call when we have an address."

"And we'll need to meet someplace so we can follow you there. We don't have a GPS unit in this thing. Any luck at Kyle's apartment?"

"No. The Santa Clara Sheriff's detectives were here yesterday, because we found an R and I of all the stuff they seized," said Gregg, referring to the Receipt and Inventory form that cops were obligated by law to leave after serving a search warrant. "But they weren't the only ones to search this place."

"How can you tell?"

"The apartment is so trashed it looks as if every rock band in the world has been staying here. The furniture is slashed, every piece of his clothing is cut up, and the word *die* is spelled out on the living room carpet with liquid drain cleaner."

"The cops didn't do that."

"No. Whoever was searching wanted to send Kyle a message of what they were going to do to him."

"So, how long before you clear there?"

"Give us an hour. We want to talk to some of his neighbors."

"That's about how long it will take us to drive down from the city. One other thing: We're going to want some Saratoga uniformed cops there if Lauren *is* right about Rhiannon being the reincarnation of Bonnie Parker," I said, referring to the female half of one of America's most famous and murderous crime duos.

"Just in case we find her and *Clyde* Vandenbosch. I'm on it."

I disconnected from the call and headed over to Nineteenth Avenue, where I turned south. If there was another route, I'd have taken it and not just because of the maniacal traffic. The freeway goes directly past one of my least favorite places in the world. I started to brood and Ash rubbed my arm, knowing why I'd become tense and silent. As we passed through the modern day necropolis of Colma, a tiny town that existed to house San Francisco's dead, I barely glanced to my left at the Cypress Lawn Cemetery. I was doing my best to ignore the fact that my parents were there under the yellowish-green grass. My most fervent wish at that moment was that I could forget them, bury them as deeply in my memory as they were in the ground.

My dad was an alcoholic defense attorney who'd never gotten over the disappointment of his son becoming a "dumb cop" and not following him into the lucrative family trade of putting felons back on the street. And he was the more lovable one of the pair now moldering in the ground. Mom was like the boxer Muhammad Ali in his prime. She could hurt you with her hands and her mouth. When I was seven years old she broke my nose with a vicious right jab and then sneeringly warned me that if I told anyone how it actually happened, she'd really give me something to cry about. I know it sounds terrible, but the nicest thing my parents ever did for me was to die in a drunken car crash before Ash could meet them. They'd have despised her for being a "hillbilly" and not "high class" like they were.

Then my blond angel came to the rescue by deftly reminding me of how good my life was now. Ash said, "How does it feel to know that you're going to walk your daughter down the aisle?"

"Happy, scared, old. How about you? How are you with the news?" I replied, my spirits beginning to lift a little.

"Don't you dare tell Colin this, but I like him. I think he's a good man and he obviously loves Heather." There was a pause before she added in a slightly scandalized tone, "We saw *that* in the Cask and Cleavage."

I chuckled at the memory of Ash's shocked reaction to Heather and Colin's torrid embrace in the bar. "God, I thought your eyes were going to pop out."

Ash giggled, too, and said, "Don't laugh. And Lord, if

my mama ever finds out about that tattoo, she'll take an electric sander to Colin's arm."

"Considering your dad is a lay deacon at the church, I don't think he'll be real pleased about it either."

"I know. Daddy would give her his best sander."

"So, note to self: Regardless of the weather, Colin wears a long-sleeved shirt when he comes to visit."

My gloomy cloud was lifted and we continued to chat about the engagement and everything it entailed as we drove southward. As we passed Lake San Andreas, I wondered how many of our fellow motorists realized that the Serra Freeway was located right next to a ticking time bomb: the San Andreas Fault. We were approaching the off-ramp for Palo Alto and Kyle's alma mater, Stanford, when Gregg called. I don't like to talk on the phone while driving, so Ash took the call. She disconnected a minute later.

"Gregg says they're leaving Redwood City now," said Ash.

"So, we're going to get there first."

"That's what I told him. He said to take the West Valley Freeway, get off at Saratoga-Sunnyvale Road, and wait there."

"In the off-ramp intersection? That sounds dangerous."

"I think he meant to find someplace off the road and park, darling," Ash said patiently. "And as long as you've used the word dangerous, how's this for news: Apparently, Rhiannon also bought a gun the same day Kyle did and from the same shop."

"Don't tell me, a twenty-two caliber revolver," I said.

"That's right. Gregg said it was a Taurus."

"Yeah, it's a Brazilian gun-maker."

"And he said it was a magnum."

"Which means the revolver is designed to be easier to handle when you're using hot ammunition like magnum loads or hollow-points."

"So, she probably didn't get it for target shooting, because those kinds of bullets are expensive."

"You're right. Look who's turning into a first-class investigator."

It was just past four o'clock when we arrived at the outskirts of the San Jose metropolitan area. Remember the old Burt Bacharach song about San Jose and how much nicer it was than Los Angeles? Those lyrics may have contained a kernel of truth back in the mid-1960s, but the fact is, with the exception of a little less graffiti on the freeway signs, most of San Jose looks exactly like LA.

However, Saratoga is the exception. The upscale, pretty town is on the southwest edge of the urban sprawl and built on the brown foothills of the Santa Cruz Mountains. We got off the freeway at Saratoga-Sunnyvale Road and I pulled into a restaurant parking lot. Then I called Gregg to tell him where we were. He and Aafedt arrived about twenty minutes later and we got out of our vehicles to stretch our legs.

Gregg said, "Saratoga PD is sending us a couple of units and a sergeant. They ought to be here soon."

"Where are we going?" I asked.

He pointed to the southwest toward the mountains. "That-a-way. Otero lives on Burgoyne Street in a neighborhood near some winery. We'll follow the Saratoga units in."

"So, what else did Lauren have to say?" Aafedt asked.

Ash and I then took turns summarizing our interview with Lauren. We were finishing our tale when the three Saratoga police cruisers rolled into the parking lot. The cops got out of their cars and the Saratoga patrol sergeant told Gregg that he'd sent a patrol unit to do a drive-through of the condo complex to see if either the Acura or Kyle's Toyota was there. Less than a minute later, the sergeant's portable radio squawked. It was the scout officer calling to report that she'd just driven past Rhiannon's residence. She'd found the Acura parked in the condo's driveway, but there was no sign of the Prius. The sergeant acknowledged the information and told the officer to pull back and await our arrival.

Everyone tried to look cool and stoic, but you could feel the excitement beginning to build. We assembled in a huddle around Gregg as he briefed the Saratoga officers on the nature of the investigation and how he wanted to approach the condo, since it looked as if Rhiannon was there. It was a rude shock when I realized the sergeant wanted to keep Ash and me far away from the condo.

But Gregg pointed at Ash and me and said, "That man was my partner in the homicide bureau longer than you've been a cop and his wife helped arrest an armed ADW suspect this morning. So either they're coming along or you and your troops can go Ten-Eight and we'll handle this alone."

That ended the discussion. A few minutes later, we were at the rear of a caravan of police vehicles headed toward the Albion-on-the-Hill gated community. Gregg stopped briefly to talk to the security guard, who then waved us all into the complex. In keeping with its name, the builders had tried to give the homes and neighborhood what they imagined was an English look. The narrow streets were paved with faux cobblestones and the two-storied townhouses were vaguely reminiscent of the famous Royal Crescent in Bath. Yet there was an elusive air of theme park to the place. The development was so self-consciously out-of-place in the arid California foothills that I half-expected to see a sign pointing in the direction of The Merrie Olde England Roller Coaster.

Obviously, Ash shared my assessment of the place. She said, "Who in the name of God would want to live on the movie set for *Mary Poppins*?"

I gestured toward the homes. "Hey, the sign out in front says that the new units are priced to sell in the low eight-hundreds. We could always sell our home in the Shenandoah Valley and move back here."

"Bite your tongue."

Burgoyne Street was the second left. There was almost no one out on the street, just a woman trimming her rose bushes and a young guy walking his shih tzu down the sidewalk. Both stared as the caravan of cop cars slowly rolled down the street. Then all the cars began to pull over to the side of the road. There was a dark blue Acura in a driveway about forty yards ahead, which meant we'd arrived at Rhiannon's house.

We parked and watched as two cops jogged around to the rear of the condo, while Gregg and Aafedt led the other two officers to the residence. We couldn't see the front door from our position, but I thought it was a good sign that we hadn't heard any gunfire. Finally, one of the uniformed cops emerged from the condo and signaled us by holding up his right hand and showing four fingers. The home was secure and we could come in.

As Ash and I approached the townhouse, we paused to look through the windows of the Acura, but didn't see anything noteworthy. Meanwhile, the Saratoga cops were returning to their patrol cars. We continued on to the house, and as I entered the living room, I saw Rhiannon. She wore jeans and a San Jose Sharks jersey and was leaning with her back against the breakfast bar in what looked like inordinately casual conversation with Gregg and Aafedt. Rhiannon glanced over at us as we came in.

I said, "Hi, Rhiannon, remember me?"

"No. Should I know you?" She scrunched her face up in an effort to make it appear as if she were trying to remember.

"We've never formally met, but I saw you watching Lauren Vandenbosch yesterday at the teddy bear show in Sonoma."

Sixteen

"I'm afraid you're mistaking me for someone else." Rhiannon gave me a chilly smile, which accessorized perfectly with her living room.

It was a cold enclosure of eggshell white and burnished metal that reminded me of a lobby in an upscale attorney's office. The walls were decorated with a trio of black-and-white Ansel Adams photos of inhospitable snowy mountain crags, each inside a silver aluminum frame; there was an ivory leather-upholstered Danish-style sofa that looked about as enticing a spot to relax as a Hindu fakir's bed of nails, and in front of the couch stood a contemporary glass and steel coffee table that only lacked a stack of old issues of *Smithsonian* and *New Yorker* magazines to complete the image of a waiting room.

I said, "No, I'm absolutely certain it was you. And you've overplayed your cool card."

"What are you talking about?" Rhiannon asked.

"You should have reacted when I mentioned your boyfriend's mother."

"Like I just told the detective. I had a brief—thank God—relationship with Kyle. That doesn't make him my boyfriend."

"Thanks for the clarification. But that doesn't change the fact that you were at the teddy bear show yesterday."

"So what if I was there? It was a nice day trip up to Sonoma. I didn't know that Oedipus's mom was going to be there."

I gestured at the stark room. "Funny, you don't seem like a teddy bear sort of person."

"Funny, you don't look like a mind-reader."

"I'm not. That must be the reason I can't figure out why you'd lie to me," I said.

Rhiannon made a *T* with her hands. "Time out. Before I say another word, I want to know who *you* are and what this is all about."

Gregg said, "Mr. Lyon is a retired homicide inspector and he and his wife, Ashleigh, are now civilian consultants for the San Francisco Police Department. And as far as what this is all about, I told you. We're investigating a murder."

"And I've already said that I don't know anything about any murder."

"Just like you told Inspector Lyon that you weren't at the teddy bear show."

Rhiannon gave him a scornful smile. "You need to listen more closely. I never denied being at that silly show. I just said he'd mistaken me for someone else."

It was apparent to me that Rhiannon was not only extremely intelligent but that she also wanted us to understand that we were her mental inferiors, which we probably were. I also suspected that the word splitting was being deliberately employed as a weapon in a mental war of attrition. She was deliberately trying to provoke us, hoping we'd become irked and focus on scoring verbal points against her, instead of getting to the crux of the interview, because she didn't want to tell us anything meaningful. So, rather than engage in a courtly semantic duel with Ms. d'Artagnan, I elected to disrupt her composure by verbally hitting her below the belt.

"Rhiannon, did you know that Kyle's mom told us that you're a cheap, gold-digging little whore and that you murdered a man in cold blood at the Paladin Motel last night?" I asked in a cheerful tone.

Rhiannon's look of superiority vanished as her eyes widened and her jaw dropped. "What? That's crazy! I didn't kill anybody."

"Yeah, but you were at the Paladin and don't bother to come up with some cunning rebuttal. You were seen, and we've recovered your fingerprints from the motel room door," I said, stretching the truth to about its maximum elasticity. I didn't know if the evidence technicians had even processed the door for latent prints yet, much less whether Rhiannon's known fingerprints were on file with a police agency. But I was certain she was the woman Kimberly had seen at Room Four. Sometimes, a homicide interview is just like playing high-stakes poker. You bluff and hope that nobody pays to see that all you're holding is a pair of fours.

"That doesn't mean I killed anyone." Rhiannon was looking panicked.

"Actually, it does, if Kyle goes through with his mommy's plan to surrender and tell the district attorney about how you put a bullet into the back of the victim's head."

"Kyle said that?" The tormented look in her eyes told me that her relationship with Lauren's devious son had been neither casual nor brief.

"There's no nice way to break this news, but yeah, he did, in a roundabout way." Then, in a more temperate voice, I said, "Rhiannon, I don't know what you think your relationship is with Kyle, but I can assure you that he doesn't love you. Otherwise, he wouldn't be setting you up to take a big fall on this murder."

The young woman glanced at Ash, who nodded in confirmation. Rhiannon reacted as if she'd just been slugged in the stomach. She covered her eyes with her hands, bent forward at the waist, and let loose with a soul-tearing wail of anguish. Ash rushed over to Rhiannon's side and helped the sobbing woman over to the couch. Meanwhile, Aafedt and Gregg gave me looks that said: *Do you think this is genuine or just a tactical use of the tear ducts?* I shrugged. The sorrow and pain looked awfully realistic to me and matched the description of the behavior of the heartbroken woman seen pounding on the door at the Paladin.

Rhiannon was hunched over in a fetal position and crying hysterically, while Ash stroked the woman's hair gently and told her soothingly that everything was going to be all right. Personally, I had my doubts that there'd be a happy ending, but if anyone could convince Rhiannon of that, it was Ash. After about five minutes, the young woman seemed to have run out of tears and was slowly regaining some control over her emotions.

Ash looked up at us and whispered, "Would you find me a box of Kleenex?"

Aafedt headed for the hallway. "I saw some in the bathroom."

The detective returned a moment later with the tissues. Ash continued to minister to Rhiannon and I sat down in one of the two suede leather chairs that faced the couch, waiting to resume the interrogation. A compassionate person would have waited a few more minutes until Rhiannon had recovered some of her emotional equilibrium. However, I didn't have the luxury of being kind. Rhiannon was upset and vulnerable, which are the best conditions for wringing the truth out of a potential murder suspect.

She blew her nose and then looked up at me with swollen and bloodshot eyes. "I'm sorry I lied to you."

I chose not to acknowledge and accept the apology for now, because that would have put us back on a more equal footing. That was something I didn't want yet. Instead, I curtly replied, "Which lie are we are talking about? Not being at the teddy bear show or not murdering that man at the motel?"

"I didn't kill anybody. I didn't. I don't know what you're talking about. Why would Kyle say I did that? Did something happen in that room?" She was babbling with fear and I was becoming increasingly certain it wasn't an act.

I glanced up at the detectives. Gregg mimed firing a pistol and I understood his silent message. He wanted me to skip the routine and preliminary collection of the background information and dive directly into finding out what Rhiannon knew about the shooting. It was a wise plan. Once Rhiannon regained her composure, there would be nothing to stop her from refusing to answer any more questions and throwing us out of her home.

In a more gentle tone, I asked, "Rhiannon, are you saying that you weren't in that room?"

"I wasn't. He never let me in. I knocked on the door and begged, but he never let me in."

She was in such a state of panic, that I thought it would be wise to confirm some basic facts. "And we're talking about the Paladin Motel on Lombard Street in San Francisco last night, right?"

The young woman nodded jerkily. "It was a filthy place. I went there to find out what went wrong. Why he'd—we were supposed to get married next April."

"Married? Kyle's mom didn't say anything about that."

"Kyle hadn't told her yet." The tears were beginning to fall again.

"Rhiannon, we know that you recently bought a revolver. Why?"

"I didn't shoot anybody."

"I understand that, but we'd like to know why you needed a gun."

"It was Kyle's idea. About once a month, we used to spend the weekend at his mom's cabin near the Sierras. We liked to hike, but I was afraid of rattlesnakes. We found one on the porch one morning."

I suppressed a shudder. I've been terrified of rattlesnakes ever since I was a kid, when I'd nearly stepped on one during a fifth-grade field trip to the Muir Woods. "That must have been very scary."

Rhiannon sniffled. "It was. So, Kyle thought it would be a good idea if we had guns. Everybody has them up there. He said he'd teach me how to shoot."

I managed to suppress my tongue before adding: *At live targets?* Instead, I said, "So, he purchased a forty-five automatic and you bought a twenty-two caliber revolver, right?"

"Yes."

"Where is your gun right now? Upstairs?"

"No. Why would I need a gun here? It's at the cabin."

"You're sure?"

"I'm absolutely certain. You can search the house if you want."

"Inspector Mauel might just take you up on that, but for the moment we'll accept that you're telling the truth. When was the last time you saw the gun?"

"About a month ago. Early August. It was the last time we went up there."

"And when was the last time you saw Kyle?"

"Tuesday night. He was acting as if everything was normal and then . . ."

"And then?"

The young woman snatched a tissue from the box. "I had the sinus headache from hell on Wednesday, so I called in sick. Later that afternoon, corporate security showed up here to give me the Spanish Inquisition. They were looking for Kyle."

"Because he'd disappeared with Patrick?"

"That damned teddy bear," Rhiannon said bleakly. "God, I can't count the number of hours we spent working on that thing."

"Interesting. We've been told that Kyle created Patrick all by himself."

"And you believed that?" Rhiannon was incredulous.

"Why shouldn't we?"

"Because Kyle may be a software genius, but he knows absolutely nothing about robotics."

"Is that your field of specialization?"

"Yes. Patrick was something we were creating together and then he . . . How could he have done this to me?"

I understood the question was rhetorical and chose not to answer it. Everyone in the room knew that ultimately Kyle wanted the money more than he wanted her. I asked, "What happened once the corporate security guys left?"

"I'd turned the phone's ringer off before going back to bed that morning, but I saw I had a message."

"From Kyle?" Ash asked.

Rhiannon nodded. "Out of the blue, he told me that he was breaking up with me and never wanted to see me again. His voice was so emotionless . . . it was like he was canceling a newspaper subscription."

"So, you tried to call him, but you quickly figured out that his phone was turned off," I said. "Then you went looking for him?"

"I didn't want him back." She sounded as if she was trying to convince herself. "But I was entitled to an explanation."

I nodded. "I'm assuming you went to his apartment. Are you the one who set off the tactical nuke in his place?"

She looked mildly offended. "What are you talking about?"

"Everything in his apartment has been destroyed and someone left a brief message for Kyle using drain cleaner on the carpet."

"Serves him right, but I didn't do it."

"But you went there."

"I may have gone to his apartment, but I never went inside. His car wasn't there, so I knew there was no point in knocking on his door."

I didn't believe her, but saw no advantage in arguing the point. I said, "Then on Saturday morning you went to the teddy bear show. Was that to see if Kyle might be there with his mother?"

"No. By then I knew that he was in hiding." Rhiannon looked down at the pile of tissues on the coffee table. "Actually, I went there to talk to her and ask for her help. Both of us love Kyle, but if what you say is true . . ."

"Unfortunately, it is. If you were on fire, Lauren wouldn't stop to throw dirt on you."

"Then it's a good thing that I was scared away by all the commotion." There was an artificial element of relief in her voice.

It sounded plausible, yet I knew I was overlooking an obvious discrepancy in the story. Fortunately, my wife had identified the incongruity. Putting her hand on Rhiannon's shoulder, she quietly said, "But a crowded teddy bear show doesn't seem like an ideal setting for a heart-to-heart chat with your former lover's mom. Why didn't you go to Lauren's house and talk to her there? It would have been much more private."

Rhiannon turned her head away from Ash's gaze. "I . . . It was . . ."

Ash continued in the same tranquil voice she'd used years ago to coax our kids into telling the truth, "You didn't, because you're a smart woman and already knew how she felt about you, right?"

"From the very beginning, his mom acted as if I wasn't good enough for Kyle," came the sullen reply.

"You're more than good enough for him, Rhiannon. A heck of a lot better than he deserves, if you ask me."

"So, why does she treat me like garbage?"

"I'm guessing that Lauren just couldn't deal with the idea of losing her son to another woman. Some mothers are like that." Ash rubbed the younger woman's arm. "So, you know what I think? I think you followed Lauren to the teddy bear show, because you were hoping that at some point she was going to lead you to Kyle."

Rhiannon nodded slightly and her chin began to tremble. "Pathetic, right?"

"You are not pathetic. You're a woman who thought that if she could just have one minute with the man she loved, that she could make everything right again."

"That's all I wanted."

"But you wouldn't have found Kyle by following Lauren anyway. Kyle had also betrayed his mother."

The young woman brightened for a second. "Good. I hope she feels as bad as I do."

I said, "Getting back to Saturday. You followed Lauren back into San Francisco from Sonoma?"

"I tried to, but I lost her car in traffic. And then Kyle called."

"What?" My voice reflected the surprise we all felt. "What did he say?"

"He told me how sorry he was, and that he hadn't meant for me to think that we'd broken up. He said that he was in terrible trouble and that he was only trying to protect me by getting me to stay away." Even now, there was a faint echo of joyful vindication in Rhiannon's voice.

I asked, "He called you on your cell phone?"

She nodded.

"And could you tell if he was using his cell?"

"No. He told me he was calling from a pay phone. Kyle

said that Lycaon security could track him if he used his cell phone."

It would have been useful to know the number Kyle had called from, but that could wait for the moment. The most important thing was to get the rest of the story. I asked, "Did Kyle say anything else?"

"He said he was moving around constantly and didn't know what to do, but that he wanted to meet with me."

"At the Paladin Motel?"

"Yes," said Rhiannon. "He told me the address and room number, but that he wasn't there yet. He told me to come after seven-thirty."

Ash murmured, "I'll bet you were happy."

"I was ecstatic. He said that he loved me and that he hoped I liked the idea of eloping."

I asked, "Here's a question out of left field: Were you driving your Acura?"

"Of course."

"And did you park it at the Paladin?"

"No. Just around the corner on a side street. The motel lot was full."

"Was Kyle's car there?"

"Yes. It was backed into a parking space."

For a speedy getaway, I thought. I said, "Did you see any other cars there that you recognized?"

Rhiannon thought for a second before saying, "No."

"Okay, getting back to your car. Would you mind if Detective Aafedt took a look at it?"

"What do you mean by *look*?"

"A quick check of the interior and the trunk."

"Why?" Rhiannon asked suspiciously.

"There are a couple of reasons. First, we had a witness who saw a dark-colored sedan fleeing the scene shortly after the murder."

"But I told you, I wasn't there when the murder happened."

"I know, but Kyle's mom has already accused you of the murder and at some point a defense attorney is going to do that, too."

Rhiannon went pale. "Oh, my God."

"Now don't panic," I said reassuringly. "You can prove that isn't true by allowing the police to search your car. That way, the detectives can testify that they didn't find any murder evidence."

"The keys are in that basket." The young woman pointed toward the breakfast bar.

Aafedt grabbed the keys and headed for the door. "I'll be back in a few minutes."

I asked, "So, what happened when you got to the motel?"

"Like I said, I had to park around the corner. I didn't like that motel." Rhiannon was unconsciously rubbing her fingers against one another as if there was something slimy on them. "The place was just scummy."

"And you got there at seven-thirty?"

"Maybe a minute or two after that. I got there way early, but it took longer than I thought it would to find a parking space."

"And what were you wearing last night?"

"Why is that important?"

"It might corroborate your story."

Rhiannon sighed and closed her eyes to think. "I had on blue jeans, a white cardigan, and my brown leather jacket."

I nodded. "Okay, so you're out of your car and walking across the lot toward the room. Did you notice anyone out and about?"

"No," she said disdainfully.

It figured that she wouldn't have noticed Kimberly. I asked, "What happened when you knocked on the door to Room Four?"

"Kyle asked if it was me, and I told him it was."

"And then?"

Rhiannon's eyes began to refill with tears. "He started to laugh like a crazy man and said that I had to be the most gullible bitch he'd ever met in his life."

"And he wouldn't open the door?"

"No." Rhiannon's breathing was growing ragged and she took the hand that Ash was offering. "I pushed on the door and begged for him to open it, but he told me that by coming there, I'd proven that his mother was right. I was nothing but a filthy whore . . . and . . . that . . . I should be turning tricks with the . . . other hookers."

"And so you left?"

I thought the young woman was going to dissolve into another crying spasm, but she held her chin up. "Not before I told him that he was a revolting little mama's boy who had certain physical shortcomings and that I was the best thing that had ever happened to him."

"Good for you. Did you say anything else?"

"No." She looked away.

"What about screaming at the top of your lungs that Kyle was going to pay in blood? Do you remember that? Our witness sure does."

Rhiannon bit her lip. "I was upset and acting like an idiot."

"I understand, but what exactly did you mean by that expression?"

"Nothing. How was I going to hurt him?"

"You own a gun."

"Which is over one hundred and fifty miles from here. I was just venting . . . making empty threats."

"Yet you felt guilty enough about those supposedly meaningless words to lie to us."

"It isn't guilt. I'm mortified. Do you know how ashamed I am of how I behaved there?"

"Of what you did outside the room or in?" I gave her a bland smile.

"I never went into that room and I didn't kill anybody." Rhiannon enunciated each word carefully.

"Okay, so at some point you left. Where did you go?"

"I walked back to my car and drove here."

"And Kyle hasn't tried to contact you again?"

"He'd better not even think of it. As far as I'm concerned, I hope he gets sent to prison," said Rhiannon.

We all looked toward the front door as it opened and Aafedt came inside. The grim-faced detective had a black peacoat draped over his left arm and held up a stainless-steel revolver in his gloved right hand. Two things occurred to me simultaneously. The first was that we were looking at the murder weapon. And secondly, that Rhiannon had missed her true vocation. She should have been an actress. We'd been duped with a few tears and a sad story. Ash understood, too. She let go of the young woman's hand and stood up.

Aafedt tilted the gun slightly. "I found this wrapped in an oily rag and hidden beneath the spare tire."

"Taurus?" Gregg asked.

"I've already checked the serial number. It's the one she bought and it looks as if it's been fired recently," said Aafedt.

All eyes were on Rhiannon, who sputtered, "I don't know how that got there!"

"Stick with that story. The jury will love it," Aafedt said.

"The last time I saw that gun, it was at the cabin." Rhiannon stood up. "You have to believe me."

Gregg said, "Actually, no, I don't. Lady, I'm done listening to your three-hankie saga of betrayal. How about the truth now?"

"I've told you the truth, and if you have any other questions, you can contact my lawyer. I'm not saying another word, because you're trying to frame me." Rhiannon pointed at the door. "Now get the hell out of my house."

Seventeen

If this were the universe inhabited by television cops, Rhiannon would have been in handcuffs faster than you could say, "Book her, Danno. Murder one." But this was the real world and we had no choice but to leave.

While it was extremely suspicious that the likely murder weapon and dark coat were found hidden in her car, and that Rhiannon had admitted to being at the Paladin Motel in the same general time frame as the murder, those facts simply weren't sufficient to establish the probable cause to take her into custody for homicide. Furthermore, she was in her home and we hadn't come there as a consequence of hot pursuit. That meant Gregg would need an arrest warrant to remove Rhiannon from the house. It's all a bit more complex than how the TV cops handle things.

Gregg paused at the door. "We're going, but keep one thing in mind: you had your chance to tell the truth and cushion your fall, but you blew it."

"I'm calling my lawyer right now." Rhiannon went over to the breakfast bar and grabbed her cell phone.

Aafedt said, "Once you're done talking to your lawyer, you might want to call a rent-a-car company. We're seizing your Acura as evidence and towing it up to the crime lab in San Francisco."

"You can't do that!" The young woman was outraged.

"Wrong, and I'd love it if you'd come out and try to stop us." Aafedt gave her a sharklike smile.

Gregg was the last one through the front door and he pulled it shut behind us. Outside, the afternoon sun was low in the sky and resting just above the Santa Cruz Mountains. It was still warm, but there was a refreshing coastal breeze that smelled of the ocean. We gathered in a group on the driveway next to the Acura.

"Where did you find the coat?" Gregg asked.

"Wadded up in a ball in the trunk. No sign of the ski mask yet," said Aafedt. Then he glanced toward the house and laughed nervously. "You know, we probably shouldn't be standing out here in the open, just in case she has another gun. We're sitting ducks."

Meanwhile, I'd recovered from the surprise of Aafedt finding the gun and now realized that something just wasn't adding up. I said, "She didn't kill Uhlander."

"Don't tell me you believe her story?" asked Aafedt.

"Most of it. I don't believe the part about not vandalizing his apartment, but I think she was telling the truth when she said that Kyle never let her into the room. Our witness statement from Kimberly corroborates that."

"Only to a certain point," said Gregg. "You said that Kimberly started talking to a john right about the same time Rhiannon supposedly left. Kimberly could have been so focused on turning a trick that she missed Rhiannon being let into the room."

"It's possible, but why?" I asked.

"Maybe she threatened to call the cops or drop a dime to Lycaon."

"And with Bronsey and the money arriving in less than a half hour, Kyle can't let her throw a monkey wrench in the works," Gregg said thoughtfully.

They were building a scenario that certainly tallied with the known facts, but I wasn't convinced. I said, "Okay, let's say she went into the room. What then?"

"That's easy," said Aafedt. "I'll bet the little weasel did some fast talking and offered her a fifty-fifty split on the money being paid for the bear."

"And Rhiannon figured two hundred thousand dollars would go a long way toward mending her broken heart," Gregg said with a bitter chuckle.

"I'm sorry, Gregg, but I have to disagree," said Ash. "That girl is in love with Kyle and my guess is that she'd have been insulted by an offer of money."

"And how do you explain the robbery?" I asked. "One minute she's screaming about killing him and the next they're working hand-in-glove to pull off an ambush? That doesn't compute, Will Robinson."

"And why would she have had two coats?" Ash quietly asked.

My wife had once more identified a significant incongruity. I swiveled to face her. "Say that again."

"Rhiannon was wearing a brown leather jacket, so where did that one come from?" Ash pointed at the coat draped over Aafedt's arm.

Aafedt looked pensive. "I see what you're saying. Kyle must have already had this coat in his room."

Ash continued to press the point. "Which means that Kyle also supplied the ski mask."

"Not necessarily," Aafedt objected. "Maybe her original plan was to kill Kyle and she was going to wear it as a disguise."

"But forgot to put it on?"

"And it didn't occur to her that wearing a ski mask on

a Saturday night in late summer might attract someone's attention and that they'd call the cops?" I added in an incredulous tone.

Aafedt sighed. "You're right, that *doesn't* make any sense. Kyle had to have supplied the mask and the coat."

"Which could also mean that Rhiannon was his partner all along," Gregg said. "For all we know, the two of them choreographed that melodramatic scene at the motel to give her an alibi."

I ran a hand through my hair. "This thing is making about as much sense as the idea of Britney Spears writing a self-help book."

We walked across the street and Gregg popped the trunk of the Impala. Aafedt slipped the revolver into an oversized evidence envelope and crammed the coat into a large paper sack. Meanwhile, I was still cobbling together my own version of the murder.

I said, "Okay, try this scenario. Could it be possible that Kyle lured Rhiannon down to the Paladin Motel, knowing she'd blow a head gasket and attract attention to herself?"

"What are you saying?" asked Gregg.

"What if it was Kyle's intention all along to frame Rhiannon for the murder? He had to make sure that she was seen at the motel—"

"And what better way to do that than to pretend to offer Rhiannon a reconciliation and then refuse to let her in the room and call her vile names?" Ash took over the narrative.

"He is the same guy who Bronsey claims hired him to gain an advantage by having his own mother terrorized and robbed," I said.

Gregg rubbed his chin. "So, you think Kyle may have planted the coat and gun in her trunk?"

"Yep. This is such a first-class quality frame-job, the son of a bitch should be working at a freaking art gallery. If you can humor me for a second, I'd like to take a quick look at the revolver," I said, putting my cane down in the trunk so that both my hands would be free.

"Sure." Aafedt tossed me some latex gloves.

"Gregg, can I borrow your little Maglite?"

He handed me the flashlight and I slipped the revolver from the envelope. I held the gun up by the trigger guard and shined the flashlight's beam at an oblique angle, which is the best method for illuminating latent fingerprints.

Gregg noticed my subsequent frown. "What?"

After another couple of seconds of searching, I turned the light off and handed it back to Gregg. "Maybe the crime lab guys will find some latents on the gun or ammunition, but it looks to me as if this thing has been very carefully wiped down with an oily rag."

Gregg understood what I meant and shook his head in bewilderment. "But why bother to do that and then hang on to the gun?"

"Exactly. She's had plenty of time to dispose of it." Slipping the gun back into the evidence envelope, I said, "This thing should have been dumped in the bay last night."

Ash glanced back at the house. "And if Rhiannon knew the gun and coat were in her trunk, why did she give you permission to search the car? That's just stupid."

"A college degree in computer science doesn't necessarily mean she's got common sense or street smarts," Aafedt suggested halfheartedly. "And she's a novice killer. She may have figured that she'd hidden the gun so well that we weren't going to find it."

"In the trunk of her car?" I asked incredulously. "Doesn't this impress you as being way too convenient?"

"Yeah, but your hypothesis puts us back at square one."

"Not really. Back at the homicide bureau, you thought the gunman was the unidentified person who ran to the Dodge Avenger." I recovered my cane and leaned on it to take some pressure off my left shin, which was beginning to ache. "You were probably right, and Rhiannon's story actually supports that theory."

Gregg cocked his head. "Keep talking."

"If you were Lycaon security and you couldn't track our wayward boy through GPS, how would you try to locate Kyle?"

"I'd have surveillance teams following his girlfriend and mom."

"Which is what they did, and Rhiannon obligingly led Lycaon to Kyle."

Aafedt nodded and pushed the car trunk closed. "So, we're back to our original theory that the Lycaon operative robbed Bronsey to teach the other company a lesson."

"Which still leaves us stalled, because you know those Lycaon rent-a-cops are going to stonewall us at the interview tomorrow," Gregg said.

"You might encourage them to cooperate if you threatened to close down the company's operations for a few days," I said in offhand voice.

The trill of a cell phone interrupted the conversation. Ash pulled the device from her jacket pocket, squinted at the tiny screen, and said, "It's Heather."

As Ash stepped over onto the parkway to take the call, Gregg said, "I'm dying to hear how we do that."

I said, "It's simple. You've got video proof that a vehicle belonging to Lycaon was parked just down the block from the Paladin Motel contemporaneous to the crime, right?"

"Right."

"You think the vehicle belongs to the security department, but for all you know, that Avenger might be the company president's car."

"Yeah . . . ?"

"So you would be well within your rights to request a search warrant for the entire Lycaon premises: workshops, parking lot, clean rooms, and even the CEO's office. After all, *you* don't know where the evidence is."

Aafedt laughed nastily, while Gregg gave me an unsavory smile and said, "Which would mean that we could completely empty the building and search wherever we wanted."

"Precisely. Plus, you'd have to keep all the employees out until you were finished with your search, to insure that no evidence was removed. If it was just you and Danny searching, why I'll bet you could shut them down long enough to hurt them where they'll really feel it."

"The pocketbook."

"Brad honey, can I interrupt for a second?" Ash called. "Heather and Colin want to know if we'd like to have dinner with them tonight at Fior d'Italia."

I glanced at Gregg. "Are we about done here?"

"We'll have to wait for the tow truck, but you can go."

Aafedt pulled his cell phone out and said, "Yeah, and I'd better get a tow en route out here and then call my wife to let her know that I'm going to be late for dinner *again*."

I said to Ash, "Tell them I'd love it and we'll see them around seven-thirty."

Ash passed the information along and then said, "Heather also told me to tell you that it isn't on Union Street anymore. It's at the San Remo Hotel on Mason."

"Got it. Oh, and I expect our daughter to be fully dressed."

"I've already made that *very* clear," my wife primly replied and then returned to her conversation with Heather.

Gregg said, "Fior d'Italia? I've always loved that place. Have a good time, but don't stay out too late."

"Why not?"

"Because you old guys need your sleep and you have to be at the Hall of Justice tomorrow morning by ten. I want you with us when we go down to talk to those sociopaths at Lycaon." Gregg extended his right hand.

As we shook hands, I said, "I'll be there with bells on . . . although that's probably a visual you didn't need."

Ash and I were in the minivan and headed back to San Francisco a few minutes later. As we waited for the red light before turning onto Saratoga-Sunnyvale Road, I said, "Guess where I'm going to go while you're exchanging teddy bear techniques with Lauren tomorrow."

"Lycaon?"

"Yep. Gregg wants me to go down there with them. You aren't interested in changing your plans and coming along, are you?"

Ash patted me on the knee. "Heavens, no. I need some teddy bear time, because this whole investigation is like walking through a freshly fertilized field."

"Yeah, it has been a little squalid."

"And I don't know how you could work homicide for as long as you did and not despise the human race."

"It's only because I had you in my life."

Fior d'Italia has been in business since 1886 and advertises itself as the oldest Italian restaurant in the United States. It might be, but that isn't as important as the fact that they serve some of the most wonderful Northern Italian cuisine you'll find this side of Tuscany. It being a Sunday night, North Beach wasn't too crowded and I found a parking space near the restaurant. The restaurant's new home was on the ground floor of the San Remo Hotel, a handsome three-storied Victorian-style building that was constructed in 1906 by a fellow named Amadeo Giannini. He's better remembered now as the man who established a moderately successful financial institution known as Bank of America.

Heather and Colin were already there and seated at one of the restaurant's tables out on the brick sidewalk. They hadn't seen us yet, so we paused for a second to watch them. Ash's hand tightened around mine as Heather laughed at something funny Colin had just said and then rested her head on his shoulder.

"Been there, done that," I whispered. "Do you remember the first time we held hands, Ashleigh Remmelkemp?"

"Of course. We were going into the old Torpedo Factory in Alexandria. You hated that artisan stuff," she said with a tiny giggle.

"Yeah, but I've absolutely loved every minute I've ever spent with you." I lifted her hand to kiss it.

"Now stop. You're going to make me cry."

"And we can't have that, because this is a celebration. Let's go and get acquainted with our future son-in-law."

We began the festivities with a chilled bottle of Asti Spumante, an Italian sparkling wine that I believe tastes every bit as good as far more expensive champagne, which probably speaks volumes about my unrefined palate. I offered a toast to the young couple and Colin scored major points by thanking Ash for the genes that had made his future bride so beautiful. Dinner was excellent, as was the second bottle of Asti Spumante. By the time we'd finished and were standing in front of the restaurant, Ash had wrestled a promise from Heather and Colin that they would spend Christmas with us in the Shenandoah Valley.

"That will allow plenty of time for your hair to get back to its original color," said Ash.

"Or I could dye it red and green. It would be festive," Heather said teasingly.

"It would be suicidal, once your grandma saw it," I said. "Listen to your mom, honey."

Heather rolled her eyes, while Colin stood behind her and mouthed the words: "Don't worry. It'll be blond."

We exchanged hugs with the young couple and a few minutes later Ash and I were in the minivan and driving westward on North Point Street. As we approached the intersection with Polk Street, I saw the scaffolding above the old brick buildings that bore the large lightbulb-illuminated letters that read: GHIRARDELLI. I sighed and realized that I had to make one more stop before returning to our hotel.

Over four years had passed since I'd been shot and crippled at Ghirardelli Square. I'd paid more than a few return visits to the tourist attraction in my nightmares, but I'd never come back in person. At the time, I couldn't. The prospect of reliving the event was too terrifying to even consider. Then we moved to Virginia, which allowed me to pretend that I'd someday go back and confront my fears. It would have been easy to drive on past, but I suspected that if I didn't go into that square tonight, I never would. I turned onto Polk Street, found a place to park, and shut the engine off.

There was a moment of silence before Ash quietly said, "I was wondering if you were going to come here."

"Yeah, I've dodged it long enough."

She took my hand. "You want me to come with you?"

"I'd love it, but I think it would be best if you stayed here. It would be too easy for me to lean on you . . . again," I said, referring to how she'd carried me through those dark days. "I'll leave the keys in the ignition."

I got out of the car and limped down the sidewalk toward the shopping complex. It was the same route I'd taken the afternoon I was shot. The square looked deserted and the chocolate shop and ice cream parlor were closed and dark. Somewhere in the distance, I heard what sounded like Gaelic music, but I couldn't be certain.

Continuing along the brick walkway, I came to the place where one man had died and my life as a cop had ended. The spot where I'd lain was marked with a large flower planter packed with chrysanthemums. The oversized ceramic pot had probably been put there to conceal my bloodstains, which was no doubt a cheaper solution than pulling up the brickwork and replacing it. Another planter marked the spot where the crook had fallen.

I stood there wondering how I should feel, other than foolish for having put this off and chilly from the breeze blowing in from the Golden Gate. Whatever meaning this place had for me was long gone and buried beneath flower-pots. Finally, I picked a mum from the planter and started back to Ash and my new life.

Eighteen

It was a typical Monday morning on the 101 Freeway headed toward San Francisco and a reminder of one of the reasons we'd decamped from the Golden State. The commuter traffic was already pretty much bumper-to-bumper where we got on in Novato, which was twenty-five miles north of the city. Traffic only got more congested the farther south we traveled. Around us, the other drivers were eating, drinking coffee, shaving, applying makeup, talking on phones, working with computers, and reading newspapers. About the only activity I didn't observe was someone paying complete attention to the fact they were guiding two tons of metal down a crowded roadway.

"I'll sure be glad to get home," Ash said with a sigh as the traffic came to a stop again.

"Me, too." Although I'd lived in San Francisco most of my life, I realized that I no longer considered it home. Suddenly, I couldn't wait to be back in our house, beside the South Fork of the Shenandoah River.

Ash turned her attention from the sluggish column of

brake lights to the teddy bear sitting on her lap. "I think I'm going to give Shannon to Lauren."

Shannon Shoofly Pie was the only teddy from Ash's Confection Collection that hadn't been sold on Saturday. This was a mystery to me, since I considered the bear's openmouthed smiling face to be an example of Ash's best work. Shannon was named after the molasses and brown sugar pie that most people associated with the Pennsylvania Dutch Country, but was also a traditional dessert in the Shenandoah Valley. The teddy bear was dressed in a wedge-shaped costume made from a rich brown fabric that looked exactly like the gooey filling.

"That's a very sweet gesture," I said.

"I just felt I had to do something. Lauren looked so sad and empty when we left her house yesterday," Ash said as she smoothed the fur between Shannon's eyes.

It was nearly nine o'clock in the morning by the time we arrived on Lauren's street. Her Outback wasn't in her driveway, which made me wonder if she'd forgotten about Ash's visit. However, as I pulled up to the curb, Lauren came out of the house smiling. She gave us a happy wave.

I leaned over to kiss Ash good-bye. "I want you to have a great time."

"And I want you to be careful." She touched the tip of my nose.

"Aren't I always? Wait, don't answer that."

"I won't. I'll see you around four."

Ash got out of the van and I watched as she gave the teddy bear to Lauren, who raised a hand to her mouth and looked as if she were about to cry. The women were exchanging hugs as I drove from the cul-de-sac. It took me twenty minutes to travel the six miles to the Hall of Justice and park. Gregg and Aafedt were waiting for me in the lobby.

"We were beginning to think we were going to have to go without you," said Gregg.

"I had to drop Ash off at Lauren's and then must have been stopped by every school crossing guard between here and the Sunset District," I replied. "When are we due at Lycaon?"

"In a half hour, so let's go."

Lycaon was down in Sunnyvale, forty-five miles south of the city, which meant that I was in for a high-speed ride down the freeway. We had to go through the police department's Southern District headquarters to get to the parking lot and I felt bad that I couldn't stop to chat with all the old acquaintances I encountered. I realized that the best I could do was smile, wave, and promise we'd talk when I returned. At least, that was my intention. However, I threw on the brakes when I suddenly saw a teddy bear I recognized. It was Bearny Fife, my furry interpretation of the bug-eyed deputy played by Don Knotts in the old TV program *The Andy Griffith Show,* and the bear stood on a shelf in an office cubicle belonging to an old friend: police records supervisor Jackie Craig. I was surprised and mystified, since I hadn't seen Jackie since leaving the department and she certainly hadn't been at the bear show in Sonoma.

Peeking into her cubicle, I saw Jackie focused on her computer. In a faux gruff voice, I said, "Hey, the city isn't paying you to waste time playing computer solitaire."

Jackie looked up and gave a joyful squeal as she jumped up from the desk to give me a hug. "Oh, my God, it's good to see you, Brad!"

"Likewise. I'm also pleased to see you have one of my bears."

"*You* made that?" Jackie looked shocked. "I noticed the tag read LYONS, TIGERS AND BEARS, but I didn't realize it was you."

"Strange as it sounds, my wife and I are teddy bear artists. Actually, my wife is an artist. I'm still learning. See the detail around the eyes and lips? That's called needle-sculpting and Ash taught me how to do it," I replied. "But what I don't understand is, how did you get him? I didn't see you at the show Saturday."

"My daughter thought it would make me laugh, so she bought it for me." Jackie picked up Bearny to admire it. "I was worried about you after the shooting. You were . . ."

"Having a colossal self-pity party."

"But this wonderfully silly bear tells me that you've got your old sense of humor back."

"Brad, we gotta go," said Gregg.

"I'm sorry, Jackie, but we've got to fly."

"Okay, but when you get back, I want you to autograph his tag."

"I promise." I gave her hand a quick squeeze.

Once we resumed our journey toward the parking lot, I asked, "So, do we have any new information on the case or Kyle?"

"Nothing on Kyle. He's gone to ground," Gregg said.

"And Rhiannon doesn't know it yet, but she's not having a good day," Aafedt said cheerfully. "The lab has positively identified her fingerprints on the motel room door."

"She had knowns on file?" I asked.

"She was arrested for Deuce back in oh-three." Aafedt used the California cop slang term for the offense of Driving Under the Influence.

"But I'll bet the lab hasn't had any luck linking her to the latents they found inside the room."

"Not yet."

"So, we have the prints and the popper. Anything on the revolver?"

Gregg pushed open the door that led out into the parking lot. "The gun is still in the fuming tank. They won't test fire it until they've checked it for latents. Oh, and that last god-awful pun was a new low, even for you."

"Why? Did it make you lose your Twain of thought?"

"No, but working with you makes me wonder if I'm losing my mind." Gregg pointed across the lot. "My car is over there."

"Where's Patrick the Polar Bear?"

"I hand-delivered him to the cyber unit this morning. The geek squad couldn't wait to get their hands on him."

As we got to the car, Aafedt opened the back door and said, "I'll sit back here. There's more room in the front seat, so it's probably better for your leg."

"Thanks, Danny. I appreciate both the gesture and knowing I'll be able to get out of the car when we arrive."

A couple of minutes later we were flying down the Bayshore Freeway toward Sunnyvale. Fortunately, there wasn't nearly as much traffic on the southbound side of the freeway as on the north and Gregg soon had the car up to seventy-five miles an hour, which meant we were running with the flow of traffic.

I asked, "Hey, were you able to get a copy of the original crime report that Lycaon filed with Santa Clara SO?"

Gregg replied, "No, and we didn't even get a chance to talk to the detectives assigned to the case."

Aafedt leaned forward and added, "Yeah, they told us that the detectives were in a meeting and couldn't be disturbed under any circumstances."

Gregg nodded. "So, we asked them to fax us the report. They said they'd do it right away, but that was almost two hours ago. Hopefully, it'll have arrived by the time we get back."

I said, "Who's your point of contact at Lycaon?"

Gregg answered, "The security director. Some guy named Victor Newton. He thinks we're coming down to talk about how the murder might be connected with their grand theft case against Vandenbosch."

"And you'll spring the subject of the Dodge Avenger on him later."

"Once we're all buddies."

"What did he sound like?"

"A pompous ass. The first thing he told me was that he used to be a captain with some PD down in So Cal and then he ran this brotherhood of the badge crap at me."

"Coming from a guy who works for a company that sells a cop killer computer game? I can't wait to meet Newt."

We continued down the peninsula and once we got to Sunnyvale, Gregg took the North Mathilda Avenue off-ramp and turned left. A couple of minutes later, we were driving along a road that ran parallel to the east perimeter of Moffett Field Naval Air Station. We passed a golf course on our left and then, ahead and on our right I saw the headquarters of Lycaon Software and Entertainment.

The complex was big, and its stark gray cement walls, dark tinted windows, and tall chain-link security fences topped with loops of evil-looking razor wire possessed all the charm of a medium security penitentiary. There was an armed guard at the gated entrance and he wasn't satisfied with merely looking at Gregg and Aafedt's badges. He insisted on copying down the information from their police IDs and my driver's license before letting us proceed into the facility.

Gregg drove through the parking lot slowly while we looked for the Avenger, but came up dry. Finally, we parked and we went inside. The lobby was as quiet as a crypt and about as cheery. Obviously, the business of making computer games wasn't nearly as much fun as playing them. The gloomy receptionist had already received instructions to usher us into an empty conference room. We sat down at a large table and waited.

Finally, Victor Newton breezed into the room. Gregg made the introductions and Newton gave a regal wave to show that he didn't object to me being present for the interview. I disliked the guy immediately. He was the very model of a modern police captain: slick, condescending, and so particular about his clothing, hair, and features that you could take it to the bank that he'd never been in a knock-down, drag-'em-out brawl with a criminal. I had no doubts that he'd fled the streets as quickly as possible, seeking safety and career advancement in an office assignment. Then, he'd moved on to a cushy and well-paying job with a company of filth-mongers.

Newton sat down across from us and said in a hearty voice, "So, how can I help you, boys?"

Gregg said, "First, I'd like to get an idea of your duties. I understand that you're the director of security, but what exactly does that entail?"

"I oversee a variety of functions," Newton said in a modest voice that oozed with self-importance. "There's plant security, combating industrial espionage, background investigations into new hires, risk management, and advising the board of directors on security issues."

"What about preventing and investigating employee in-house theft?"

"Well, of course . . . we do that, too."

"Which brings us to the reason why we've come down here. As I told you over the phone, Mr. Newton, we're investigating a robbery and murder that happened on Saturday night and we're pretty certain those events are a direct outgrowth of the charges you filed against Kyle Vandenbosch."

"We'd like to learn more about the crimes you believe he committed," Aafedt added.

"Well, actually that's a closed issue now." Newton gave us a tight-lipped smile.

Gregg sat back in his chair. "Really? As of this morning there was a million-dollar warrant for Vandenbosch's arrest."

"That's been resolved. We . . . uh . . . contacted the sheriff's department this morning and advised them that we no longer wish prosecution against Mr. Vandenbosch."

I shot Gregg a glance that said: *And now we know why*

the sheriff's detectives weren't available to take your call. At the same time, I was trying to figure out what might have provoked Lycaon to withdraw its criminal complaint. Maybe management was worried that a real homicide wasn't the best publicity for a software company that produces games glorifying mass murder.

Gregg asked, "Why did you that?"

"That information is confidential." Newton studied his nails.

"Fine, but there's nothing to prevent you from telling us about the circumstances that caused you to file the crime report in the first place."

"I'm sorry, but that's quite impossible. We don't discuss personnel issues with anyone."

"That's good, because I'm not interested in personnel issues. Grand theft isn't a personnel issue. What did Kyle steal from Lycaon?"

"Unfortunately, we've deemed that it *is* a personnel issue." Newton's tone was almost haughty.

"Yeah, but murder isn't and I'd just like a little information from you."

"I really wish I could help," Newton said and started to rise from his chair. "So, if we're finished . . ."

"As a matter of fact, we aren't." Gregg opened his briefcase and removed a manila folder. He pulled some papers from the folder and slid them across the table. "I'd suggest you sit down, Mr. Newton, and take a good long look at this document before trying to give us the bum's rush."

Newton slowly lowered himself back into the chair. Squinting at the paperwork, he said, "It's an affidavit for a search warrant."

Gregg nodded encouragingly. "Good, you got that on the first guess. Now check out the address of the place we're going to ask for permission to search."

The security director's face began to go pale. "You can't . . . The entire plant? No judge will issue this."

"Actually, I think a judge will, especially if we track down the one whose time was wasted issuing Kyle's arrest warrant," Gregg said merrily. "But I'm certain that whoever reviews this affidavit will see that I've drawn a clear chain of events that began here on Wednesday afternoon and culminated with a man being executed on Saturday night in San Francisco."

"And after we get the warrant, we'll come back here and shut this place down until we find the information you're hiding," said Aafedt.

"So, what'll it be?" asked Gregg.

"I need to talk to my supervisor first."

"Nope. You'll leave and never come back. You either agree to talk now, or we're going to the Santa Clara County Courthouse to find a judge."

Newton swallowed nervously. "You don't understand. I could lose my job if I answer your questions."

"Better the unemployment line than the chow hall line at Folsom," I said.

"What are you talking about?"

"You're willfully withholding and concealing information about a murderer. That makes you an accessory-after-the-fact, which means you could potentially receive the same punishment as the killer," Gregg explained.

"But I'm just following my supervisor's instructions."

"If I were you, I wouldn't put too much hope in the Nuremberg I-was-only-following-orders defense," I said the last part in a bad German accent. "You know why?"

Newton looked down at the tabletop and didn't answer.

I continued, "You're the throw-down. When this all unravels, your bosses are going to disavow any knowledge of your activities. They'll perjure themselves, paint you as a loose cannon, and let you go to state prison to save their own miserable hides. You work with them. Tell me I'm wrong."

Newton glanced up at me and then his gaze dropped

back to the table. He sighed and said, "What do you want to know?"

Gregg opened his spiral notepad and clicked his pen briskly. "Thank you for your voluntary cooperation, which is how I'm going to write it in my report, Mr. Newton. Now, tell us all about Patrick the talking polar bear."

Nineteen

"Did you find it?" Newton's tone was pitifully eager.

Gregg gave him a faux indulgent smile. "I know you've been away from cop work for a while, so here's a quick refresher on police interrogations: I ask the questions and you answer them. Not the other way around."

"But there isn't much I can tell you."

Aafedt checked his watch. "Wow. You went from helpful witness back to being a codefendant in less than ten seconds. That's a new world's record. Let's go get the search warrant, Gregg."

The security director held his hands out imploringly. "Look, you've got to understand that I don't know one-quarter of what they're working on at any given time in this place. So, the first time I ever heard about the cyber teddy bear project was on Wednesday afternoon, when it all got dumped into my lap."

"What happened?" Gregg asked.

"It started with someone activating two fire alarms in

the robotics facility. Per our normal policies and procedures, we evacuated the building."

"Something tells me you didn't find a fire."

"No, and when we checked the security videos, we saw that Vandenbosch had tripped both alarms."

"Why did he do that?"

"As we later discovered, it was to create a diversion, so that he could steal the prototype bear. He had it inside a canvas bag and walked right out the front door with it. It was a complete breakdown in our security procedures." Newton's voice was bleak.

"Which your bosses blamed on you, right?"

"It took almost a half hour for the airhead who runs the robotics facility to even notice that Vandenbosch had disappeared with the bear. But, yes, I was held responsible."

"What happened after that?"

"We locked down the plant, but by that time, Vandenbosch was long gone."

"So, Patrick was created here?" I asked.

"Of course. Why would you ask that?"

I glanced at Gregg, who gave a tiny nod signaling me to continue with the questioning. I said, "Vandenbosch has been telling people that he used his own money to create the bear in his home."

Newton gaped at me as if I'd just suggested that he'd enjoy being back in a black-and-white and patrolling a gang-ridden neighborhood. "That's ludicrous. The company has spent millions of dollars developing that toy."

"And you can prove that?"

"Absolutely. Vandenbosch tried to cover his tracks, but we've still got the hard copies of the schematics, a photo log of the project, and the testimony of all the other people working in the robotics lab."

"How did he try to cover his tracks?"

"One of the first things I did when we began our investigation was have my best IT person secure Vandenbosch's computer. I figured it would contain valuable evidence."

"Wise move."

"Unfortunately, that's when we found out that Vandenbosch had loaded extremely sophisticated logic bombs into all of the computers in the robotics facility's network."

"Sorry, but I'm not familiar with that term. What's a logic bomb?" I asked.

Newton looked miserable. "Basically, it's a program that sits in a computer until an execute command is given. Then it destroys all the data on the hard drive. Vandenbosch activated them right about the same time he pulled the fire alarms."

"Does that mean the software programs that Kyle designed for Patrick are gone?"

"The experts have told me that, given enough time, they might recover some of it." Newton didn't sound hopeful.

"So, he wasn't just covering his tracks. He went into scorched-earth mode. Had Kyle been having any problems with anyone at Lycaon?"

"None that we were aware of."

"But you admit that up until Wednesday you weren't in the information loop. For all you know, there might have been trouble brewing for months," I said.

"What are you getting at?" Newton was interested and leaned forward.

"We've been told that Lycaon basically tried to steal the bear from Vandenbosch and refused to offer him any compensation."

"Whoever said that was either lying or badly misinformed. I've since heard through the corporate grapevine that Vandenbosch and his project partner were going to receive six-figure bonuses once the cyber bear went into production."

Although I already knew the answer, I asked, "And who was his project partner?"

"Rhiannon Otero. She's a robotics expert."

"Is she here today?" Gregg asked, reinforcing the pretense that we hadn't already interviewed Rhiannon.

"No, she called in sick this morning."

"That's a shame. It would have been useful to talk to her." Gregg wrote something in his notebook. "Was she here on Wednesday?

"No, she called in sick that day, too."

"Suspicious, don't you think?"

"Of course." Newton bristled a little.

"What kind of relationship did they have?"

"I understand they were dating."

"Even more suspicious," said Gregg. "Have you talked to her?"

"Late Wednesday afternoon. She was at home in her pajamas. Our assessment of her was that she didn't know this was going to happen."

"And she couldn't tell you where Vandenbosch was?"

"No. She even called his cell while we were there, but he wouldn't answer."

Gregg leaned forward to rest his chin on his fist. "Okay, let's go back to earlier that afternoon. The crap has hit the fan and you're standing there in front of your bosses, right?"

"Yes." Newton sighed and I could tell he was reliving an unpleasant scene.

"And I'm assuming they gave you the mission of recovering the bear. I'll bet your bosses stressed how important it was to get the bear back quickly, before Vandenbosch could sell it to one of your competitors, right?"

"We assumed that's why he'd stolen the prototype robot. The board made it clear that the clock was ticking and they wanted fast results."

"And that your job was on the line if you didn't recover the bear."

"That was implied."

"Did your bosses also say that they'd cover your pay if

you were forced to accidentally break something like a door . . . or someone's arm?"

"They told me that they'd cover all my expenses. I'm not naïve. I understood what that meant." Newton then added in a huffy voice, "But I want *you* to understand something, too. I never broke any laws, nor did I instruct any of my personnel to do so. I've always been a by-the-book cop."

Gregg started to laugh and threw one arm over the back of the chair. "Oh, Newt, you were doing *so* well and then you had to go and ruin everything by lying to us."

"I'm not lying. Everything we did was legal!"

"Does that include breaking into Vandenbosch's apartment on Wednesday afternoon and trashing the place?" Gregg noticed the flicker of surprise that crossed Newton's features and added, "Oh yeah, we know all about that."

"We didn't break in. The door was open and the apartment was already like that."

"How convenient for you."

After a quarter century in law enforcement, my natural instinct was to automatically mistrust anything a police administrator said. Yet, I believed Newton. It was easy to imagine how panicked he must have been on Wednesday afternoon. I couldn't picture him wasting time vandalizing Kyle's apartment when his lucrative position hung on retrieving the bear.

Then another disquieting thing occurred to me and I said, "No, Gregg; how convenient for *Kyle*."

My old partner looked at me. "What are you thinking?"

I resisted the urge to slap the tabletop in frustration when I realized that we'd been fooled again. "It's another freaking frame job! Kyle knew that the very first place that Lycaon security would go was his apartment. So, he trashed the place himself—"

"Because he knew the neighbors would notice the security guys going into the apartment and assume they committed the vandalism while searching for the bear," Gregg finished the statement for me.

"And it worked. It's what *we* thought happened," said Aafedt.

Newton looked confused. "But what did he hope to gain by doing that?"

I replied, "To put your company on the defensive. I'm pretty certain Kyle's original plan didn't include a murder, but he did figure he'd end up being sued in civil court by Lycaon."

"And?"

"He was going to sing the blues about how he'd been persecuted by the wicked capitalist pigs and their thugs. I imagine his version of the story was going to be that he was there at the apartment when you arrived and just managed to escape with his life."

"Who would have believed that?" Newton demanded.

"His mother, for starters. That's the tale he told her. And he also hired a PI to threaten her using the Lycaon name, to corroborate the persecution story. We all know that the story might have played well to a certain kind of northern California jury."

"My hat is off to this kid," said Gregg. "He's been three steps ahead of everyone from the very beginning."

"That's because he's planned this entire thing out like one of his computer games," I said. "Mr. Newton, what did you do when you finished at Vandenbosch's apartment?"

"Like I said, we went to interview Ms. Otero."

Gregg said, "You keep saying *we*. Who was the other person that was with you that day?"

"His name is Cory Eldritch. He's my special investigator," said Newton. "He's a former cop from my old department."

"Is Mr. Eldritch here today?"

"Yes."

"Good, because we'll want to talk to him at some point." Gregg consulted his notebook for a second and said, "Did you go anyplace else once you finished questioning Otero?"

Newton nodded. "Into San Francisco. Otero told us about Vandenbosch's close relationship with his mother and we hoped he might be there."

"Did you contact his mother?"

"No. We could see that she was alone and we didn't want to let her know we were watching her house."

"You could see her? How?" Gregg asked suspiciously.

"She was in a room upstairs, and the curtains were open. The lights were on and we could see her working on something."

"And how long did you watch her?"

"Until about ten P.M. She turned the lights off shortly after that."

"Meanwhile, you were waiting for Kyle's wireless provider to call and tell you they'd done a GPS locate on his phone. Right?" I asked. "You didn't have a search warrant, so how'd you persuade them to violate their right-to-privacy rules?"

Newton looked embarrassed. "We're . . . uh . . . one of their software vendors. I don't have any details on what was said to secure their cooperation."

"Call me a cynic, but I'll bet it was probably, 'We'll deposit the payment in your off-shore account right now.' I hope the money was well spent."

"It wasn't successful. Vandenbosch's cell phone hasn't been turned on since Wednesday. We assume he knew we would try to track him that way."

"So, you were dead in the water. Did something change on Thursday or Friday?"

"Not really."

"Even though you'd assigned stake-out teams to follow Rhiannon and Kyle's mom?" I added encouragingly, "Don't look sheepish. It's exactly what I would have done."

Newton suddenly looked weary. "But you would have had trained professionals doing the surveillance. I have the Keystone Kops . . . wannabes who work security, because they can't pass the police selection process."

"Still, you tried to put the women under round-the-clock surveillance."

"That was the plan, but my teams always lost contact with their targets."

"Meanwhile, your board of directors was screaming for results."

"Yes. That's when I decided to discontinue the surveillance on Vandenbosch's mother, and Eldritch and I would focus on following Otero."

"And what day was that?"

"Saturday morning."

Gregg asked, "How did your surveillance work out?"

Newton shrugged. "We kept close obs on her throughout the day, not that she went many places. Just shopping at the fashion park in Cupertino and then home. Oh, and she stopped to pick up some Thai food."

"How long did you watch her?"

"Until about twenty-three hundred hours," said Newton, using military time for 11 P.M.

"That's damned interesting," I said in an artificially hearty voice. "You had Rhiannon under surveillance all day, yet you didn't see her drive up to Sonoma or back to San Francisco and stop at the Paladin Motel. So are you a Keystone Kop, too, or just a freaking liar?"

Twenty

Newton inhaled sharply and shot a panicked glance at the door.

"And there's your answer," Aafedt growled.

"Let's try for another one. Who drives the black Dodge Avenger with the California plates of seven-ocean-charles-ocean-zero-two-six?" Gregg's voice was colder than a Martian winter.

"It's mine." Newton's voice was barely audible.

I sat back in my chair and gave the security director an evil grin. "My, my. I think we just took a giant step closer to identifying our gunman in the ski mask."

"I had nothing to do with that murder." Newton sagged into the chair.

"But you were out there," said Gregg.

"Yes."

"Were you armed?"

"No. I never carry a gun."

"Good, then you won't mind standing up and assuming the position so my partner makes certain that wasn't another lie." Gregg turned to Aafedt. "Pat him down for weapons."

The security director stood up and put his hands against the wall as Aafedt conducted a thorough weapons search. However, Newton was telling the truth. He was unarmed.

Once Newton was again seated, Gregg asked, "Was Eldritch with you on Saturday night?"

"Yes."

"Then call him and get him in here ASAP. And don't even think about trying to warn him, unless you want me to drag you out the front door in handcuffs."

"I'll try. But he may not want to talk to you."

Gregg turned to Aafedt. "Danny, jet out to the main gate and make sure Eldritch doesn't try to escape."

Aafedt gave the security director a glare and then jogged from the room. Meanwhile, Newton had pulled his phone from its holder on his belt and was pressing Eldritch's number. Staring at us with frightened eyes, he told the special investigator to come to the conference room.

Disconnecting from the call, Newton said, "He said he's on his way."

"Good, and in the meantime you can tell us what you were doing at the Paladin," said Gregg.

"I am not responsible for that murder."

"What about Eldritch? Did he do it?"

"He *said* he didn't do anything wrong."

"You weren't there?"

"No, I was in the car. I never got out of the car."

"Which was parked behind the liquor store down the block?"

"Yes."

"And Eldritch was at the motel looking for Vandenbosch."

"Yes."

"Was your special investigator armed that night?"

"I don't know. He could have been."

"And when you heard all the gunfire and he came running back to your car, did it maybe occur to you to ask him if he was involved?" Gregg's tone was laden with irony.

Newton was wiggling in his chair like an anxious toddler. "I think it would be best if I invoked my right to remain silent now."

"Fine, the interview is over. You can leave or stay, I don't care which, so long as you keep your mouth shut while we're talking to Eldritch."

"I'm not under arrest?" There was a faint trace of relief in Newton's voice.

"Only because I don't feel like spending half the day booking you and writing the paper. I'll get a warrant and come back later. So, Newt, are you going to go or stay?" Gregg demanded.

"I'll stay for now," Newton mumbled.

"Okay, but keep one thing in mind. If you do anything to interrupt the interview, I'm going to book you and make sure that all the inmates find out you're a cop."

The door opened and Cory Eldritch came into the conference room. He had the unmistakable look of a burly ex-cop: dressed in that haphazard combination of Levi's Dockers, an inexpensive sports jacket, and an out-of-style tie that passes for professional work apparel for California police detectives. Eldritch scanned the room and the look on his face said he smelled trouble. I didn't get the sense he was dangerous, though, just frightened. Suddenly, I wasn't so certain he was our killer.

"You wanted me, Mr. Newton?" he asked his boss.

"Please sit down, Mr. Eldritch. I'm Inspector Mauel from the San Francisco Police Department and we need to talk to you," Gregg said.

"What's this all about?" Eldritch was still standing in the doorway and suddenly looked ready to bolt.

Without thinking, I said, "Cory, your boss has just set

you up big-time to take the fall on a One-Eighty-Seven. We think he's lying, so we need your help."

"I knew it. I told you, you stupid bastard! Didn't I tell you? But you wouldn't listen!" Eldritch snarled at Newton, who cringed.

"What did you tell him?"

"That we should have gone to police headquarters that night. But, oh, no!" Eldritch flung his arms skyward. "Slick Vic had one of his patented brainstorms and I'm such a freaking idiot, I went along with him."

"Maybe it isn't too late to undo the damage. Right, Gregg?"

He nodded. "That's right. Your boss has decided to become a defendant. So, we're still looking for a helpful witness."

"Then sign me up, because I'm suddenly feeling *very* helpful." Eldritch pushed the door shut behind him and sat down at the table as far as he could from Newton. "You're awfully quiet, Vic. Not that I'm complaining."

"Mr. Newton can't say anything. If he does, Inspector Mauel is going to arrest him."

Gregg said, "Before we get started, I need to make a quick call to let another detective know that you aren't going to be trying to escape through the front gate."

"Mr. Newton implied that you might bail," I explained.

"Mr. Newton is going to wish I had," said Eldritch.

Once Gregg had concluded the call, he gave me a subtle nod that I should continue in the role of primary interrogator. I knew he was hoping that Eldritch would view me as a more sympathetic audience, since I'd warned him about Newton's machinations. We'd know in a minute.

"Cory, my name is Brad Lyon. I used to work homicide for SFPD, but now I'm medically retired." I held up my cane. "However, I was called in as a consultant on this case and I'd like to ask you some questions. I'm hoping you can help us rectify some misinformation we've received."

Eldritch glared hatefully at Newton and then looked back at me. "Am I under arrest?"

"Nope. You're here voluntarily. You can end this interview any time you'd like and walk out of here."

"Ask your questions."

"Let's start with the most obvious one. Did you shoot and kill that man at the Paladin Motel on Saturday night?"

"Absolutely not."

"But you were there?"

"I was there, but I didn't shoot anybody."

"Do you own a handgun and have a concealed-carry permit?"

"I own several handguns and I have a valid CCW permit. And I already know your next question. Yes, I was armed that night. I was carrying this Glock forty cal." Eldritch casually pulled his jacket open with his right hand to reveal a black semiautomatic pistol in a hip holster. "I'm assuming you're going to want to test it at your ballistics unit."

"Do you have a problem with that?"

"None whatsoever. Would you like me to remove it from the holster?"

"Please, and I'll take it," said Gregg.

Eldritch slowly took his gun from the holster and handed it to Gregg, who unloaded the weapon and slipped it into his briefcase.

I said, "Okay, here's a fun question. Did Mr. Newton shoot and kill that man?"

Eldritch gave Newton a malicious smile and there was a long pause before he said, "No, he was in his car."

I said, "I applaud you for your honesty. I don't know if I would have done the same if I were in your position. Next question: Do you know who killed the man in that motel room?"

"No, but I can tell you that Kyle Vandenbosch was in that room along with at least three other people."

"Excellent, and we'll get to that in a second. But I want

to cover some foundational material first. We know that you're trying to recover a robotic teddy bear that was stolen from your facility by Kyle Vandenbosch. Correct?"

"Correct."

"Who was your surveillance target on Saturday?"

"Vandenbosch's girlfriend, Rhiannon Otero, who's also a Lycaon employee. We'd been monitoring her outgoing cell calls and knew she'd been trying to contact Vandenbosch."

"Where does she live?" Although I knew Rhiannon's address, I decided to throw in a random bait question to ensure that Eldritch was telling the truth.

"Saratoga. Her place is off of Pierce Road."

"And you were working with your boss. Who was driving that day?"

Eldritch pointed at Newton.

"What kind of car does he drive?"

"A black Dodge Avenger. It's a company car."

"When did you start the stakeout?"

"Fairly early. We got to Saratoga around six A.M. At around seven she left in her car."

"The dark blue Acura?"

Eldritch nodded. "That girl drives like a maniac, but we managed to keep a visual on her all the way up to Sonoma."

"That's a long drive. You must have been hoping she was going to meet Vandenbosch."

"We were, and Slick Vic was yammering about how he was so relieved that he'd be able to tell the board that *he'd* solved the case."

The door opened and Aafedt came back into the conference room. He took a seat near the door.

I asked, "So, what happened in Sonoma?"

"Otero parked her car and went into this big freaking teddy bear show in the main square."

"A teddy bear show?" I feigned mild surprise, not wanting him to know that I'd been at the event.

"I was surprised at how many people were there. Anyway,

Vic stayed Code Five on the Acura, while I followed her into the Plaza." Code Five was the California police radio code word for a stakeout. "Otero wandered around aimlessly and eventually ended up in front of the city hall. That's when I saw why she'd come to the show. Vandenbosch's mother was there."

"She's a teddy bear artist, right?"

"Yeah, she had a booth."

"Did Rhiannon try to make contact with her?"

"No, she hung back. I could tell she didn't want to be seen."

"So, you figured she was Code Five, hoping that Vandenbosch would show up."

"Exactly, but she didn't stay there very long. There was some sort of ruckus at Mrs. Vandenbosch's table and Otero took off shortly after that."

"What kind of ruckus?" I asked, silently praying that Eldritch wasn't about to spring a verbal bear-trap and accuse me of not being honest with him, because he'd seen me at Lauren's table.

Eldritch shrugged. "I don't know. I was trying to keep my distance and there were a lot of people there, so I couldn't really see. I heard somebody say that a guy wearing a bear suit had knocked Mrs. Vandenbosch's table over."

Although my expression was relaxed, inside I heaved a huge sigh of relief. I shot a momentary glance at Gregg. There was a ghost of a smile on his lips and I could picture a cartoon strip thought bubble above his head that said: *You dodged a bullet there, cowboy.*

I said, "I'm assuming you followed Rhiannon after she left the city hall?"

"Yeah. She began walking up and down the streets around the Plaza. At first, I thought maybe she was window shopping, but then she pegged on Mrs. Vandenbosch's car," Eldritch said.

"Which you recognized?"

"It's a Subaru Outback. We saw it parked in her driveway on Wednesday night."

"What did Rhiannon do then?" I asked.

"She went back to her car and drove it over to a position where she could keep an eye on the Outback. We figured she was going to follow the mom."

"How long did you guys stay there?"

"Almost seven hours."

"Rhiannon, too?"

"She left once to go to a fast-food place and use the restroom, but came right back."

"And at some point, you guys all began caravanning back to San Francisco."

"It was shortly after five. Vandenbosch's mother got the Outback and drove back over to the Plaza to pick up her stuff. Otero followed and we did, too."

"Where did they go after that?"

"South out of town and then they cut over to the one-oh-one freeway."

"What happened when you got to the city?"

"We assumed Otero was still following the Outback, but suddenly she whipped this U-turn and headed in the opposite direction."

"Did you think you'd been burned?" I asked.

"Yeah. My boss, the surveillance expert, was right on her rear bumper and we almost hit her," said Eldritch with a sneer. "Somehow, we managed to do a turnaround and keep her in sight."

"Where'd she go?"

"The Paladin Motel on Lombard Street. Otero did a slow drive-through of the parking lot and that's when we spotted Vandenbosch's Toyota. Vic was so excited, I thought he was going to wet his pants."

I glanced at Newton, who appeared to be pouting. I asked, "What happened then?"

Eldritch replied, "There wasn't a parking space at the

motel, so Otero pulled back out onto Lombard and then turned onto a side street. We figured she was looking for a place to park."

"Meanwhile, you guys parked at the liquor store down the block. What was your plan?"

"That I'd recon the place, make contact, and recover the bear."

"Alone? Mr. Newton wasn't going to go with you?" I asked in mock astonishment.

"Of course, by myself." Eldritch gave his boss a withering look of contempt. "The official story is that Slick Vic has a bad knee and can't run. But back at our old PD his other nickname was the Banana Peel. He's yellow and slippery."

Twenty-one

"Considering it's my last day here, do you mind if I violate Lycaon company policy and smoke?" Eldritch asked.

Although I hate the smell of cigarette smoke, I knew it was important to reward him for his candor thus far. I said, "Go ahead, but I don't see anything you can use as an ashtray."

Eldritch pulled a package of Camels from his jacket pocket and lit one with a chrome-plated lighter. He took a long drag from the cigarette, flicked some ash on the tabletop, and replied, "Don't need one. You guys have no idea of how much I despise this place . . . and myself."

"Why did you come to work here?" Gregg asked.

"Because I'm stupid. All I looked at was the big paycheck. I should have given some thought as to whether I wanted to spent forty-plus hours a week with a bunch of Dr. Moreaus."

"Who?" Gregg looked puzzled.

"*The Island of Dr. Moreau* by H. G. Wells," I said. "He turned people into animals."

"Which is exactly what Lycaon's computer games do." Eldritch pointed at his boss with his cigarette. "Now Vic there, he fits right in with this crew. Look at him wrinkling his nose at my smoke. Well, let me tell you something. This smoke is freaking Chanel Number Five compared to the toxic crap they're pumping out on those computer discs."

I waited until he'd taken another pull from the smoke, before saying, "So, getting back to the Paladin. You'd just gotten out of Mr. Newton's car and . . . ?"

"I walked down the street to the motel. I didn't know what room Vandenbosch was in, but I was pretty certain Otero would be back, so I scouted around for an OP," said Eldritch. The initials stood for Observation Post. "There was kind of a dark alcove behind the manager's office, so I ducked in there."

"And did Rhiannon show up?"

"Yeah. She came in on foot and went up to one of the doors and knocked on it."

"Did you see the room number?"

"Not from the alcove. Later, I saw it was Room Four."

"What happened after Rhiannon knocked on the door?"

"Nothing at first. The door didn't open and Otero started yelling, but I was too far away to hear if she was actually talking to anybody."

"Did the door ever open?"

"No, and then she began to go utterly Fifty-One-Fifty." The numeric code was cop argot for behavior that was violently insane. "She was screaming and pushing on the door."

"Then?"

"Then she took off in the same direction she'd come from."

"Did she ever come back?"

"Not while I was there. I didn't see her again."

"So, you've now identified Kyle's room. What did you do next?"

"I called Vic and told him that it would be best if he got the cops out here. Vandenbosch had a million-dollar warrant for his arrest, so they could kick the door down. I didn't have any legal authority to do that." Eldritch crushed the smoldering cigarette out on the tabletop.

"That's true. But obviously your boss said no. Why?"

"Vic said that if we got the police involved, the bear would be logged into evidence and there was no telling how long it would be before the company got it back."

"And Lycaon wanted Patrick returned immediately, because they had a production timetable to meet, right?" I asked.

"Yeah."

"Did Mr. Newton have any suggestions as to what you should do?"

"It was classic Slick Vic. He told me to improvise, and that failure wasn't an option. Then he hung up."

"What did you take that to mean?"

"That he expected me to force entry into the room, but was making damn sure he could cover his ass in case things went bad." Eldritch shook another cigarette from the pack.

"Now while you were standing there, was anything happening at the motel?"

Eldritch looked toward the ceiling and thought for a moment. "There was a hooker out on the sidewalk trolling for johns and some tweaker-looking guy came out of a room at the other end of the motel. He drove off in an old Mazda RX-Seven."

"But there was no sign of activity from Vandenbosch's room?"

"Nothing." He lit the cigarette. "I was getting myself psyched up to take the door when a car came rolling into the lot and parked."

"What kind of car?"

"A light-colored Chevy Celebrity. This mope got out

and stood there for a moment and then this other hinky-looking guy carrying a gym bag came into the motel lot from the west side."

"The gym bag must have grabbed your attention."

"Oh, yeah. We knew that Vandenbosch had smuggled the bear out in a canvas bag. But it was dark and I couldn't be certain this was the same one."

"Had you ever seen either of these men before?"

"No."

"Could you identify them if you saw them again?"

"I think so."

"What did they do?"

"They stood there for a second, eyeballing Room Four and talking. Then they went up to the door and knocked." Eldritch flicked some more ash onto the table. "The door opened and someone let them in."

"So, at that point you confirmed the room was occupied. What did you think was happening?" I asked, trying to ignore the cigarette smoke.

"Christ, I didn't know. Maybe the guys had come to buy the bear. But, for all I knew, Vandenbosch was on a serious crystal meth jag and these were two of his tweaker compadres."

I nodded. "So, what did you do?"

"I should have gone back to the car and told Vic it was a no-go, but that would have meant listening to him moaning about how I'd failed the team."

"Meaning him."

"Of course. So I decided I'd creep up to the door and try to hear what was going on inside."

"That took some guts, especially since your backup was cowering in a car over a half-block away." I glanced at Newton, who looked affronted.

"Thank you. Anyway, I managed to get up to the room and tried to gently press my ear against the door. But I accidentally pushed the door and it kind of bumped against the frame."

"What happened then?"

"Nothing at first. I thought maybe they hadn't noticed it inside. There was what sounded like a male voice and then the shooting started."

"How many guns?"

"At least two. They were blazing away at each other like it was the North Hollywood bank robbery," said Eldritch, referring to the famous televised gun battle between the LAPD and two heavily armed crooks that happened back in 1997. "I fell back fast and took cover behind an old Coke machine."

"Did you pull your weapon?"

"I won't lie to you. I cleared leather. Anyone would have in my position. But I never fired my gun." Eldritch extinguished the second cigarette on the tabletop.

"Okay, what happened after that?"

"The bullets were still flying and then I heard the door slam open and someone ran from the room. I took a peek around the corner of the soda machine, but only caught a glimpse of some guy running for his life."

"Was it one of the two men you saw enter the room?"

"I'm assuming it was, but I don't know. Right after that, there was a second or two of quiet in the room and then there was another shot. I'm thinking the gunfight has started up again, so I ducked back behind the Coke machine." Eldritch hooked a thumb at Newton. "Meanwhile, this moron is trying to call me on the phone to find out what's happening, as if the freaking gunfire wasn't a big enough clue."

I chuckled and asked, "So, what happened then?"

"I was shutting my phone off when someone else came out of the room and ran right past the Coke machine. It happened so fast and I was so scared, all I could do was scrunch into the corner and hope he didn't see me."

"Fortunately for you, he didn't. But you got a look at him, right?"

"Yeah, but all I can tell you was that he was completely dressed in black, including a ski mask. He ran eastbound toward Lombard."

"Could you tell if he was armed?"

"He might have had something in his hand, but I can't say for sure. It was dark and I was trying to keep an eye on the room. I figured Vandenbosch was coming out next."

"Because his car was still there."

"Yeah. He came blasting out the door carrying the canvas bag and a gun in his . . ." Eldritch paused to think. "Left hand. And he was fumbling with his car keys in his right."

"What did you think was in the bag?"

"The robot."

"Did you consider drawing down on him and holding him for the police?"

"With at least one other armed suspect running around that freaking motel and no way of calling the cops? Sorry, I can think of easier ways to commit suicide. Besides, my mission was to get the bear, not Vandenbosch."

"So, what did you do?"

"You want to know how stupid I am? I hate the company I work for and I hate my boss even worse. Even so, I holstered my gun and charged the guy to make a grab for the bag."

"Commitment to duty is a harder addiction to break than heroin," I said quietly.

Eldritch sighed. "I suppose. Anyway, he never saw me coming. I rammed him from behind, kneed him in the groin and grabbed the bag. There was a struggle and Vandenbosch dropped his gun. Then I stomped on his foot and that finally made him let go of the bag."

"And then?"

"And then I ran for my freaking life with the bag. I still

can't believe he didn't shoot me in the back, but I guess I got around the corner of the building before he could find his gun and get a shot off."

"What happened when you got back to the car?"

"Vic took off out of there at warp speed and he almost went spastic when I told him about the shooting. Suddenly, he was moaning about how the board wasn't going to be happy, and I'm thinking: I risked my life and that's the only thing you can say, you little putz?"

"Did you know that someone had been murdered in that room?"

"Not definitely, but I could do the math. I'd seen three people come out of that room and neither of the two guys who went in there were dressed in the black outfit with the ski mask. So, I figured there was at least one person dead in there."

I decided it was time to drop a big stone in the verbal pond and watch the ripples. "And when did you discover that Patrick wasn't in the gym bag?"

Newton's eyes narrowed and there was a touch of dread in Eldritch's voice. "How did you know?"

I sat back in the chair and interlaced my fingers over my chest. "We recovered the bear from the motel parking lot. The first guy out the door dropped it, but you couldn't see that because of the parked cars."

"So, you already know what was in the gym bag."

"Yep. What happened when you opened the bag and found four hundred thousand dollars?"

Eldritch's jaw dropped. "Is *that* how much there was in there?"

"We have good reasons to believe so. You didn't count it?"

"No, I didn't want to touch it. We were sitting in this shopping center parking lot looking at all that money and I told Vic that we had to go to the police immediately."

"Why?"

"Why?" Eldritch looked at me as if I'd just gone soft in the head. "I was a witness to a robbery-murder and was in possession of physical evidence of the crime to the tune of, apparently, four hundred freaking thousand dollars. Aside from the fact that it was the right thing to do, if we didn't come forward we might become prime suspects."

"Thank you, I was hoping you'd say that." I glanced at Newton, who'd assumed an air of indifference. "What did your boss think of your idea?"

Eldritch's rasping laugh sounded more like a growl. "Vic told me that we needed to think this through. He said that if we went to the police that it would create major publicity problems for Lycaon—as if I'd lose any sleep over that."

"What else did he say?"

"He told me that he figured Vandenbosch had set up a deal to sell the bear to one of Lycaon's competitors and that the guys I'd seen going into the motel room were the buyers."

"As a matter of fact, he was right," I said.

"Then Vic told me that whatever company it was that lost the money was never going to report it as stolen. If they did that, they'd also be admitting to receiving stolen property and industrial espionage."

"So, what did he propose you do with the money?"

"Split if fifty-fifty and keep our mouths shut about what happened that night."

"In effect, he suggested you guys steal the money. Correct?" asked Gregg.

"Yeah, but he went into this double-talk spiel about how it wasn't really theft and that this was like an informal bonus for all the work we'd done."

I whistled. "That's one hell of a bonus. What did you think of that plan?"

Eldritch glanced at Newton. "I told him that I wasn't a damn thief and that we had to go to the police."

The security director folded his arms and looked as if he was about to say something. Then he glanced at Gregg and seemed to change his mind.

I said, "But you didn't go to the police. Why?"

Eldritch glared at his boss. "Vic said to wise up. He said *he* could live without the money, but life might be a little difficult for me in jail. I asked him what the hell he meant by that and he told me that if we went to the police, he'd tell you guys that I'd admitted to having shot someone at the motel."

"That must have blindsided you."

"Yes and no. Vic has always been a whore. He'll do anything for money."

"Still, you weren't expecting him to move from graft to extortion."

"No."

"It sounds like he had you over a barrel."

"Tell me about it. I wanted to kill him right then and there, but that wouldn't have solved anything . . . except maybe make the world a little bit cleaner."

"So, you went along with his plan, but it was against your will."

"I didn't have any choice."

"What did he do with the money?"

"We drove back down here and he put the gym bag into his office safe. He said that he'd give me my share once the excitement died down. I told him I didn't want any money, but he kept saying it was only fair that I be rewarded for being a good team player."

"That sounds very generous, but I think Mr. Newton was probably more interested in protecting himself by making you a coconspirator. Is the money still in his safe?"

"As far as I know."

"Has he said anything about it to you since then?"

"No, but this morning he winked at me, which seriously creeped me out." Eldritch pretended to shiver. "It's as if he thinks we're buddies or something."

"No, Mr. Eldritch, he was just sending you a signal that he owned you. Tell me, have you heard anything about Lycaon dropping the charges against Vandenbosch?"

"That's news to me."

"Any idea why your board of directors would do that?"

Eldritch shook his head. "The only thing I can figure is that Vic told them his version of the shooting—without mentioning the money—and warned them that if we continued to investigate, the company's name might come up in connection with the murder."

I turned to Newton. "A moment ago, you looked as if you wanted to say something."

The security director stuck his chin out. "I do. He's told you a pack of lies and I'm done protecting this goon. The fact is, he *did* tell me that he shot someone in that motel room. And as far as the bag of money is concerned, the last time I saw it was on Saturday night when he got out of my car."

"You little—" Eldritch began to rise from his chair and I could see the blood in his eyes.

Gregg pointed at him and said, "Sit down and chill."

I waited until Eldritch was seated again and then said, "Now before we go any further, Mr. Newton, do you remember that you invoked your rights?"

"Yes, but I'm not going to sit here and listen to this two-bit hoodlum impugn my integrity and dump the blame for *his* crimes onto me. I want to clear my name."

"And I've got a foolproof way of doing that. Let's all go to your office and you can open up the safe for us." I leaned forward and rested my elbows on the table. "If we don't find a bag of money, then that will conclusively prove you're telling the truth."

Newton suddenly looked queasy. "I . . . well . . ."

"Oh dear, Vic. It looks like you were so focused on trying to be clever that you just screwed yourself. The money *is* in the safe, isn't it?"

"I want to remain silent again. I want an attorney."

Gregg cut in, "And we want that evidence. Look, you aren't going to be allowed to leave the building with the money. So how about we do a little horse-trading?"

"I'm listening," Newton said petulantly.

"You *voluntarily* give us the gym bag, with all four hundred thousand dollars in it, and we won't file on you for grand theft and accessory after the fact." Gregg made it sound as if the offer was against his better judgment, but we both knew the DA would probably never file those charges on Newton. The evidence was too thin on the accessory charge and in order to allege the grand theft of the four hundred grand, there had to be a genuine victim.

"And you'll write the report so that I don't look so . . ."

"Crooked? Not only no, but hell, no. I'm not going to lie for you. Now, make your decision, because this offer becomes null and void in ten seconds."

Newton sighed. "All right. I'll go get it."

"And Inspector Aafedt will go with you, just to keep you honest."

"Keep him *honest*? What, do I look like a miracle worker?" said Aafedt as he followed Newton from the room.

Gregg turned to Eldritch. "And you'll be free to go once I've got your contact information."

Eldritch gave Gregg his driver's license and grumbled, "And as usual, nothing *ever* happens to bastards like Newton. Hell, the board of directors will probably give him a raise."

"Inspector Mauel had to cut that deal. He didn't have any other option," I said.

"I know."

"But you have some. If I were you, I wouldn't quit. Wait for Vic to fire you and then sue him and Lycaon for wrongful termination and retaliation against a whistle-blower."

"I'm not a whistle-blower."

"Of course you are. You tried to prevent a member of

the Lycaon management team from stealing four hundred grand and what happened when you tried to stop him?"

A light dawned in Eldritch's eyes. "I was falsely accused of murder and fired."

"Exactly, and Vic was representing Lycaon when he did those things. A company, I might add, which has very deep pockets. You shouldn't have any trouble finding a slash-and-burn attorney to represent you."

"And I hope you sting them for a couple million," said Gregg, returning the license to Eldritch. "I'll send you a letter when you can come and pick your gun up."

I followed Eldritch out the door and went into the hallway to get some fresh air. Meanwhile, Gregg's cell phone rang and he answered it. The conversation was brief and by the end I could tell Gregg was excited.

Disconnecting from the call, he joined me in the hallway and said, "That was the cyber forensics lab and they said to get back up there immediately."

"What else did they say?

"Only that Patrick has a very interesting story to tell . . . and it ain't 'Goldilocks and the Three Bears.' "

Twenty-two

Unfortunately, we couldn't leave for San Francisco immediately. We had to count the currency in the gym bag and issue Newton a receipt. That's when we uncovered yet another shabby scam in an investigation already chock full of deceit. Many of the bundles of hundreds near the bottom of the bag were actually camouflaged stacks of one-dollar bills, with a couple of Ben Franklins at either end. Newton swore he hadn't touched the money since it had gone into the safe on Saturday night and was so panic-stricken at the discovery that we were inclined to believe him. We also thought it extremely unlikely that Bronsey was responsible for the chicanery, if for no other reason than he was terrified of Lizard Eyes.

It was pretty clear what had happened. The buyers had assumed that Vandenbosch wouldn't stand around and count out the entire four hundred thousand dollars before handing over the bear, so they'd taken a calculated risk and shorted him. By our count, there was "only" two hundred and ten thousand dollars in the gym bag, which is still more money than most felons make in a lifetime of crime. It was nearly noon by the time we started our drive back up the freeway to San Francisco.

Upon our arrival at the Hall of Justice, Aafedt went to the homicide bureau to secure the bag of money in an evidence locker. Meanwhile, Gregg and I took the elevator up to the crime lab. The cyber forensic investigation unit was located in a stuffy and windowless office that smelled faintly of French fries. There were six computer workstations in the room, five of which were vacant.

All the computer experts were around the cubicle where Patrick lay facedown on the desk. The bear's back was open and several data cables connected the robot to the diagnostic computer. However, the techs weren't looking at Patrick. Instead, they were staring at an oversized monitor, as if hypnotized. On the screen were images of what looked to me like multicolored pie charts and a list of data files scrolling upward so fast that it was impossible for me to make out an individual entry.

Gregg tried to introduce me to the cyber lab's supervisor, Julie Nguyen, who was seated at her desk and peering at the screen with the same rapt fascination as her subordinates. Never taking her eyes from the screen, Nguyen acknowledged my presence with an absentminded "nice to meet you," and then said, "Inspector Mauel, this robot is incredible. Whoever designed Patrick's software is a genius."

"And a coconspirator in an ambush murder, so don't start building him an altar. What do you have for us?"

"This robot's functions are controlled by a microcomputer with a seven-hundred-and-fifty-gig hard drive, ten gigs of RAM, and it has voice and face recognition software, and—"

Gregg cut her off. "Which all might be interesting if I understood half of what that meant. You said you had major news about the murder."

Nguyen finally managed to pull her eyes away from the screen. "I do. This robot has a miniature television camera and microphone installed behind the right eye and it digitally records everything it sees and hears while operational."

"And Bronsey turned Patrick on before he connected it to the phone line to test it," I said.

"Please tell me that we have a video recording of the murder." Gregg's voice was eager.

"I won't go so far as to say that," said Nguyen. "We've recovered video and audio data from what we believe is the Paladin Motel at the time of the murder. However, its evidentiary value is . . . equivocal."

"Just what exactly does that mean?"

"It would probably be easier for me to show you than try to explain." Nguyen double-clicked her mouse.

The diagnostic graphics display vanished from the screen and at least two of the computer wonks let out tiny groans. Aafedt came into the office and joined us at the workstation as Nguyen used her keyboard to type a computer command. Suddenly the monitor showed a crisp black-and-white static image of Merv Bronsey's face. The PI was looking mighty shocked. There was a blurred and shadowy figure behind Bronsey, whom I assumed was Joey Uhlander. A small information window in the lower right-hand corner of the screen showed Saturday's date and a time of 20:03:32.

"I've cued the recording from the moment the robot was activated on the night of the murder," said Nguyen.

"Not that I want to see them right this minute, but are there earlier recordings?" Gregg asked.

"There were at some point, but the files were intentionally deleted."

"Any chance you can recover them?"

"Absolutely, but it will take time and we knew you wanted us to focus on this first."

"Good work. Now, why don't you go ahead and hit play."

Nguyen clicked on a rightward facing arrow icon above the digital clock display in the information window. On the monitor screen, Bronsey's face abruptly unfroze and I heard the robot say, "Hi, my name is Patrick Polar Bear and I'm your friend. What's *your* name?"

Bronsey intoned, "Jesus H. Christ."

"Hi, Jesus H. Christ. Do you want to sing a song?" Patrick asked.

"No, my name is . . . uh, Larry," said Bronsey, wisely deciding to use an alias.

The bear said, "I'm sorry, I guess I didn't hear you right the first time. Hi, Larry. Did you know your name rhymes with berry?"

"Yeah, I guess it does."

"Do you like strawberries?"

The sound quality of the recording was every bit as good as the picture. A young man's voice was now audible and Bronsey's gaze shifted to someone behind the bear. The voice sounded like Patrick's, yet it was cold and imperious and I assumed it belonged to Kyle. He said, "The clock is ticking, you fat oaf. Tell Patrick you want to play hide-and-seek and then stand him on the floor."

Bronsey's expression became hard with anger, but he obeyed. He told the robot that they were going to play a game and Patrick reacted with a realistic sounding *whoop* of joy. Then the PI's face slid quickly upwards and vanished. There was a dizzying shift of imagery on the screen and then the view stabilized. I realized we were looking at the room from a height of about two feet. The battered old dresser was straight ahead and part of the bed frame was visible to the right.

Kyle spoke again. "Tell Patrick to find me."

Bronsey asked, "How?"

"You are more stupid than my teddy bear, do you know that? It already knows we're playing hide-and-seek, so tell it to find me."

"Patrick, go find Kyle," Bronsey said.

"Okay, Larry. This is a great game and I really like playing with you." It was a weird counterpoint hearing the bear speaking in such a kindly tone, while the man that had given Patrick his voice was behaving like a vicious jerk.

Nguyen clicked on an icon to pause the recording. "Now, this is incredible, because it demonstrates that Patrick is, for want of a better term, cognizant. The robot has a memory and *knows* who Kyle is."

"As Mr. Spock would say, *Fascinating*. Now, please restart the video," Gregg was obviously trying to keep the frustration from his voice.

Looking slightly insulted, Nguyen clicked on the play icon. The image on the monitor began to jiggle back and forth slightly as the bear walked in the direction of the dresser. Once the robot was past the end of the bed, it made a right turn and started walking toward what I presumed were Kyle's legs. I couldn't be certain, but it looked as if Vandenbosch was wearing Nike tennis shoes and jeans.

Meanwhile, from out in the crime lab corridor, I heard a woman's tinny voice echoing from the Hall of Justice's public address system. She said that Inspector Mauel needed to contact the front desk immediately. Nguyen heard the summons, too, and looked up at Gregg, who folded his arms to signal that he wasn't going to move until he'd viewed the rest of the recording.

On the monitor screen, I could see that Patrick had come to a halt in front of Vandenbosch's knees. The robot said, "Hi, Kyle. I found you. Now it's my turn to hide."

"Satisfied?" Although we couldn't see Kyle, it was obvious he'd addressed the question to Bronsey.

The PI replied, "Cool your jets, Junior. You know the deal. Now, we hook this thing up to the phone."

"Well, hurry!"

"Kyle, did you hear me? I'm going to hide now and you have to find me," Patrick said joyfully.

"Oh, shut the hell up, Patrick!" Even though I knew Kyle was yelling at an inanimate object, I felt a surge of anger.

"I'm sorry, Kyle," the bear whimpered.

"Check out Billy Bad Ass, the computer nerd. He's so scared, he's shaking like a freaking leaf," Bronsey sneered and someone—probably Uhlander—giggled.

Kyle shouted, "You shut up, too, or the deal is off! I'm in charge here!"

"Relax, Vandenbosch." Bronsey sounded placating. "We'll run whatever this test is and then you can have your money and we'll take the bear."

"Then get busy."

The screen blurred as someone picked up the bear and moved it. After about three seconds, the video image came back into focus and the scene had shifted to the back corner of the motel room. I could see part of the bathroom sink and a tiny bit of the alcove that served as a closet. The camera's view seemed to be at just below normal eye-level, which led me to conclude that Patrick was now standing on the night-stand. However, there was no sign of Kyle and I suspected he was deliberately staying off-camera.

There were some muffled sounds and then Bronsey mumbled something under his breath that sounded like, "Here they are."

After a second or two of silence, Kyle demanded, "What the hell was that?"

"How should I know? The hookers are always trying to get into the rooms here," Bronsey snapped.

A man dressed in dark clothing and a ski mask abruptly emerged from the bathroom. He held a revolver in a two-handed grip and seemed to point it at Patrick, although I knew he was actually aiming the weapon at Bronsey. There was the sound of a sharp intake of breath.

Meanwhile, Kyle was still hidden from the camera's view. In a voice quavering with fear, he said, "Okay, okay, throw the bag on the bed and then take your guns out slowly and put them on the floor."

"It's a freakin' rip-off," a man's voice hissed.

"Be cool, Joey," said Bronsey. "Vandenbosch, you're making a huge mistake."

"I don't think so, lard ass. You see this? You see THIS?"

"Yeah."

"It's a forty-five. Come on, talk some trash to me *now*, tough guy!"

"In a quieter voice, Bronsey said, "Be cool, Joey. Be cool. Just go with the program. Just . . . aw, shit . . .""

Based on Bronsey's account of the shooting, I had no doubt that it was Uhlander who unexpectedly moved into the foreground of the picture and blocked our view of the masked robber. At that same instant, the gunfire began. It was deafening, but not loud enough to mask the gargled scream of a man in pain. I knew it was Uhlander, who'd been accidentally shot in the back by Bronsey.

The camera's view shifted with a violent jerk and I caught a momentary glimpse of Bronsey's hand shoving a staggering Uhlander towards the masked robber and Kyle, who was finally visible on screen. Then the screen became an erratically dancing blur as Bronsey bolted from the room with Patrick in his hand. I could tell when he got outside. There was a tremendous increase in background noise from the vehicle traffic out on Lombard Street. Yet I could still hear Bronsey's sharp and ragged intake of breath as he tripped and fell.

Suddenly, the screen was no longer blurry. It was simply dark and I realized that Bronsey had just dropped Patrick and the bear was now lying facedown on the parking lot pavement. There was a scuffing sound, some distant voices, and then another crack of a pistol. A few seconds later, I thought I could hear the rapid footfalls of someone running from the room, but it might have been my imagination.

Nguyen clicked on the pause icon and said, "There's nothing after that. The robot is designed to turn itself off after thirty seconds, if no one is interacting with it. The next image is of Mr. Lyon and a CSI."

"Gee, Bronsey neglected to mention that he used Uhlander as a human shield to get out of there. Talk about a bottom-feeder," said Gregg as his cell phone began to trill.

As he answered the telephone call, I said, "Ms. Nguyen, right before the final gunshot, I thought I heard maybe two people talking. Is there any chance you can isolate those sounds and amplify them?"

"Absolutely. We knew that there were pedestrians out on the sidewalk, so we assumed that was the origin," said Nguyen, as she double-clicked on an icon and then used the keyboard to type a command.

The image on the monitor flickered as Nguyen reset the digital video sequencing. This time there was no background noise from the traffic on Lombard Street and what I heard utterly chilled my blood. We'd heard Kyle's voice enough already to identify him as the person who said, "Mom, please don't kill him!" I also recognized the voice that answered him. It was Lauren Vandenbosch, and she snarled, "Shut up and get out of the way, Kyle. He can identify us." Nguyen had the volume turned way up, so the gunshot that instantly followed was deafening.

"Oh my God," I whispered, realizing that I had driven my wife to a rendezvous with a killer.

"They need us down in the lobby ASAP." Gregg disconnected from the call. Then, seeing my face, he said, "What?"

"The person wearing the ski mask was Kyle's freaking mom." Aafedt pointed at the monitor. "You can hear it. Kyle begged her not to off Uhlander, but she shot him because he was a witness."

Gregg turned back to me and looked nearly as sick and frightened as I felt. "Jesus Christ. Ash is at Lauren Vandenbosch's house right now."

"After Lauren lured her there with a freaking dog-and-pony show story about how she just wanted some teddy bear artist companionship. And I'm so damned stupid, I bought it." Suddenly, my fear was replaced by a more savage combination of emotions and my fist tightened around my cane. In an icily calm voice, I continued, "If they hurt her, I will kill them both, just as slowly as possible. They'll be begging for death by the time I finish."

Nguyen blanched and slowly pushed her chair away from me.

"But as far as Lauren knows, she's not a suspect in the murder, so maybe she won't do anything," Aafedt said hopefully.

Gregg hung his head. "I hope you're right, Danny, but . . . the reason they need us to respond Code Three to the lobby is because someone dropped off a teddy bear at the front desk. And there's an envelope pinned to it that's addressed to me."

Twenty-three

"I'll call dispatch and get patrol units en route to Vandenbosch's house," said Aafedt as he snatched up the phone from Nguyen's desk.

"And along with the physical description, tell them that Ash is wearing blue jeans and a white long-sleeved shirt with a bunch of tabby cats appliquéd on it," I said, knowing the responding cops would need the information.

"What the hell is appliqué?" asked Aafedt.

"It's an embroidery technique that she taught me this past winter on her sewing machine. She was so patient, and I was like sewing my fingers together and . . ."

"Don't worry. Everything is going to work out all right," said Gregg, pulling me by the arm. As we left the office, he called out to Aafedt, "Meet us downstairs when you're done."

We rode the elevator to the ground floor and rushed to the lobby, which was crowded with people waiting for copies of police reports and other services. Two uniformed cops stood next to the metal-detector kiosk at the building's entrance and one of them waved to us. My heart shot into my throat as I saw what was on their metal worktable. It was Shannon Shoofly Pie, the bear that Ash had given Lauren. There was a business-sized envelope safety-pinned to the bear's costume and on it was printed "TO INSPECTOR MAUEL, SFPD" in oversized block capital letters and red ink. I knew the choice of color was deliberate.

The older of the two cops said, "We've already run it through the scanner. It's just a teddy bear, but the envelope looked suspicious. That's why we called."

Gregg asked, "Did anyone see who dropped it off?"

"No. One of the records clerks found it when she came back from lunch. It was on that low wall near the door."

His partner added, "We checked the video from the security cameras and it looks as if a male transient dropped it off at thirteen-thirty-one."

"Almost a half hour ago," said Gregg, checking his watch.

"Which means Vandenbosch paid some vagrant to make the delivery," I said.

"We didn't touch the envelope," said the older cop. "We figured you'd want to process it for latent fingerprints."

"We don't have time for that." I picked up the teddy bear and unpinned the envelope from the costume. "Besides, we know who sent this letter."

I tore the envelope open and pulled out a sheet of white printer paper that had been tri-folded. Opening the letter, I immediately suspected that Kyle was the author of what I knew was a ransom demand note. The message had been produced on a computer word processor and was printed in bold red capital letters with the excess of underlined phrases you'd expect to find in a bombastic manifesto written by an insignificant and emotionally immature twit like Kyle. As Gregg and I began to read the letter, I found some of my fear giving way to annoyance when I saw that the super genius had misspelled my wife's first name.

The text read:

TO SFPD INSPECTOR MAUEL:

WE HAVE KIDNAPPED ASHLEY LYON. AS
PROOF, HER HUSBAND CAN IDENTIFY THIS
BEAR AS THE ONE ASHLEY HAD THIS MORN-
ING. OUR HOSTAGE IS ALIVE AND SAFE <u>FOR
NOW</u>. SHE WILL STAY THAT WAY, IF YOU GIVE
US PATRICK AND DON'T TRY ANY CUTE COP
GAMES. <u>SO, DON'T BE STUPID</u>! DON'T TRY TO
HIDE A GPS TRANMITTER INSIDE PATRICK,
BECAUSE <u>WE WILL FIND IT</u> AND <u>ASHLEY
WILL DIE</u>! NO HELICOPTERS OR SURVEIL-
LANCE CARS. <u>WE WILL SEE THEM</u> AND <u>ASH-
LEY WILL DIE</u>. I WILL CALL YOUR OFFICE
TELEPHONE <u>THIS AFTERNOON</u> WITH FUR-
THER INSTRUCTIONS. WHEN I DO, <u>JUST SHUT
UP</u> AND LISTEN. WE ARE IN CONTROL.

" 'We are in control.' I'll bet that arrogant little wimp
had to get his mommy's permission before writing that," I
said, handing the letter to Gregg. "And now I realize why I
didn't see Lauren's Outback this morning. It must have
been in the garage."

"They had to get Ash into the car without the neighbors
seeing."

"Exactly. This also explains why Lycaon suddenly withdrew all the criminal charges they'd filed against Kyle."

Gregg nodded. "He's offered to sell Patrick back to
them."

"Yeah, but I'll bet it was his mom's idea." I slapped my
cane against my palm. "Lauren has been behind the scenes
like a freaking puppet-master from the very beginning and
I never even suspected. And then I delivered Ash to the
killer's house and drove away."

"She fooled all of us, Brad. But we're going to get Ash back safely. I promise you."

Aafedt trotted up. "We have units en route Code Three. Is that . . . ?"

Gregg held up the letter. "Yeah, it's a demand note from Kyle. They want the robot as ransom."

"The uniforms aren't going to find anyone at the house," I said. "Lauren has had five hours to move Ash. They could be anywhere by now."

"Danny, I need you to roll out to Lauren Vandenbosch's house right now and personally supervise processing the crime scene," said Gregg. "Job number one is locating her credit card and ATM card numbers—"

"I'll issue an alert on them in the credit data systems."

"Precisely. If she uses them, I want to know when and where."

"I'm on it." Aafedt turned and headed for the door that led toward the police parking lot.

Gregg grabbed Shannon Shoofly Pie. "Now, we'd better get up to my office. There's no telling when that bastard is going to call and I have to start letting the bosses know that we have a hostage crisis on our hands."

I sighed, "And I have to figure out some way to tell Heather and Chris that their mom has been kidnapped . . . and it's my fault."

We went back upstairs to the homicide bureau, and as we entered Gregg's office, his desk phone rang. He grabbed the receiver but after a moment or two of conversation wore a look of disappointment.

Hanging up, he said glumly, "That was dispatch. The patrol units are at Lauren's house. The Outback is gone and there's nobody there."

"I didn't think there would be."

"There's also no sign of a struggle."

"*That*, I wasn't expecting. The place should be in shambles, because Ash would have fought them tooth and nail."

"The officer said it looked like they were having coffee. Maybe she was drugged. I'll call Danny right now and make sure he collects the cups and looks for signs of any pharmaceuticals. GHB is pretty easily available on the streets," said Gregg. He was referring to Gamma-hydroxybutyric acid, a chemical compound famous as a "date rape" drug.

"GHB tastes too salty. Ash would have noticed it. More likely it was Rohypnol," I replied, naming another popular sedative used by sexual predators. "And I can't dodge this any longer. I've got to call Heather." I sat down at my old desk and stared at the cell phone in my hand for almost a minute before I could work up the courage to press my daughter's wireless number.

Heather answered on the first ring. "I love caller ID. Hello, Mama!"

It suddenly felt as if my heart was being torn from my chest by a giant pair of pliers. I managed to rasp, "Actually, it's your dad, honey. I . . ."

"Dad, what's wrong?"

"We just found out that your mother was kidnapped this morning and it's all my fault. I'm so sorry," I blurted out.

"What? How?"

"Lauren Vandenbosch was the one wearing the ski mask. She killed Uhlander."

"And, oh my God, Mama was supposed to spend the day with Lauren. Did you . . . ?"

"Yes. Yes, honey, I dropped her off this morning and then went to play the brilliant detective while my wife was being abducted. We don't know where your mom is . . . or . . ."

"She's alive. I know she's alive, Daddy. Have they made contact with you yet?"

"Yes. They dropped off a demand note about an hour ago. The Vandenbosches want the robot, or they say they're going to . . . kill your mom." I took a deep breath. "God, how do I tell Chris? How do I tell him that I caused this?"

"Daddy, you are not responsible for what happened," Heather said sternly. "And don't worry about telling Chris. I'll call him on our way in to the station."

I glanced over at Gregg, who was on the phone and rapidly jotting down notes on a yellow legal pad. "I have the feeling Gregg's office is about to become a kidnapping operation command post. The suits might not let line-level troops like you in."

"I'd like to see them try and stop us. You hang on, Daddy. Colin and I will be there in less than a half hour."

As I disconnected from the call, I heard that Gregg was no longer talking to Aafedt. He said in an aggravated voice, "Look, Captain, why don't you come on down here and personally explain to Brad Lyon why you won't release the evidence. I'm certain he'd love to hear all about your policies and procedures. Oh, that's *not* what you're saying? Then send someone down here *right now* with that freaking robot!" Gregg slammed the receiver down and then hurled the notepad across the office. "I swear to God, there must be some requirement that you have a full frontal lobotomy before they give you captain's bars."

I pushed myself from the chair to retrieve the notepad. "Has the department decided to pay the ransom?"

"Screw the department. I made the decision and it's a no-brainer. We give them the robot and get Ash back. If we lose the opportunity to prosecute Ma Barker and her egomaniacal son, then so be it."

"Thanks, partner." I handed him the notepad.

"You're welcome. How did Heather take the news?"

"Obviously, she's scared, but it also sounds as if she's ready to kick some ass."

"Imagine that. A member of the Lyon family spoiling for a fight? Who'd a thunk it?"

I smiled for the first time since watching the video in the crime lab. "She and Colin are on their way up here."

"They'd be calling him in anyway. I've requested SWAT

and the hostage negotiation team," said Gregg. "Oh, and I also got ahold of Lieutenant Garza. She's en route back here, Code Three. She told me to tell you that everything is going to be all right."

"I hope so. I—"

The office door opened and Nguyen came in, carrying Patrick in both hands. The cyber criminalist carefully stood the robot on Gregg's desk, next to Shannon Shoofly Pie. Then Nguyen looked at me. "Mr. Lyon, I heard what happened and I'm so sorry. We'll all be praying for your wife."

I barely nodded in response. It was a kindly sentiment, but also an unintentional reminder of how often I'd seen such prayers go unanswered. Apparently, my expression betrayed that bleak thought. Thinking that she'd somehow said the wrong thing, Nguyen mumbled an apology and slipped from the office.

Not long after that, Gregg's office started to fill up with detectives and uniformed cops. Gregg began handing out assignments. Then the SWAT commander arrived, dressed in his black military fatigues and baseball cap. He advised Gregg that his unit would be ready to roll in less than ten minutes. Meanwhile, I sat there feeling useless.

Then Heather and Colin arrived and joined me at my old desk.

I asked, "Did you talk to Chris?"

"Yes, and he's trying to get a flight out from St. Louis tonight. He'll call me when he knows," said Heather.

"How'd he take the news?"

"He's scared, but he knows you'll get Mama back safe."

My daughter rubbed my arm and that was almost enough to shatter my thin veneer of stoicism. Ash did the same thing to me when I was agitated. Gregg's phone continued to ring and the room went silent with anticipation each time he snatched up the receiver. Then we'd relax when we saw that it wasn't Kyle calling.

Suddenly, the phone in front of me rang. Without thinking, I answered it, saying, "Robbery-Homicide, Inspector Lyon."

"Brad, it's Danny. I'm calling on this line to keep Gregg's clear."

"You're apparently the only one that's thought of that," I replied as Gregg's phone rang again.

"Has he called?"

"Not yet. Do you have anything?"

"I don't know. Maybe motive. I'm going through Lauren's financial paperwork right now and, for starters, we don't need to waste our time requesting a locate order on her credit cards. She can't use them and she knows it."

"Why?"

"Lauren has maxed every one of her cards to the limit, and then some." I heard the rustle of paperwork in the background and then Aafedt continued, "From what I can see, she owes at least thirty grand on the plastic alone."

"Alone? There's more?"

"I think the cards are just the tip of the iceberg. It looks as if she mortgaged herself to the hilt to put that little monster of hers through Stanford. And she hasn't been repaying the loans. There are so many 'final notice' letters here, I'm beginning to think the Day of Judgment is at hand." Aafedt suddenly realized that it was the wrong joke at the wrong time, and quickly added, "Jeez, Brad, I'm sorry."

"It's all right. Is there anything else?"

"Yeah. There's also a notice that her county property taxes are delinquent. Bottom line: It looks as if she was going to lose this house and soon."

"And you collected the coffee cups?"

"It was the first thing we did and we've already rushed them to the lab. We'll keep looking and I'll call if we come up with anything else."

"Thanks, Danny." I disconnected from the call and brought Gregg up-to-date on what Aafedt had discovered.

Three o'clock passed, and then four o'clock came and

went. I was becoming increasingly frightened that we weren't going to hear from Kyle and knew that I wasn't the only one feeling that way. Gregg was staring at the phone as if willing it to ring and Heather paced the office, while practicing karate punches. Meanwhile, Colin sat by the side of my desk and was disassembling and then reassembling his forty-five automatic. Then, at 4:13 P.M., Gregg's phone rang.

"Homicide Bureau, Inspector Mauel." Gregg instantly reached over and pressed the button for the speakerphone so that we could all hear the call.

"—and listen, stupid!" It was Kyle and I could clearly hear the sound of traffic in the background. He was outside and possibly driving.

"Hello, Kyle." Gregg almost sounded kindly.

"I said, shut up! I'm doing the talking!" There was more fear in Kyle's voice than menace. "Have you got Patrick?"

"Right here on the desk in front of me. We're ready to deal when you are."

"Then let me tell you how this is going to happen. First, if I even think I see a cop, the lady dies."

Heather's jaw tightened and her hand drifted subconsciously to the pistol on her right hip. Meanwhile, I was replaying Kyle's words in my head. There was something passive and almost ambiguous about how he'd phrased the threat. He didn't say he'd kill Ash, only that she'd die. I couldn't be certain, but perhaps that meant he wasn't one-hundred-percent committed to the kidnapping.

Gregg said, "I understand. We will stay out of the area."

"Next. I don't want a cop delivering Patrick. Get someone else. Some regular person."

"Kyle, we can't just grab some civilian and tell them they have to deliver a ransom to an armed kidnapper."

"Just do it!" Kyle snapped. "If you send a cop, I'll go and you'll never see that woman again."

This time the phrasing was even more vague. It was clear to me that Kyle was trying to intellectually distance himself from both the crime and his victim.

"Okay. We'll find someone," Gregg said in a none-too-hopeful tone.

"And don't try to put any homing devices in Patrick. I know that robot from top to bottom and I'll find it."

"We won't do that. You made that very clear in your letter. May I ask you one thing?"

"What?"

"If we act in good faith and give you the robot, when do we get Ashleigh back?"

There was a long pause before Kyle replied: "I guess you've just got to trust us on that. Monster Park. Jamestown Avenue entrance at the gate. Five o'clock."

Kyle hung up and then there was the hum of a dial tone. Monster Park was the current name of a fifty-year-old San Francisco landmark: Candlestick Park, a sports stadium that stood near the bay. Geographically, it was only about six miles south of the Hall of Justice, but with the rush hour traffic it could take a half hour or more to drive the distance.

Gregg turned the speakerphone off as an investigator burst into the office.

The detective said, "He was calling from a pay phone near the intersection of San Bruno Avenue and Mansell Street."

Gregg grimaced. "So, he's already in the area. If we start moving units into the neighborhood, he'll see it."

Colin snapped the magazine into his pistol. "And you'd better warn the Air Bureau to keep their choppers clear of the area."

"I volunteer to deliver the robot," said Heather.

"I'm afraid that isn't possible, Detective Lyon," Gregg said gravely. "I said that we'd play the game according to Kyle's rules and we will . . . for now."

"But—"

I interrupted my daughter. "And even with the blue hair, you look way too much like your mom. Besides, I'm making the delivery."

Twenty-four

Once Gregg got off the phone with the Air Bureau, he asked me, "You're sure about this?"

"Yeah, and not just because I'm feeling as if I have to redeem myself," I said. "This may be our best shot at a peaceful resolution to this thing."

"How so?"

"If you move beyond his bluster and listen to his actual words, you can hear that the kidnapping wasn't Kyle's idea."

"He's definitely spooked," said Gregg. "Maybe he's discovered that killing people in real life isn't as fun as in a video game."

"I don't know." Colin shook his head. "The little puke sounded pretty definite."

"That's because you were listening to the sound instead of the message, son." I pushed myself to my feet. "Think back on the words and expressions he used. They're mushy. He's mushy. Kyle is already mentally disassociating himself from the crime."

Heather's eyes narrowed. "You're right. He never referred to Mama by her name."

"Exactly. Kyle's not even aware of it, but he's trying to rationalize the kidnapping by depersonalizing your mom. But he won't be able to do that if he has to talk to the kidnap victim's loving husband."

"Then before we go . . ." Gregg took out his key ring and unlocked the bottom drawer of his desk. Opening the drawer, he pulled out a small semiautomatic pistol in a nylon ankle holster and offered it to me. "Just in case."

"I appreciate the thought, but an *ankle* holster? If this goes to hell, I don't think Kyle is going to give me the time to sit down so I can get to my gun."

"Then stick it in your jacket pocket." Gregg still held the gun out.

"There's no point. I won't use it. If Kyle dies, then so will Ash."

"Will you at least take a portable radio?"

"Of course, but I'll leave it in the van when I get out to give Kyle the bear." I checked my watch. "The other thing I'm going to need is a black-and-white to give me a Code-Three escort at least part of the way. With the traffic, I'm going to have to use the breakdown lane on the freeway."

"And it probably wouldn't be a good idea to have the CHP chase you to the rendezvous." Gregg put the gun back into the drawer. Pulling his portable radio from its charger and handing it to me, he said, "I'll grab a patrol car and notify the highway patrol that we're going to be breaking some traffic laws."

Turning the radio on, I said, "I'll stand by at the handicapped parking slots and follow you."

"Fine, but I want your promise that you're going to be damn careful. I don't want to be the one explaining to Ash how you got hurt." Gregg slapped me on the shoulder.

Heather grabbed the robot and we all trooped from the

office. Once downstairs, I ignored the pain in my left shin and limped as fast as I could from the building and to the parking lot. I unlocked the doors when we were still fifteen yards from the van and Heather rushed ahead to put the robot on the passenger seat. Just before I climbed into the minivan, Colin shook my hand and my daughter gave me a tight hug. Then they sprinted toward the police parking lot and their unmarked car.

Once I was behind the wheel and shut the door, I took a deep breath and was unprepared for what happened next. The atmosphere inside the vehicle was still slightly fragrant with the delicious smell of the gingerbread-scented lotion Ash had rubbed into her hands just before going into Lauren's house. The aroma almost swept me away in a tsunami of anguish, fear, and guilt. However, I roughly reminded myself that this wasn't the time or place for a self-pity party. I started the van, turned on the emergency flashers, and peered into the rearview mirror, waiting for Gregg to arrive.

A few seconds later, a police cruiser came tearing around the corner of the parking lot. The car's overhead emergency lights were flashing and the headlights were wigwagging. Then the car skidded to a stop as Gregg waited for me to back the van up and then pull in behind him. My old partner gave me a thumbs-up and then we pulled out onto Bryant Street.

One of the very first things I discovered was that boxy minivans don't corner well at high speeds. Nor are they particularly fast. What's more, some drivers assumed that I was merely trying to take advantage of the path that Gregg was blazing and attempted to cut me off so that *they* could escape the gridlock by following the police car. Meanwhile, I was leaning on the van's horn and giving my command of Anglo-Saxon expletives an aerobic workout.

We finally worked our way through the city streets to the on-ramp to the 101 Freeway, where the commuter traffic in the southbound lanes was nearly immobile. Gregg made no effort to merge into the traffic. Sounding his car's siren, he remained in the right-hand emergency lane and I had to jam the van's accelerator to the floor to keep up with the cruiser. It was smooth sailing until we got to the Cesar Chavez Street off-ramp, where the traffic was so congested that our progress was reduced to little better than walking speed. I got as close as I could to the black-and-white's back bumper as Gregg slowly forced his way through the solid mass of vehicles. The dashboard clock read 4:36 P.M.

Four minutes later, a gap opened and we were soon rocketing down the emergency lane again, but I knew it was only a temporary respite from the gridlock. The interchange connecting the 101 Freeway and the Southern Embarcadero Freeway was just ahead and our speed was once more reduced to a crawl. Furthermore, we needed to make a lane change to the left so that we didn't end up on the ramp that would take us southwest toward the other side of the San Francisco peninsula and away from the stadium.

We tried to edge our way into the correct lane, but some middle-aged guy driving a BMW convertible actually closed his distance with the truck in front of him so that Gregg couldn't make the merge. Gregg hit the siren, but the driver of the Beemer stared straight ahead, as if oblivious to the deafening electronic yelping.

That's when my old partner decided to use his patrol car as an icebreaker. Using the cruiser's heavily reinforced front push-bumper, Gregg slowly edged up to the BMW and began carefully shoving it sideways toward the adjoining lane, where cars were swerving to avoid a low-speed collision. Meanwhile, the driver of the convertible was shaking his fist and, although I couldn't hear him, I knew he was screaming. Once there was enough room for us to get into the correct lane, Gregg waved at the choleric driver and I followed the black-and-white through the newly created hole. The dashboard clock read 4:47 P.M.

When we got south of the freeway interchange, Gregg turned off the police car's siren and we resumed our high-speed journey in the breakdown lane. We passed a highway sign that said the Monster Stadium exit was only a mile and a half ahead and I heaved a tiny sigh of relief. It looked as if I was going to make it to the rendezvous in time.

Gregg radioed, "Okay, partner, I'm going to continue south and do a turnaround at the next off-ramp. We'll be standing by at McLaren Park."

I keyed the transmit button of the portable radio. "Copy that and I'm turning the radio off now. I don't want to run the risk of our boy hearing it."

"Ten-four, and if we haven't heard from you by seventeen-fifteen, we're coming in like the Second Armored Division."

"I appreciate the sentiment, but negative. Kyle will probably be late, because he's going to want to make absolutely sure we haven't set up a trap. I'll call when we've made the exchange"

"I suppose you're right. But if we haven't heard from you in a half hour . . ."

"You have my permission to charge. Been nice working with you again, partner," I said, as I guided the minivan onto the off-ramp for Monster Stadium.

"Same here and good luck," said Gregg.

I stopped for a red light at the end of the ramp and used the opportunity to turn off the portable radio and hide it under my car seat. The light turned green and I drove toward the stadium, passing a huge, flashing marquee-style sign that said the 49ers would be playing the St. Louis Rams there next Sunday. Turning onto Jamestown Avenue, I went down the road until I came to the parking attendant kiosks at the entrance of Monster Park. The tall chain-link fence gates were closed and locked. The van's dashboard clock read 4:58 P.M.

There was no one else there; however, I'd expected that. Knowing that Kyle was probably watching me at that very moment, I turned the engine off, grabbed Patrick and my cane, and got out of the minivan. Even though it was a sunny day, it was windy and almost unpleasantly cool.

I checked my watch. The time was now 5:01 P.M. Just three minutes had passed since I'd arrived, but it felt much longer. I leaned against the side of the minivan to temporarily take some of the weight off my left leg. Then I checked my watch again. It was 5:02 P.M. Jamestown Avenue was empty and I was growing more nervous by the moment.

In an effort to avoid slipping into panic mode, I forced myself to role-play the impending meeting with Kyle. My first inclination was to threaten the little scumbag and his mother with death if Ash received so much as a scratch. It would have been satisfying for me to see the fear in Kyle's eyes, but I knew it was the wrong approach. I just wasn't certain why.

Then it struck me. Some of the recurring phrases that Kyle had used in the demand note and later on the telephone were the key. He repeatedly called other people stupid, told them to shut up, and had a pathetic thirst for telling the police that he was the boss. My guess was that Kyle was merely repeating what he'd heard from his mother throughout his life. In fact, Lauren was still telling him to shut up. She'd delivered the command to her son moments before murdering Uhlander.

Remembering my own torturous childhood and the emotional wreckage wrought by trying to reconcile the fact you were being bullied by someone who was supposed to love you, I felt a distant kinship with Kyle. That didn't mean I was prepared to pardon his behavior, however. He was a grown man and it was well past time someone gently reminded him of that.

It was 5:12 P.M. when I saw a car approaching from the same direction I'd come. As the vehicle got closer, I could see it was a pale green Toyota Prius, which had to be about the most ridiculous-looking and environmentally-friendly getaway car I'd ever seen. The car came to a stop about twenty yards away and Kyle glared at me through the windshield. I could tell he knew who I was and that he was trying to make a decision on whether he should abort the rendezvous. Meanwhile, I continued to lean against the minivan with Patrick in my arms, doing my best to keep a sad yet serene look on my face.

Finally, Kyle put the car into park, but didn't shut the engine off. When he got out of the Prius, I saw that he seemed to be dressed in the same clothes I'd briefly seen him wearing in the video shot on Saturday night. The other thing I noticed was the .45 automatic in his right hand.

Kyle took a few steps toward me and pointed the big gun at me with a palsied grip. "You're a cop! I ought to kill you right now!"

"Since I know that you're going to kill my wife, you'd be doing me a favor, Kyle."

"I told you that if you cooperated, she'd be all right."

"If it were up to you, I might believe that. But it isn't, and I've already seen what your mother does to witnesses." I glanced meaningfully at the robot.

"What are you talking about?" Kyle took another couple of shuffle steps towards me, while keeping the pistol shakily pointed at my chest. Now that he was closer, I could see he was unshaven and that there were dark circles under his eyes.

"Patrick recorded the gunfight. Even though you begged her not to, your mother killed that man in cold blood."

"We didn't have a choice." Kyle tried to sound bellicose, but I could see the horror in his eyes as he recalled the murder.

"Of course you had a choice. You just elected not to

make one, because you're way too comfortable taking orders from your mommy," I said in a mildly scoffing tone. "Grown men don't behave that way. They make their own choices."

"I make my own decisions!"

"Really? So, was it your idea to break off the relationship with Rhiannon?"

Kyle sagged slightly. "I . . ."

"Yeah, that's what I thought. Rhiannon was in love with you, Kyle. And you loved her, because you were talking about getting married. Yet you threw it all away simply because your mom told you to."

"Mom was only looking out for my own good."

I gave him a pitying look. "Do you honestly believe that? Here's a news flash, Kyle: It had nothing to do with your welfare. Your mom was jealous of Rhiannon. More importantly, a man your age looks out for his *own* good. Hell, I'll bet the idea to steal Patrick wasn't even your idea."

"Mom said she was going to lose the house and that we had to do something." Kyle took another couple steps closer and slowly lowered the pistol to his side.

"So, she forced you to break the heart of the woman you love, steal from your employer, destroy your career, and as a bonus, got you involved in an ambush murder. And this was for your own good?" I chuckled bitterly. "Thank God your mom wasn't trying to ruin you."

"It didn't work out the way she thought it would."

"Which is a clue that what she's doing is selfish and wrong. Yet, you're still following her orders like a little four-year-old . . . who's terrified that he'll be beaten and told he isn't loved if he doesn't obey. Which was exactly what happened when you were a kid, wasn't it?"

Kyle's body stiffened and his eyes met mine. He looked ill.

I sighed and continued in a softer tone, "My mom was

the same way. She was a control freak and she played the same manipulative mind games with me that your mother does with you."

"No, that's not the way my mom is," he said feebly.

"Right. Look, Kyle, I know you didn't have a happy childhood, but it has been a long one. It's time to grow up and cut the puppet strings. Would you have killed that man on Saturday night?'

"No."

"If your mother hadn't told you to, would you have planted the murder weapon in the car owned by the woman you love?"

"No." Kyle swallowed hard.

"And would you have kidnapped an innocent woman so that you could sell Patrick back to Lycaon?"

Kyle shook his head.

"And if your mom says there's no other way, are you going to stand by and let her kill my wife simply because we made the mistake of trusting her?" When there was no immediate answer, I continued. "Kyle, I'm begging you, just like you begged your mom in that motel room: Please, don't kill Ashleigh. For once, make your own choice and do the right thing."

"You don't understand."

"I do, and I know that what I'm asking is hard. At least tell me where my wife is."

"I can't." Kyle swiped at his eyes with the back of his left hand and then raised the pistol and pointed it at my face. "Give me Patrick."

Realizing that I'd failed to sway him, I tightened my grip around the robot's torso. "Not happening, Peter Pan. You'll have to kill me and you won't be able to pawn responsibility for that off onto your mom."

He kept the weapon pointed at me and I could see sweat beading up on his forehead. His trigger finger was quivering and I found myself holding my breath as I wondered how much and long it would hurt before the bullet finally shut off my brain's circuitry. Then I caught sight of a pearl gray import sedan flying down Jamestown Avenue and heading directly toward us.

Kyle cast a quick glance over his left shoulder when he saw that I'd noticed something behind him. By now, the car—which I could now see was a Honda—was less than a hundred yards away and we both realized that the approaching sedan was traveling far too fast to stop in time. I tossed Patrick on the ground and actually broke into a reasonable facsimile of a gallop toward the safety of one of the parking attendant kiosks.

Obedient to a suicidal fault, Kyle didn't instantly flee for his life, but paused to pick up the robot. By the time he'd gathered Patrick into his arms and stood up to run, the speeding Honda was looming over him. The only reason he wasn't smashed and sent flying through the air toward the stadium was that the Honda swerved away at the last second and only struck him a glancing blow. Still, it was a hard enough collision to send Kyle crashing to the asphalt like a limp marionette. Patrick flew almost ten yards farther, and the robot's head and one of its arms came off when it smashed to the pavement.

Meanwhile, the swerving maneuver had caused the Honda to go out of control. Skidding sideways, the car slammed into one of the chain-link gates, which collapsed atop the now stationary sedan. The Honda's motor continued to roar as its horn began blaring.

I half-limped, half-skipped over to the minivan and grabbed the portable radio, "Two-Henry-Sixteen, I need backup and paramedics now! We've had a major injury accident with at least two people severely injured."

The dispatcher immediately acknowledged my call for help. At the same time, off to the west, sirens began yelping and howling like a big pack of robot coyotes. I went over to the Honda to check on the driver and shut the engine off before a fire developed. The left front door was jammed from the collision and the female driver was slumped forward over the steering wheel, her face buried in the fabric of the now deflated airbag. Using my cane to carefully break out the passenger window, I gently pulled the woman's head back from the steering wheel. I was shocked to see it was Rhiannon. She was unconscious and had sustained a nasty jagged gash on her forehead. The first in a line of black-and-whites and unmarked police cars sped into the parking lot as I reached into the Honda to turn off its motor.

Gregg jumped from his car before it came to a full stop. "What the hell happened?"

"I wouldn't give Kyle the bear and he was about to kill me when Rhiannon tried to turn him into a hood ornament. She was aiming to kill him, but changed her mind at the last moment," I replied.

"Rhiannon? What was she doing here?" Gregg turned to look at the Honda.

"For all we know, she was Code Five on Lauren's house and followed him from there. Maybe this was the first opportunity she had to make good on that promise."

"What promise?" Gregg asked.

"That Kyle would pay in blood."

Lieutenant Garza came running up from another detective car. "Are you all right?"

"Fine. How many traffic laws did you break getting here this quickly during rush hour from Fresno?"

"Lots, but that's what you do when your first training officer calls for backup."

"Thanks, Bobbie." I stumped over toward where Heather and Colin knelt over Kyle, who was motionless. "Is he dead?"

Heather looked from the injured man. "No, but he's got major trauma and I don't think he's going to be talking anytime soon. Did he tell you where Mama is?"

"No. That was one of the reasons I wasn't going to give him the bear."

"Daddy, what are we going to do?"

"We're going to find your mom. I have an idea where to start looking."

Twenty-five

A paramedic van rolled up and came to a stop near the Toyota. The medics jumped from the vehicle and one of them rushed to examine Kyle, while the other went over to Rhiannon. We all moved over to the side of the minivan to give the paramedics room to work. Meanwhile, more and more cops arrived. Next, a television station van came tearing down Jamestown Avenue. They'd obviously been monitoring the police radio frequencies and knew that a major operation was under way.

I said, "Bobbie, you're going to have to prevent them from broadcasting any video of the scene. If word of this somehow gets back to Lauren, she'll kill Ash."

"I'll stop them if I have to break their freaking camera," said Garza as she ran toward the van, which had come to a stop about thirty yards away.

Heather asked me, "So, where do you think they took Mama?"

"Out of the city. That would explain the lengthy time lag from the actual kidnapping to the delivery of the demand note," I replied. "I dropped your mom off at Lauren's just before nine o'clock and it's safe to assume that she was subdued and moved from the house shortly thereafter."

Gregg said, "Yet the bear with the demand note wasn't dropped off at the station until just after one-thirty."

"That's maybe four hours after they kidnapped her," said Heather.

I nodded. "And there's no reason for that long of a delay, unless they drove Ash a significant distance."

"But I don't see how that can help us, sir," said Colin. "You can cover an awful lot of ground in four hours."

Another paramedic van rolled up, its emergency lights flashing and siren wailing.

I waited until the siren was turned off before answering, "That's true, but we can narrow down the possible destinations to a very short list. For instance, Lauren would need to take Ash someplace where she wasn't going to be seen dragging her kidnap victim into a building."

"You're right," said Gregg. "You'd need someplace private."

"Someplace like that cabin up in the Gold Country," I said. "Didn't she say it was in Volcano?"

"Yeah."

"What county is that in?"

"El Dorado," said one of the newly arrived uniformed cops.

"No, it's Amador County," said Gregg, pulling his phone from his jacket pocket. "I'll have dispatch call their sheriff's department and see if they have anything on file about Vandenbosch."

"And if not, they need to check their tax assessor's files," I said. "They've had that cabin since Kyle was a kid, so they ought to have an address somewhere."

Garza came jogging back from her brief confab with the TV reporter. She said, "We're good for now. They'll sit on the story and video until we give them the okay . . . or until some other station breaks the news."

"So, the clock is still ticking," I said, watching the new team of paramedics go over to help treat Kyle.

"Unfortunately," Garza sighed. "Who is Gregg talking to?"

"Dispatch. He's having them call Amador County SO to see if they have an address on file for Vandenbosch. I think Lauren might have taken Ash to a cabin somewhere near Volcano."

"Where the hell is that?"

"It's an old and mostly abandoned gold rush town in the Sierra foothills near Jackson, about a three-and-a-half-hour drive from here. The problem is, we need to get there fast." I checked my watch. "It's five-thirty-one now and I'd imagine that Lauren will be expecting Kyle to arrive no later than nine."

"Wouldn't he call her?"

"Not if she was concerned there was a trace on the cabin's phone." I hesitated for a second before continuing. "Bobbie, can we get a chopper here, now? But let's get one thing straight—I'm going."

"Of course you are . . . and I don't feel like arguing with your daughter and her partner either. So we'll need two choppers," said Garza, pulling her phone from her pocket. "I'll have them land here in the parking lot."

"You're taking both choppers out of the city? The brass will have a fit, especially when they find out you took a civilian along for the ride," I warned.

"The brass can kiss my butt." Garza turned to Colin. "Sinclair, check with the uniforms and see if someone has a pair of heavy-duty bolt cutters in their car."

"I've got a set in my trunk. They come in useful when we're serving dope search warrants," said Colin.

"Good. Then cut the lock on that gate, so we can get

into the parking lot." Garza pointed to one of the entrances to Monster Stadium.

"Yes, ma'am."

Colin and Heather went to open the gate, as Garza began pressing the numbers into her phone. Meanwhile, I limped over to where Patrick's decapitated and broken body lay on the asphalt. The robot's head was several yards from the torso. I bent to pick up the fur-covered cranium and found it was surprisingly heavy. Torn wiring, heavier data cables, and part of the metal skeleton protruded from the bottom of the head, looking like a caricature of human viscera. I peered into Patrick's dead blue eyes and tried to comprehend how something so cute and innocent had been the cause of so much tragedy. Then I reminded myself, the bear hadn't caused this. As always, it was evil and selfish people who were at fault. Meanwhile, I heard a metallic snapping sound and glanced over to see Heather and Colin pushing the gate open.

Gregg's excited voice jerked me from my morose reverie. "We've got an address!"

"What?"

"An address. I talked to the night watch commander from Amador SO. The county tax assessor employees had already gone home, so he broke into the office and looked up the information." He waved his notepad.

"Is the cabin in Volcano?"

"Yeah. In fact, the watch commander knows the place. It's just east of town, back in the hills, on some side road. He's going to send a deputy in an unmarked vehicle to see if the Outback is there."

"If the place is that isolated, Lauren is going to notice a strange car." I tried to keep the fear from my voice.

"Don't worry. We talked about that and you can apparently see the front of the cabin from a hilltop that's about two hundred yards away. The deputy is going to scope the place with binoculars and then pull back. And before you say anything, all the communications will be done via phone. He's also calling in the local CHP office and the regional SWAT team, just in case." Gregg pointed at Patrick's head. "What are you going to do with that?"

I tossed the head once in my hand. "I know it's evidence, but I'm going to take it with me. Lauren is going to want proof this is over."

Garza snapped her phone shut and walked over to us. "One chopper has an ETA of two minutes. The other is refueling now and will be here in ten minutes."

As Gregg brought Garza up-to-date on what he'd learned from the Amador County Sheriff watch commander, I walked over to Heather, who'd just signaled me with a tiny wave. She stood with Colin next to their unmarked car.

"What's up, honey?" I asked.

"Chris just called. He's on his way to St. Louis to catch a flight to Oakland," said Heather. "If there aren't any delays, he'll be here just after midnight."

"Hopefully, we'll have good news for him by then." I tried to sound more confident than I felt. "How's he doing?"

"He's frightened, Daddy."

"That makes three of us. The choppers will be here soon." I glanced at Colin. "I know you're a member of the SWAT team. Do you want to bring anything special with you on the flight?"

"Just this." Colin reached into the backseat of the car and pulled out a brutal-looking black submachine gun with a laser-sight.

Off in the distance, we could hear the thrumming sound of a helicopter approaching fast and from the north. Then the airship rushed into view and I was relieved to see it bore the blue seven-pointed star of SFPD and not the logo from a TV station. The police helicopter circled the stadium once to make sure there weren't any nearby telephone or power lines, and then landed in the parking lot, about thirty yards away.

Garza trotted up to me and shouted to be heard over the deafening whine of the chopper's turbine engine. "Do you want to wait for the second helicopter so that we can all go together, or do you and Gregg want to head out now and we'll catch up?"

"Has he heard anything back from Amador SO?" I asked.

"No. Too soon."

"Then we've got to roll the dice and go."

"That's what I figured you'd say."

I turned to Heather and Colin. "I'll see you in just a little while in Amador County."

In no time at all, we were over the bay, flying low and fast. So low, in fact, that it looked as if we were about to slam into the gray water, but we were near Oakland International Airport and had to stay low so that we kept out of the flight paths of the passenger jets. Then we were back over land again and our elevation began to increase.

About ten minutes later, the observer officer turned in his seat to tell us that the second helicopter, carrying Heather, Garza, and Colin, was on its way. I was glad we'd decided to go on ahead. I didn't hear it, but Gregg's phone rang as we were flying over the Central Valley.

There was a short, shouted conversation and then Gregg disconnected from the call and spoke loudly into my ear, "The Outback is there."

I felt simultaneously relieved and terrified. I replied, "We can't land too close to the cabin."

"There's no place to land up there anyway. We're supposed to set down in Jackson, about thirteen miles away. The regional SWAT team is getting ready to deploy. They're going to establish a loose perimeter, just to make sure Lauren doesn't go mobile," said Gregg.

I reached up to tap the observer officer on the shoulder and yelled, "What's our ETA?"

He half-shrugged and loudly replied, "Twenty minutes or so."

Ahead and in the distance was the grayish-brown bulk of the Sierra Nevada Mountains. It was just after 6:50 P.M. when the helicopter began to descend into a narrow valley hemmed with forested hills. Raising myself slightly so that I could look out the windshield, I saw the red-and-blue flashing lights of two police cars marking a high school football field as the LZ. We were on the ground less than a minute later. The Air Bureau cops wished Gregg and me good luck as we clambered from the aircraft.

A lanky and gray-haired Amador Country Sheriff's captain met us as we hurried toward the patrol car. Shaking hands with us, he introduced himself as Mitchell Tewksbury and told us that he was in command of the hostage rescue operation. There wasn't any fresh news. The SWAT team was in position, but they'd seen no activity around the cabin.

Once we were clear of the rotor blast, I realized how warm it was in Jackson. It had to be in the mid-eighties and I took my jacket off before getting into the patrol car. Gregg insisted I take the front passenger seat, which I appreciated. My left leg was stiff and achy from the cramped conditions in the helicopter.

Tewksbury slid behind the wheel of the cruiser and appeared to notice for the first time that I was carrying a teddy bear's head in my hand. "What the devil is that?"

"Believe it or not, it's a robot teddy bear's head. Patrick was his name and he was a sweet little guy." After a moment, I added, "And it's also ironclad proof that the damn human race can turn anything into a motive for murder . . . including something as lovable as a teddy bear."

Twenty-six

The other patrol car remained at the football field, awaiting the arrival of the second chopper. Meanwhile, we sped through Jackson with emergency lights and siren on, although that didn't seem necessary. There weren't many vehicles on the road in the small and charming Gold Rush town. Then we turned east onto State Route 88. Once we were clear of town and racing up into the piney hills, the sheriff's captain switched off the overhead lights and siren.

Tewksbury glanced over his shoulder to tell Gregg, "Your department emailed us the photo of Lauren Vandenbosch. We've already had copies made and distributed to the SWAT team."

"Excellent," said Gregg. "And did they also pass along the clothing and physical description of the hostage?"

"Better than that. Your Detective Aafedt sent us her DMV photo, too," said Tewksbury. "Now, it's your homicide investigation, but my tactical operation. How do you want to work this?"

"Not that I'm trying to be pushy, but I'm the one you

need to talk to," I said. "After all, it's my wife that's been kidnapped."

"You're the victim's husband?" Tewksbury asked incredulously. "Inspector Mauel led my watch commander to believe that you were his partner."

"I used to be until I got shot and needed this," I said, holding up my cane. "It's true I'm not a cop anymore, Captain Tewksbury, but I *am* going into that cabin to rescue my wife."

"Like hell." Tewksbury's jaw tightened. "We'll do this operation by the book."

"Nine times out of ten, I'd agree with you. But this time the book solution is the wrong one. For starters, Lauren Vandenbosch isn't your typical brainless killer. She executed a man in cold blood and set up an innocent woman to take the fall. Meanwhile, she had us completely fooled into thinking she was being victimized by a thug whom she'd actually hired," I said.

"So, how does that connect with the hostage rescue operation?"

"Once Lauren realizes her son isn't coming back to that cabin, she'll turn into a suicide-by-cop looking for a place to happen."

Tewksbury squinted. "But her son is alive."

"He is, but Lauren isn't going to believe anything a hostage negotiator says. She's going to assume we offed him. Then she'll murder my wife and come out guns blazing so that you guys can finish her off."

There were several seconds of silence and I could tell that Tewksbury was processing this new information. At last, he said, "Let me make this clear in advance that I'm not agreeing to anything . . . but, what exactly are you proposing?"

I took a deep breath and slowly exhaled. "I think there's a chance that if I walk in there unarmed and basically offering up my life, she might believe me when I tell her what happened to Kyle."

"And then?"

"I'll give her the chance to surrender and go to the hospital to be with her son before she's booked into county jail." I glanced back at Gregg. "Do you see any problems with that?"

"None," said my old partner.

Tewksbury said, "But why do you think she'll listen to you?"

"Because I'm going to make Lauren understand that if she surrenders, she stands a fighting chance of walking for the murder," I said, "by providing her with a version of events like what her defense attorney will present in trial: She's a sweet middle-aged woman, who's made teddy bears for over twenty years. A jury is going to want to believe—"

"That she was led astray by her greedy son, who designs violent computer games," Gregg cut in.

"Precisely."

"It might work," Gregg mused. "She *has* had Kyle doing all the dangerous stuff. Call me a cynic, but Lauren might elect to throw Kyle under the bus and then feel good about herself because she comes to visit him in prison."

"But what if she doesn't take the deal and then goes sideways?" asked Tewksbury.

"Then I'll make sure I'm the first and only person she shoots. Your SWAT team will make dynamic entry and smoke her."

"Look . . ." Tewksbury began.

"Before you tell me no, what would you be doing if it was your wife in there?"

The sheriff's captain sighed. "The same damn thing. You gonna want a ballistic vest?"

"No. I've got to go in there looking completely defenseless."

"Do you think you can keep her diverted while we move the entry team as close as possible to the front door?"

"Count on it. I'll sing all three verses of the Monty Python 'Lumberjack Song' if that will keep her attention, but I want your promise that you won't delay making entry—not even for a second—if she begins shooting," I said.

"You have my word," said Tewksbury.

"And Gregg, if this goes south, I'm depending on you to explain what happened, to Ash and my kids."

"You have *my* word," said Gregg.

We rolled through Pine Grove, which was the proverbial wide spot in the road. A few moments later, we turned left onto Pine Grove–Volcano Road—the roads don't have real imaginative names up in the Gold Country. It was a narrow two-lane highway that ran upward through the increasingly steep pine-covered hills. When we reached the top of the ridge, I understood how Volcano had gotten its name. The town lay nestled at the bottom of a bowl-shaped valley that looked a great deal like a volcanic cone. Back during the Gold Rush, thousands of people had lived in Volcano, but the highway sign said the population was now ninety-seven.

We drove down into the valley, through the picturesque old mining hamlet, and then turned onto Rams Horn Road, which began to take us back up the other side of the basin. Once we reached the top, Tewksbury made a right turn onto a dirt driveway. Another quarter mile brought us to an angular contemporary house with huge plate windows and surrounded by pines. The gravel driveway was full of sheriff department SUVs, CHP cruisers, and a Department of Forestry paramedic van. Obviously, this was the incident command post.

Parking the car, Tewksbury said, "Wait here for a minute, while I tell the SWAT team what's going to happen."

"Where is Lauren's cabin?" I asked.

"On the other side of the ridge." The sheriff's captain pointed to the hillside behind the house. "We're going to

go back to Rams Horn Road and I'll drop you off at the end
of her driveway."

"How long a walk to the house are we talking about?"

"Not bad. Maybe a hundred yards."

"Well, hurry up and make your arrangements, before I
decide I've lost my nerve."

Tewksbury gave me a wry smile. "Somehow, I don't
think that's real likely. I'll be back soon."

"Soon" turned into ten minutes, but I'd expected that. I
suspected that Tewksbury was arguing with the SWAT
team commander, who probably thought the plan was insane. To be fair, the plan *was* crazy, but sometimes that's
what the situation demands. In any event, there was nothing I could do to influence that debate; I could only hope
that Tewksbury didn't change his mind.

Gregg said through the metal mesh screen, "Ash is going to be there and everything is going to work out all
right."

"Yeah, but just in case . . ." I got out of the cruiser and
dug my wallet-cum-badge-case from the back pocket of
my slacks. Opening the back door, I handed the billfold to
Gregg. "My old inspector's badge is in there. Tell Heather
that I want her to carry it when she finally gets promoted to
the homicide bureau."

"I'll see to it."

"And if I do come back, I'd better not find any charges
on my credit card to some Internet porn website."

Gregg chuckled. "God, I miss working with you."

Finally, the sheriff's captain returned to the patrol car
and got in. Firing up the cruiser's engine, Tewksbury said
to me, "Everybody in the command post admires the size
of your *cojones,* but they also think you're nuts."

"That's pretty much our assessment of him at SFPD,
too," said Gregg.

"Are you sure you don't want a hideout gun?" Tewksbury asked. "I've got a little five-shot Chief's special . . ."

"I'd love one, but no. If Lauren finds that I'm armed, she won't listen to anything I have to say."

We went back to Rams Horn Road, turned left, and Tewksbury drove about a half mile down the hill before pulling over next to a rutted one-lane dirt road with such a dense canopy of pine boughs overhead that it looked like a tunnel. I got out of the car and shook hands with Gregg. Then, carrying the robot's head in one hand and my cane in the other, I began walking down the driveway.

It was cool and shady on the road and the air was redolent with the aroma of pine. As I limped down the road, I tried to decide just how I was going to initiate the conversation with Lauren. Then I tried to figure out what I'd do if it turned out that Ash was not inside the cabin. *Die, probably,* I thought.

I rounded a slight curve and there was Lauren's house. It was one of those tall, redwood A-frame cabins so popular in the 1960s. However, it also looked as if that was the last time anyone had performed any serious maintenance work on the home and property. The redwood boards were in dire need of refinishing, one of the porch rail beams was missing, and the yard was overgrown with tall weeds.

There was a light on inside the cabin. Lauren had parked the Subaru so that the station wagon's back hatch was almost flush against the topmost of the three wooden porch steps leading up to the front door, which told me that Ash must've still been unconscious when Lauren arrived in Volcano, and that she'd dragged my wife from the car to the cabin. Envisioning that scene, my hand tightened involuntarily around my cane and I roughly commanded myself to stay calm.

I reached out to touch the hood of the Outback. The metal was cool, which meant the vehicle had been parked here for hours. Then I began to mount the wooden stairs, knowing that the sound had to be audible inside the house.

"Kyle, is that you?" Lauren nervously called from the other side of the decrepit front door.

"No, Lauren. It's Brad Lyon. I've come to get my wife."

"If you take one step closer to the door, I'll kill her right now." I heard a round being chambered into a shotgun. Lauren wasn't bluffing.

I froze in place, while experiencing dual surges of joy and terror. My wife was inside the cabin and alive, but if I made even a tiny error in judgment, Ash would die.

"Lauren, it's all over, and Kyle needs you very badly," I said in a weary and regretful voice.

"I want my son released from jail and brought here, right now!"

"Your son isn't in jail. We can't bring him here. He's in the hospital in pretty bad shape."

There was a tiny pause as Lauren digested the news. Then she shrieked, "The police shot him! You shot him!"

"No, Rhiannon found him and hit him with her car. I was there. I saw it. She ran him down like a dog," I said, hoping to subtly channel some of Lauren's rage toward the woman she already loathed.

"Don't lie to me. I'm not stupid!"

"That's the last word I'd use to describe you. In fact, you're one of the smartest people I've ever met. And if I was lying, do you think I'd have come up to the front door like this?"

"Where did Kyle supposedly get run down?" Lauren's voice was no longer just angry. She was frightened for her son.

"At Monster Stadium, right after I'd given Patrick to him." The answer was like a docudrama movie: mostly imaginary, but based on real events. I added, "The robot was destroyed, too."

"Even if that's all true, you've got the police out there!" she snarled.

"Of course, the police are here. In fact, the only reason the SWAT team hasn't already filled your house with tear gas and come inside to play submachine-gun hide-and-seek is because I convinced them that you *aren't* a merciless killer." I paused for a second before continuing with my fantasy interpretation of the events, "You're just a very loving mom who was trying to help her son and things got out of control."

"Oh yeah, as if you believe that. I'm supposed to accept that you *really* understand, and have forgiven me? You must think I'm an idiot."

Realizing that Lauren's emotions weren't going to be manipulated as easily as I'd hoped, I switched tactics. "Hell, no, I haven't forgiven you. If I had the chance, I'd kill you like a cockroach. However, we've both got something the other wants."

"What's that?"

"Let me in and we'll talk. The longer I stand out here, the more likely it is the SWAT commander will decide I'm not getting anywhere and order an assault," I lied.

"What do you possibly have that I could want?"

"Your life. Your freedom. You could very well go free on all the charges if you make the smart decision now."

There was a brief pause. When Lauren spoke again, I could tell that she'd moved away from the front door. "Open the door slowly and come in. But if you try anything stupid, I'll kill you and then your wife."

Twenty-seven

Tucking my cane under my left arm, I opened the door, which squeaked on its hinges.

Lauren snapped, "Leave your cane outside!"

I propped my cane against the porch rail and limped inside. The living room was mostly in shadows, except for a diffuse cone of yellow light emanating from a lamp on an end table. Lauren stood near a threadbare sofa and she was aiming what looked like an old pump-action twenty-gauge shotgun at me. Smaller than a police shotgun, it was a firearm intended primarily for bird hunting, but at this range it could kill a Lyon, too.

"What's that in your hand?" she demanded.

I held up the robotic bear's head. "Proof that Rhiannon ran Kyle down."

"You could have done that yourself."

"I'm not as devious as you are, Lauren."

"Come inside and shut the door, slowly."

I did as I was ordered and then I saw Ash. She lay sprawled and motionless on the wooden floor near the stone hearth of the fireplace and I had to peer at her chest to make sure she was breathing. My wife's hands were resting on her stomach and secured together at the wrists with bonds made from silver duct tape. The heavy-duty tape also bound her ankles. But what rocketed my terror level up into the stratosphere was that she still wasn't awake. Lauren had drugged Ash nearly ten hours ago, which was more than enough time for most sedatives to wear off. Yet my wife remained completely unconscious, which almost certainly meant that she'd received an overdose of the drug.

Ash needed medical attention *now* and I suddenly realized that I wasn't going to have the luxury of time to convince Lauren that surrender was her best option. That meant coming up with a hasty and probably suicidal new plan. I limped a couple of steps closer to Lauren, until we were just a few feet apart.

Then she brandished the shotgun. "That's as far as you come."

"It's as far as I want to come. I just wanted a better look at my wife."

Although I was trying to keep an impassive demeanor, Lauren saw the fear in my eyes and said, "She's fine. I took her gag off hours ago."

Knowing it would strengthen her bargaining stance, I resisted the urge to blurt: *No, she's not fine, you freaking psychopath. She's been overdosed.* Instead, I bounced Patrick's head once in my hand and replied, "Gee, am I supposed to say thank you?"

Her eyes flicked from the robot's head to my eyes, yet the gun remained aimed at my midsection. "Don't get smart with me. I could have killed her."

"That's true, but here's some advice: From now on, your story is that you prevented Kyle from killing her."

"What are you saying?"

"Oh come on, Lauren. As brilliantly as you've plotted this thing, please don't tell me that you haven't given *this* scenario some thought." I bounced Patrick's head in my palm again and Lauren's eyes involuntarily followed the movement.

"If you're suggesting that I betray my son . . ." She took a step forward and now the muzzle of the shotgun was a scant foot away from my abdomen.

Doing my best not to wet my pants, I said, "Hey, somebody has to be thrown to the wolves and it's in your best interest if it's Kyle. You know why?"

"You seem to know everything. Tell me."

"Because his attorney is going to portray Kyle as one of Professor Pavlov's poor little salivating puppies."

"What are you talking about?" Her eyes narrowed.

"The lawyer is going to say that you physically and emotionally abused Kyle throughout his childhood, which resulted in him becoming conditioned to obeying you without question." I tossed Patrick's head in my palm again. "And I'll bet that lawyer will even be able to find at least two or three liar-for-hire academic experts to bolster that claim."

"That's ridiculous."

"No, actually that's a clever defense, especially since Kyle will get up in the witness box and testify to how you've utterly dominated his life."

"My son would never do that!" Her face was growing pale with rage.

"Wrong. Even with a gun in his hand and me at his mercy, Kyle made sure I understood that this was all your doing. Take it from me. He's going to give you up, Lauren. He's weak," I said regretfully.

I made as if to bounce the robot's head in my palm once again. This time, however, I threw it to my left and across my body. As I'd hoped, Lauren's eyes instinctively followed the flight of the white furry skull. That's when I made a two-handed grab for the shotgun and wrenched the barrel upwards and to the left, away from Ash. Lauren jerked on the trigger and the gun went off only inches from my left ear.

Stunned by the deafening blast but otherwise unhurt, I tried to keep my hands on the pump action so that Lauren couldn't chamber another round into the weapon. She was shrieking obscenities at me and sent a vicious kick at my groin. I half-blocked the blow and attempted to yank the gun away, but she clung to the weapon with an iron grip. Then there was another loud discharge and it took me a second to realize that the shotgun hadn't caused it. It was the much louder detonation of a stun grenade. Having heard the shot, the SWAT team was making entry into the cabin.

In an instant, the living room was full of people wearing black uniforms and Kevlar coalscuttle helmets. One of the SWAT members shot a short burst of pepper spray into Lauren's eyes and I suddenly had sole possession of the shotgun. Unfortunately, I was so close to Lauren that some of the ricocheting spray hit me in the face. It felt as if someone had just stuck a blazing road flare into my eyes. Meanwhile, Lauren was gang-tackled and she screamed in fear and pain.

Actually, I assume she was tackled, because I couldn't see much through the swimming haze of burning tears. I handed the shotgun to a dark form that I could just barely discern as a SWAT guy and then dropped to my knees and blindly crawled toward Ash. When I found her, I pressed my ear up close to her mouth and nose. She was breathing, but her respiration seemed very shallow and far too slow. Now it wasn't just the pepper spray that was causing my tears.

Cradling Ash's head in my arms, I bellowed, "We need paramedics in here, now!"

A few seconds later, there was someone next to me. Pulling my arm, she said in a gentle yet firm voice, "I'm a paramedic. You have to let go of your wife."

"But—"

"You've been pepper-sprayed and we can't run the risk of that stuff migrating into your wife's eyes."

"Daddy, you have to let them work. They'll take good care of Mama." I felt Heather's hand on my shoulder.

Reluctantly releasing my grip on Ash, I said, "Okay, but help me into the kitchen, so I can wash this crap out of my eyes."

"Come on, sir," said Colin, slipping his hand under my arm.

I was assisted to my feet and as I lurched toward the kitchen, I could hear Lauren wailing and sobbing about how badly *her* eyes hurt.

Gregg said to her, "We'll wash them out when we get down to county jail. Then we'll book you for murder and as many other felonies as I can think of."

"Kyle killed that man! He threatened to murder me too if I didn't go along with the kidnapping!" Lauren sobbed.

"Your son got run down by a car because he stayed loyal to you and it took all of fifteen seconds for you to decide to rat him out? Lady, the EPA ought to declare your soul a toxic waste dump," Gregg sneered.

"You don't understand. My son is a monster! If you need any proof of how evil he is, just look at the vicious computer games he's designed," she implored with a sniffle.

I caught myself before I could tell Lauren that if Ash died, I hoped the jury would buy her story. If she were free, it would make it that much easier for me to hunt her down and kill her. However, the cardinal rule for getting away with murder is to keep your mouth shut before and after the event.

"Jeez, get her out of here before I'm sick," said Lieutenant Garza.

Lauren was still crying and protesting her innocence as the SWAT team dragged her from the cabin. Heather and Colin led me into the kitchen and I bumped gently against the counter. Then I heard the sound of water splashing into a sink. I reached out with my hands to find the faucet and then bent over to allow the cold water to wash my eyes. It was agonizing at first, but I forced myself to endure the pain. The sooner I washed away the pepper spray, the sooner I could return to Ash's side.

I heard footfalls on the kitchen's linoleum floor and then Gregg said, "You are one hell of a cop, partner."

Spitting out some water, I replied, "How is Ash?"

"Okay, I think." Gregg tried to sound reassuring, but I could perceive the doubt in his voice. "They're getting ready to transport her to town and then airlift her to Sacramento."

"Has she regained consciousness?"

"Well . . . no."

"I've got to go with her. Give me a towel or something," I said.

"There isn't going to be any room in the air ambulance, but we'll get you to the hospital. Don't worry," said Garza.

"And you haven't rinsed your eyes enough, Daddy," said Heather, pushing gently on my shoulder.

Bowing to the inevitable, I stuck my head under the faucet again. This time it didn't hurt so much. Meanwhile, I heard the distinctive metallic clicking sound of an ambulance gurney being either elevated or lowered. Pulling my head from the water, I again tried to go into the living room to be with my wife.

Blocking my path, Garza said, "Brad, you saved Ash's life, but now you need to let the paramedics do their job."

"And you still have enough pepper spray on you to make *my* eyes sting," said Gregg.

"Daddy, I'm scared for Mama, too. But we'd just be in the way," Heather added.

"Okay, but I want someone to promise that I'm not going to sit around here for another thirty minutes waiting for a ride back to town," I snapped. I realized that everyone meant well, but I was becoming frustrated.

Captain Tewksbury stuck his head around the corner. "You've got it. I have two patrol units standing by to transport your group into town."

"Thanks, Captain," I said, and then stuck my head back under the faucet.

Although my ears were still ringing from the gunshot and the stun grenade, I heard a truck engine roar to life and then the howl of a siren over the sounds of the rushing water. The paramedics were taking Ash to Jackson to rendezvous with the air ambulance. I rinsed in the cold water for another five minutes or so. When I stopped this time, Gregg handed me a roll of paper towels. I dried my face and hair as we headed for the door, pausing only for a second to retrieve my cane from the porch.

The sheriff's deputies drove at such a breakneck speed back to Jackson that we almost overtook the paramedic van as it arrived at the small community hospital. I was relieved to see that an air ambulance was already on the helipad, with its engine idling. However, I had to watch from a distance as Ash was wheeled out to the chopper on the gurney and put inside the craft. Then the helicopter's engine began to race and a few seconds later the air ambulance rose into the twilight sky.

"Where are they taking her?" I asked.

One of the deputies replied, "Sutter Medical Center in downtown Sacramento."

"Time's wasting. Let's roll."

"Sorry, partner, but we can't go." Gregg held out his right hand. "We have to interview Lauren and then process the cabin for evidence. Call me when you hear anything."

"I will and give my best to Danny," I replied, shaking his hand. "Oh, and you have my permission to give me a swift kick in the ass if I ever ask to go to another homicide scene with you."

Turning to Garza, I extended my hand, but she brushed past it to give me a hug. "Thanks for being the best training officer a cop could ever have. Now, go and take care of that lucky wife of yours."

I joined Heather and Colin in the sheriff's cruiser and we took off. It was almost fifty miles to the hospital, but the deputy covered the distance in just over forty minutes. By the time we arrived at the emergency room entrance of Sutter Medical Center, the helicopter had already landed and Ash was in a treatment room. Fortunately, since we'd arrived with an Amador County cop, there weren't going to be any of the usual hassles over whether the hospital could release information to me about my wife's medical condition—not that there was anything to report yet. We were ushered into the staff's break lounge and told to make ourselves comfortable.

Over two hours passed in mostly nervous silence before a doctor came in to tell us that Ash had briefly regained consciousness and was going to be all right. The identity of the drug used to sedate my wife was still a mystery, so the hospital was going to admit her overnight for observation. I hugged Heather as she buried her head in my neck and began to sob with relief. Colin joined us for a group hug and then I grabbed the phone to call Chris, but remembered he was still airborne. I left a message on his voice mail and then telephoned Gregg with the wonderful news. As I spoke with my old partner, I could hear Garza *whoop* for joy in the background.

It was nearly midnight before they moved Ash to a room in the Intensive Care Unit. A nurse came to lead us upstairs. Suddenly shy, Colin remained outside in the corridor, while Heather and I went into the room.

Even knowing she was going to make a full recovery, the sight still hit me like a kick to the stomach. Dressed in a pale blue hospital gown, Ash was lying on the bed and obviously still asleep. She had an IV attached to one arm and was hooked up to all sorts of medical monitoring equipment. Heather crept up and kissed her mother softly on the forehead. Ash didn't stir.

"Chris's flight is going to be landing soon. I have to call the PD and have someone pick him up," whispered Heather. She gave me a peck on the cheek and left the room.

Limping over to the chair beside the bed, I sat down and gently took Ash's hand. After a few seconds her fingers tightened slightly around mine. I looked up and saw that her blue eyes were open and she was looking at me blearily.

"Honey, what happened? Where am I?" Ash whispered in a groggy and raspy voice.

"You're in a hospital in Sacramento, my love," I said as my eyes began to fill with tears. "It's a long story, but Lauren Vandenbosch drugged and kidnapped you."

"Why?"

"Because she was the person in the ski mask at the Paladin. She killed that man and she was going to kill you. We almost figured it out too late . . ." I looked down for a second, ashamed that my failure to solve the puzzle had nearly cost Ash her life.

"I'll bet you saved me."

"I had a lot of help. Heather and Colin and Gregg."

"Why are your eyes so red?"

"I got pepper-sprayed," I said, which was partly true. "Again, it's a long story and there'll be plenty of time to tell it later."

"Uh-huh . . . Where's Heather?"

"Calling Chris to tell him that you're okay. He'll be here in a couple of hours."

"Chris . . . is in Missouri." I looked up and saw that her eyes seemed slightly unfocused. Ash was beginning to drift.

"I know, honey, but he caught a flight out. He'll be here soon."

"That's nice. I'm very tired."

"Go back to sleep, honey."

"I want to go home, Brad. Back to the Valley."

"I know. So do I. Rest, my love, and we'll go home soon."

"I will, but . . . Brad?"

"Yes?"

"If I'm . . . asleep when . . . Heather . . . comes back, will you please . . . tell . . . her something?" Ash was on the verge of going to sleep again.

"Anything. What?" I kissed her hand.

Ash yawned and closed her eyes. "Please tell her . . . that she and Colin . . . have to . . . come to Remmelkemp Mill . . . to get . . . married, because . . . I don't ever want to . . . come back here again."

"Neither do I, love. I may have been born and raised here, but my home is in the Shenandoah Valley and my life is making teddy bears with you."

There was a hint of a smile on Ash's face as she drifted into slumber. I held her hand for a while and once I was certain that she was fast asleep, I released it so that I could look in the nightstand drawer. I found what I was looking for: a notepad and pencil. Sitting back down, I began to make some rough sketches of a teddy bear with a Karl Marx beard and wearing a groom's tuxedo. Later, when Ash felt better, I'd share my idea for a wedding gift and I knew she'd want to begin work immediately on her half of the ensemble. It would be a teddy bear dressed in a bridal gown and it would look like our daughter . . . sans the blue hair.

A TEDDY BEAR ARTISAN PROFILE
Penny French

One of the things I really enjoy about writing these books is inserting some of the actual teddy bears that my wife Joyce and I own into the tale. For instance, in Chapter Two, Brad buys a bee-costumed bear from artist Penny French as a birthday gift for Ashleigh. Been there, done that. The bumble-bear and the artificial tree he's climbing are on display in our home, as are nine more of Penny's sweet creations. Sometimes I wonder if I shouldn't just arrange for a monthly allotment from our bank account to Penny's, because we can't seem to get enough of her wonderful Back Mountain bears. We're also honored to count her as one of our friends, and she is one of the funniest people I've ever met.

Penny lives with David, her husband of forty-seven years, in Trout Run, Pennsylvania. She made her first teddy bear back in 1970, when her two-year-old son wanted a Winnie-the-Pooh bear for Christmas. Money was tight and Penny couldn't afford to buy a bear, so she decided to make one.

"I spent seventeen cents to get a copy of *Woman's Day* that had a teddy bear pattern in it, and used an old coat lining for my material. Then I used a small piece of red knit fabric to make a little shirt." Penny recalled. "My son loved the bear! After that, I began to make more bears for my nieces and nephews and other family members."

For the next sixteen years, Penny made the bears exclusively for family and friends. Then in 1986, she took the plunge and became a full-time teddy bear artist. Up until that time, she'd been modifying commercial and other people's patterns to create her bears, but now she began developing her own designs and was surprised by her own creativity.

"It was like opening Pandora's box," Penny said with a chuckle. "Except the box was full of warm and sweet and fuzzy things, instead of creepy stuff."

Warm and sweet and fuzzy things, indeed. Penny's bears radiate a tangible aura of kindness and joy. Joyce and I aren't the only ones who hold that opinion. In the winter of 2006, one of Penny's bears won the People's Choice Award at the prestigious Teddy Bear Artist Invitational show in Binghamton, New York.

When asked about the creative process that goes into making a bear, Penny told me that she views fabric the same way a sculptor envisions a figure within a block of stone. She can somehow "see" a bear's face in the mohair or plush fur, and it's her goal to bring that vision into existence. And like so many other bear artists I've spoken to, Penny doesn't consider a teddy bear finished until you can look into its eyes and see life. However, she is also quick to clarify that she doesn't give the bear its "soul," she merely helps make it manifest.

Metaphysics aside, Penny is a bear-making machine. It takes her six to eight hours to make a bear and she creates on average one a day—a fact I find mind-boggling. It also provides some insight into just how popular her stuffed animals are among collectors and fur fanatics. Another amazing thing is the constantly changing variety of bears you'll find at her booth. The reason for this is that Penny tends to produce small limited editions of her bears, which allows her the freedom to experiment as fresh designs occur to her.

"I get bored and I want to explore new ideas," said Penny. "Yet there's a fine line. I'm always looking to redefine my work, but I also want people to be able to recognize my bears."

Penny needn't worry about that. Whether it's one of her spectacular angel bears, a magical Celtic Santa bear, or one of her cute little girl bears in a party frock, Penny's creations are immediately identifiable. They mirror her infectious humor, warmth, and sincerity.

Penny attends teddy bear and craft shows throughout the northeastern and mid-Atlantic regions of the United States. If you'd like to learn more about her event schedule and her bears, she can be contacted via email at davidfrench @kcnet.org.

Afterword

I'm sad to report that there is no annual teddy bear show in Sonoma's lovely and historic Plaza. If there was, my wife and I might be induced to return to California to attend it. But like Brad and Ashleigh, we'd only go back to the Golden State for a brief visit. We have a blissful life here in the Shenandoah Valley.

As in the past, I've mixed some genuine folks up with my fictional characters. Donna Griffin, Mac Pohlen, Karen DiNicola, and Rosalie Frischmann are all real teddy bear artists and Joyce and I are honored to have their creations on display in our home. Susan and Terry Quinlan are also real, as is their incredible teddy bear museum in Santa Barbara, California. If you want to find out more about the museum, please visit www .quinlanmuseum.com. On a technological note, both the Japanese scientist and his remarkable humanlike androids that I obliquely referred to in Chapter 13 are authentic, too. Dr. Hiroshi Ishiguro is the director of Osaka University's Intelligent Robotics Laboratory and one of the world's foremost pioneers in this field.

Finally, I want to thank all my readers who've either sent me photos of their teddy bears or brought their furry treasures to my book signings. I'm humbled that you'd share such a joyful part of your life with me.